COME BACK TO BED

KAYLEY LORING

COME BACK TO BED

USA TODAY BESTSELLING AUTHOR
Kayley Loring

2023 Cover design by Najla Qamber Designs
Proofreading by Jenny Rarden

CHAPTER 1
BERNADETTE

FROM: DOLLY KEMP <doloreskemp123@yahoo.com>
TO: BERNADETTE FARMER
<thisisbernadettefarmer@gmail.com>

Bernadette my dear—greetings from Prague! I think you would love it and be so inspired here. There is art everywhere, and I want to buy all of it. Everything is gorgeous and delicious (especially the beer and sausages). Marty and I are having a ball.

Speaking of sausages and balls—I'm sure you have enjoyed <u>not</u> hearing us fooling around next door for the past three months. LOL Numerous guests at five-star hotels all over Europe have not been so lucky.

I hope you are well, and I have a favor to ask of you.

My lawyer nephew needs a place to stay for a while and will be living in my apartment until he finds one of his own.

His name is Matt McGovern, Esq.

He is my younger sister's son.
Matt spends most of his life at work or out on the town, so you probably won't even know he's there.
Can I trouble you to give him your spare key for my flat tonight? I know you are a private person, so I didn't give him your phone number. I told him to buzz you at 4A around 7:30 p.m. If that is inconvenient for you, you can email him at: iammattmcgovernsemail@gmail.com to plan a better time.
You have similar personal email addresses—isn't that cute?!
Thank you for taking care of my plants.
I still don't know when we will be returning, but you may continue to pay rent at the discounted rate until then.
xx DK

Well, crap.

It was fun having the floor to myself while it lasted.

And by "fun," I mean blissfully uneventful and quiet.

Dolly Kemp is my landlady and neighbor. She owns both condos on the fourth floor of the Upper West Side townhouse we live in, sublets the smaller one to me, and charges me less when she's out of town because I water her plants while she's gone. She is a retired investment banker and an enthusiastic art collector, a senior citizen who has a far racier wardrobe and love life than I do. Since I don't know exactly how old she or her younger sister are, her nephew could be anywhere from midtwenties to early fifties.

Here's hoping he's a shy fifty-something intellectual property lawyer who listens to classical music and does crossword puzzles to relax when he's at home. I don't know if that person actually exists anywhere on earth in the twenty-first century, but that's my idea of a good neighbor. Polite, quiet, and almost never at home.

I myself am a twenty-seven-year-old homebody who deeply values what little time I get to spend in my apartment. Being the well-paid executive personal assistant to a very successful (and moderately sexy—okay super sexy) recently divorced artist means that I spend most of my days doing whatever he needs me to do for him, whenever and wherever he wants me to do it. And no, none of those things ever involve sex. Unfortunately. Unless you count the time he asked me to pose partially nude for a painting, but I may as well have been a naked bowl of fruit as far as he was concerned. A really demure, secretly horny bowl of fruit.

Being a homebody in Manhattan is like being a vegetarian in a meat market, but when your life revolves around another person in the way that mine does, in a city of eight and a half million other people, you really need that room of your own. Even when you spend most of your time in that room thinking about your boss. Even when you spend most of your time in any room thinking about your boss.

Today, world-renowned artist Sebastian Smith has tasked me with stretching canvases, ordering paints from Japan and brushes from China, responding to interview requests, and updating his website, all of which I have been able to do from his four-bedroom converted loft in Tribeca. He himself has spent the day driving around the Hudson Valley for inspiration, and while I'd always prefer to see his face and hear his voice, it does make for an easier work day. I should easily make it home before seven thirty, so I shoot Dolly an email saying just that.

I get off at the 79th Street station instead of 86th because the sun hasn't gone down yet and it's a gorgeous mid-March early evening after a full week of rain. I always enjoy people-watching as I walk up Broadway, but it's especially fun now that New Yorkers are starting to show some skin again.

I really love my Upper West Side neighborhood. I am the only single under-thirty-year-old in the art world that I know of who chooses to live up here. It's old-school—a little mellower than downtown—and with its relatively unpretentious residents and neighborhood feel, it's the closest I can get to my home state of Vermont without leaving Manhattan. And okay, yes, I also moved here because of *You've Got Mail*, and I hear "Dreams" by The Cranberries in my head whenever I walk around here. Don't judge me. Call me crazy, but at this point in my life I'd rather be safe and living in Nora Ephron's charming but not-at-all-cool late-90s fantasy world than do ecstasy at an after-party where the DJ is some model with a famous parent and a bottle of Heineken costs more than the Uber ride it took to get there.

I cut across to 85th to check out the floral offerings at my local green grocer, but my attention is diverted by the cutest damn Boston Terrier I've ever seen. She has a pink collar, is staring right at me, and I swear it's love at first sight for both of us.

I don't want to brag or anything, but dogs love me. Like, every dog I've ever met. To dogs, I'm basically a five-foot-seven jerky treat with a voice and hands. I march straight over to that black and white beauty and drop to my knees. She keeps licking her chops as she stands up on her hind legs, resting her paws on my thighs and hopping up and down.

"Ooooh you're so cute! Look at that face! Look at that sweet, sweet little face! Ohhhh, what's your name, happy girl? You're a pretty girl, aren't you? What's your name?" I turn my question to her owner. "What's her name?"

I stand up as my eyes follow the leash up to the big strong hand that's holding it and the man in the suit and coat who is attached to the hand. He is so ludicrously gorgeous, I just burst out laughing. This must happen often when people look at him, because his facial expression betrays absolutely no sense of surprise. In fact, he is completely stone-faced. Like a handsome statue. A handsome statue in a modern-cut suit and slim tie and trench coat that is probably worth more than everything I own, who is talking on the phone through his earbuds and has no intention of answering my very important question about his dog's name. He just stares at me while continuing to engage in his phone conversation about contracts and clauses or something.

Whatever!

Seriously though—what is he thinking? Who just stands around outside a grocery store looking that handsome, unless… I look around for a camera crew. Am I interrupting a photo shoot or a movie set? Nope. Unless it's a hidden-camera reality show about people reacting to cute dogs and annoyingly attractive strangers.

He is expressionless as he continues to watch me while talking on the phone. I kind of want to slap his face because it's so obnoxiously good-looking. Inside, though, my vulva is dimming the lights and queuing up "Let's Get It On" by Marvin Gaye. *Calm down, vulva! It's just some guy on the sidewalk. You'll never see him or his sweet dog again.*

I bend down to rub the dog's head again, whisper "I love you" to her, and then continue on my way back home.

I have about fifteen minutes before Matt McGovern, Esquire is supposed to show up, so I check my mailbox. I never expect to actually receive anything besides marketing crap, but there's a squishy mailer stuffed in there, and I stare at it for a few seconds before casting my mind back to five nights ago when I ordered a sexy dress in a Pinot-induced online shopping frenzy. I sometimes have to attend gallery openings and parties with Sebastian (for work, not as a date), and I keep buying sexy dresses online while under the influence, with every intention of wearing them. Then I return them and show up to events in a black cardigan, really expensive jeans, hoop earrings, and red lipstick, because that's the level of sophistication that I'm comfortable with.

I run up the stairs to the fourth floor, taking two at a time… Okay, I do that for one floor and then walk up the rest of the way. I don't want to be all sweaty when I'm trying on this dress. Also, I may be having a heart attack.

As soon as I'm inside my apartment, I tear off my coat, top, and bra, rip open the package, and pull out the folded burgundy red dress. I remember thinking that it would go well with my dark auburn hair, but I don't remember the plunging V neck or the stupid zipper in the back. Sighing, I remove my socks, shoes, and jeans, already knowing that

I'll be returning this sleeveless number on my way to work tomorrow.

I have no idea how much time has passed since finally getting this dress on and staring at myself in the mirror. It took about a month to zip it up in back because it's so tight, and then I decided I should at least see what it looked like with the right shoes, and then it seemed necessary to find the right lipstick before taking it off and packing it up again, and now my intercom is buzzing and I can just tell from the way the guy presses the buzzer quickly, two times, that he's impatient. So, I don't have time to change out of this dress. I grab my keys and tell the buzzy intercom guy that I'll be right down to let him in.

I remove my heels while taking the stairs and then slip them back on before reaching the front door. Through the glass and decorative iron grate, I can see that the man is tall and probably not fifty-something. When I open the door, I stare up at someone who is as surprised and confused to see me standing here as I am to see him.

It's laugh-out-loud handsome stone-faced suit guy. He is just as handsome and stone-faced as he was the first time I saw him. I still feel the need to laugh when he gives me a quick, expressionless once-over.

"*You're* Bernadette Farmer?"

"Yes. And you're…" I feel like I should ask for some sort of identification, but he's so freakishly handsome and serious, I don't know why he'd bother standing here staring at me if he weren't Dolly's nephew. Unless, of course, he's a serial killer who's about to murder me. If so, this would be a great outfit to die in.

"Matt McGovern. Dolly Kemp is my aunt."

He just stands there studying me for what feels like a year. An actual year, starting with winter as his coal dark eyes search my face, his jaw frozen in place; a late-spring thaw as his liquid gaze trickles down the front of me; sudden blazing hot summer as it returns back up over my curves; and see how the leaves now turn from red to gold to brown and then die off instantly when he meets my stare again. Unblinking. Like a cowboy in one of those old westerns my dad and I used to make fun of but I secretly fantasized about banging Gary Cooper in the back of a saloon.

When I was a child, I was trained to see a person or object as a collection of lines, shadows, shapes, and contours, but when I look at this guy it's like I'm blinded by my physical response to the overall effect of his…everything.

He's an assault to my retinas.

Or maybe he's just an asshole.

Either way, I want to slap him.

Also, I may have just had a very quick, tiny orgasm.

Like an orgasm zap. Is that a thing?

Feeling the need to take control of this situation, I thrust my hand out to shake his, but he's got a huge duffel bag hanging from one shoulder, a cross-body satchel, an overstuffed garment bag, and guitar case in one hand, leash in the other.

"Hi," he says. He makes no effort to shake my hand, which is fine. That's when I finally look down and see the beautiful Boston Terrier, who is shifting around on her paws, wagging her whole body, licking her lips, and snuffling and slobbering a little bit. She is so much happier to see me than Matt McGovern is. I don't recall Dolly mentioning there would be a dog staying in her apartment, but the building is pet-friendly, and I have no complaints.

"And we meet again! Hello, sweet thing!" I sing to the dog as I start to bend forward and then think better of it as I realize I'm already showing about seventy percent more cleavage than I'm generally comfortable with. "Uh. Come on in. I have the keys for you." I step aside, holding the door open for them.

His eyes stay locked on my exposed cleavage for about one full second before they return to my face, which is probably very pink and feels like it's contorted and having a mild spasm on one side.

"You're Dolly's neighbor?"

"And tenant, yes."

He nods his head once, adjusts the handles of the duffel bag on his shoulder, and then leads his dog across the threshold. "I thought you'd be a lot older. Like, seventy."

"I get that a lot. Sorry to disappoint you."

He stops once inside to survey the foyer. My new canine friend assesses the smells.

"Are you just visiting New York or new in town?"

"Neither." He doesn't offer any more information.

"Okay. So this is the foyer. Those are the mailboxes!" I wave my hands like the candelabra in *Beauty and the Beast* and I'm about to belt out "Be Our Guest."

"I won't be here long enough to get mail."

"Alrighty, then. Marco the super lives in unit 1A over there."

He just eyes the stairs.

"No elevator, right?"

"Yeah, it's a pre-war walk-up. Built in 1920."

"We're on the fourth floor?"

"Yeah, you'll be in apartment 4B. It's three flights of stairs. You get used to it."

"After you," he says.

"Do you want me to take..." I hold my hand out, offering to take the leash.

"I got it."

I watch his lips, waiting for them to form the word "thanks," but those lips are glued shut. They honestly do look like they're made for kissing, but I sort of just want to tell him to kiss my ass, throw Dolly's key on the floor, and run back to my apartment so I can get out of this damn dress.

I mean...New Yorkers have always had a bad reputation for being rude and impatient, but I rarely come across anyone here who's actually this cold and impolite. I'm not exactly Little Miss Sunshine, but I do pride myself on being a nice person who gives people the benefit of the doubt. He's probably just stressed about moving. So, I will give this handsome asshole nephew of my landlady another chance.

"May I ask your dog's name?" *Again.*

"It's Daisy."

"Awww, Daisy!" I coo. "Such a sweet pretty name for such a sweet pretty girl! How old is she?"

"Five."

"Five! Perfect! Awww, that's the perfect age! Awwww!"

Daisy looks up at me, spins around, hops, and makes a weird little cartoon alien gopher sound that matches the pitch of my "aww."

I'm in love.

Matt McGovern clears his throat while focusing on the second-floor landing like getting up there is the most important thing in the world right now and wouldn't it be just great if we could make that happen immediately? He doesn't jerk his head and whistle sharply to indicate that I should get going, but he may as well.

"Right. Well. I'm sure you're eager to get to your new apartment."

"It's just temporary."

"Yeah. So you said." He waits for me to take the lead up the steps. I don't know if he's being a gentleman or if he plans to stare at my ass, or both, but I have never been so self-conscious about how I move while walking up stairs. It feels like my hips are swaying too much. I don't want him to think I'm trying to move seductively, but I sort of have to sway my hips to lift my knees in this tight dress. Oh God—what if he thinks I changed into this dress for him?

"Um. I was just trying on this dress that I ordered online when you buzzed me. I kind of forgot you were coming when I saw the package, so I put it on. I don't usually dress like this at home. I mean, I just got home from working all day. I don't usually dress like this for work either. Or ever, really." I'm babbling. What is it about exceptionally handsome silent assholes that makes people babble? I am usually so comfortable with silence. "I don't usually get much time to shop, so when there's a sale online, I go a little nuts. I think I'll have to return this. It's not really me."

"You should keep it," he mumbles.

"What?" I don't turn around. My hand stays on the rail and my eyes stay glued to my feet so I don't fall over.

"Keep it. It's a nice dress. You look good." He somehow manages to say those words in such a way as to make it sound like he is in no way giving me a compliment.

"Oh." I don't say "thank you" because I'm pretty sure he doesn't want to be thanked, and I'm also quite certain that we already hate each other. This makes me laugh, for some reason. Again. It's hilarious how much this person seems to offend me. I have never felt this kind of hostility toward someone I've just met before. Now I just want to keep talking as much as possible because it obviously annoys him.

"So you're a lawyer?"

"Uh-huh."

"Dolly didn't tell me much about you, other than your name and your esquireship. Is that what it's called? An esquireship?"

"Nope."

Two more delightful flights of stairs to go!

"Anyway, there are eight units in the building, two on each floor. There's a laundry room in the basement. It's a pretty quiet building. Everyone's nice but keeps to themselves. Old people, working people, blah blah blah. You won't be here long enough to get to know them anyway. Mrs. Benson on the third floor has a poodle, but that's the only other dog in the building. I occasionally hear him barking, but not much." I lower my voice before continuing. "Mrs. Benson is so sweet, but she has these dinner parties that are a total disaster. You know, she tries to have the kind of Upper West Side intellectual dinner parties you see in movies, but her friends and family just get drunk and argue with each other. So, if she corners you and invites you—well, you've been warned."

"Thanks."

"What else? I watered Dolly's plants on the weekend,

so if you could water them on Sunday, that would be great. The water pressure in the showers here are pretty good, but they're never quite as hot as I'd like."

One more floor!

"Dolly said you'll probably be out and about most of the time."

"She did?"

Gasp! A response!

"She said you're usually either at work or out on the town."

"Usually, but I don't have a dog-walker in this neighborhood yet, so I'll have to come home more."

"Oh right. Where are you moving from?"

"SoHo."

"Oh yeah? I'm in SoHo a lot. My boss is in Tribeca, so I'm downtown most of the time. Do you work downtown?"

"Yes."

"Really? That's so interesting. Tell me more!"

He doesn't tell me more. I didn't expect him to. I finally glance back at him and see something that I don't expect at all—he's smiling. He looks totally amused.

I am so startled by the complete transformation of his face that I lose my balance. I swipe at the air, blurt out about five swear words, and feel myself falling backwards in slow-motion. And then I'm leaning back into Matt McGovern's strong, sturdy body. He has taken a step up and calmly wrapped his arm around my waist, one leg firmly set to the side of mine to keep me in place. He's still holding on to Daisy's leash and seems to be in no danger of losing his balance himself.

"I got you," he says in a deep, quiet voice that actually does make me feel safe.

Until I look up and see him staring down at me with those eyes that aren't black as coal so much as they're dark chocolate, but I'm the one who's melting.

I grab on to the handrail and pull myself upright and steady. "Thanks," I say. "I just lost my balance."

"I know."

"I mean, I'm usually pretty good at walking up stairs."

"I hear you get used to it."

"It's just this stupid dress is so tight. I'm definitely sending it back."

"Shame."

"Aaaand fourth floor—ladies' lingerie!" Oh God. I've gone from being the kooky lady who falls backwards to the old guy who makes dumb jokes in elevators. I must be having an allergic reaction to his pheromones. That's a thing, right?

I point to my front door and then his. "Mine. Yours. I'll get the lock for you." I remove Dolly's spare key from my keychain and unlock the door to 4B, leaving the key in the door. "Don't forget to grab that when your hands are free. The spare key for the exterior door is in that tray on the console table."

"Thanks. Appreciate it."

"Sure thing." I start making my way over to 4A and the bottle of Pinot Noir that I will be polishing off momentarily.

"Do you usually talk this much?"

I turn back to him and the annoying smirk on his annoying gorgeous face. "No. Not at all."

"Good."

"Do you usually talk more than this?"

He places the duffel bag, garment bag, and guitar case on the floor and shrugs. "A bit."

"Are you usually this big of a dick?"

"Nah, it's kind of a new thing for me."

"Well, I think you've found your calling."

He picks Daisy up, pulls the key out of the lock, and goes inside the apartment.

"Okay, enjoy your stay! It was wonderful to meet you —Daisy!"

The door shuts and I'm alone in the hallway, shaking my head and reaching my hand behind me because I can somehow still feel his chest pressed up against my back.

The most interesting thing about the past ten minutes—I didn't think about my boss once.

CHAPTER 2
MATT

Well, that was unexpected.

Wish I could say it's a welcome surprise. Not like it's that much of a surprise that Aunt Dolly didn't mention her neighbor's an attractive young woman. If she had, I probably would have found myself an Airbnb. Dolly never liked Vanessa. I always wondered why she kept talking about "Bernadette next door" and how I should meet her. Why do I need to meet a seventy-year-old artist nerd, I'd think.

I leave my stuff on the floor in the front hallway, hang my coat in the closet, and loosen my tie. I can't wait to get out of this suit. I only wore it because I had a lunch meeting with other lawyers today. The rich tech and math geeks I work with usually get uncomfortable when I wear a suit to the office, the general counsel that I report to hates it when I dress better than him, and I've gotten so used to my downtown style I think I just act differently when I dress like a typical corporate lawyer. Like a big dick, apparently.

Daisy's hard at work, sniffing around.

"What do you think, girl? This is where we'll be staying for a few weeks, maybe."

I've only been to visit my aunt here once, and I don't recall getting the full tour. It's a good-sized space—bigger than our place. I mean—bigger than the place I've been living in with Vanessa for the past three years and paying a hundred percent of the rent for, like a fucking idiot. I follow Daisy down the hall to the living room. Her nosy, judge-y nature aside, Aunt Dolly has always had exceptional taste in almost everything.

The art and furniture in this room is stunning without being intimidating. Sort of like Vanessa. Which is why I never understood how Dolly could be so against my relationship with her. Even now.

Fuck.

I pull my phone out of my back pocket to check my messages. Still nothing from Vanessa. At least I went a good fifteen minutes without checking my texts or her social media accounts. Guess all it took for me to turn into an obsessed teenage girl was getting dumped by the woman of my dreams. No big deal.

It's only been four days since I've seen her.

Four days since I hired guys to move the few large objects that I consider to be mine into a small storage unit.

Two months of her not acting like herself.

Two months since she let me touch her in bed.

One month of her insisting that "it just isn't working for us anymore."

One month of me asking if there's someone else and her saying, "There isn't an 'us' anymore. I just need space. I just need to find myself again."

She just needs time and space to find herself again, and I'll give it to her.

She'll call.

I haven't failed.

It's not over yet.

"Right, Daisy?"

Daisy ignores me. She's too busy investigating smells in my aunt's bedroom.

"Let's stay out of this room," I tell her as I peek inside. It's basically a big, tasteful boudoir, pretty much what I'd expect of my mom's long-divorced, sexed-up older sister. "Come on, Daisy. Out. Let's find our room."

Our room is the guest room, on the opposite side of the hallway. It's a pretty small room, painted bright white and just wide enough for a queen-size bed and a bedside table. But it's the painting on the wall above the bed that makes the room magnificent. A heavy square canvas about four feet wide all around. Abstract, muted blues, white, and gold blending into each other, just a hint of seascape. It kind of looks like marble, but there's a warmth to it. It seems alive and changeable. I have no idea why I like it so much, I just do.

I check the signature in the lower right corner. ***B. Farmer***. Bernadette Farmer?

What do you know.

The less-than-seventy-year-old artist nerd has got talent.

A bod and talent and some kind of fragrance that I've never encountered before and more than one screw loose, so far as I can tell.

I can't help but wonder what she's doing on the other side of the wall right now. Taking off that dress? Scheming to steal my dog? Both, probably.

Daisy circles my legs and barks her approval of our new digs.

"Yeah. It'll do for now." I pick her up and let her drench my face with saliva. Honestly don't know what I would have done the past few days without her. "I'm gonna have to find you a dog daycare, huh, girl?"

As soon as I let my parents know that we'd moved out of our apartment, I got an email from Aunt Dolly insisting that I stay at her place. That's how it goes in my family—I tell my parents there's an issue, they say they're sorry to hear it and ask if there's anything they can do, I say no, and then we stop talking about it. My mom emails her sister, and then Dolly offers up her opinions and solutions for everything. It's efficient and effective.

I figured it would be nice for Daisy to be near two big parks for a change, but I'm not going to be able to come home at lunch to walk her like I could sometimes do when we lived downtown. If we don't move back in with Vanessa, this could be a good opportunity to find a ground floor unit with some backyard space.

But it's too soon to think about that just yet.

I go back out to the hallway to bring my stuff to the guest room. I could text Vanessa to ask if there was anything else of mine that I missed, but I'm determined to get her to make the first move. After three nights in a hotel with my dog, the least she could do is text to ask where we've been staying.

I can hear Bernadette's front door shut and realize a few seconds later that I've been holding my breath. She doesn't knock on my door. Fortunately. Don't know why she would. Other than to baby-talk at my dog again.

Suddenly, a yappy dog starts barking downstairs, and Daisy joins in on the fun. Must be Mrs. Benson's poodle. Daisy's scampering back and forth along the front door, her flat nose to the ground. Poodle must be barking at the door directly downstairs.

"Hey! Shush." I raise my finger to her and give her my best alpha voice. "Daisy, quiet." I pick her up and take her to the guest room and shut the door. She quiets down immediately, and I am one proud dog daddy. The poodle downstairs, though, keeps barking.

When I'm back in the front hallway to pick up my bags, I hear a faint knock. It's so faint and hesitant that I can't quite tell if it's on my door or Bernadette's. Three louder knocks confirm that someone's outside my door, and I have to wipe the grin off my face before opening it.

"Hi," says Bernadette Farmer. She's still wearing that dress, her arms hiding behind her back, one foot crossed behind the other, looking up at me sheepishly. She wrinkles her nose. "Sorry about the poodle."

"Should have known you had something to do with that."

"I just knocked on Mrs. Benson's door to see if she could help me with something, but she's not at home."

"Fascinating. Thanks for the update." Lavender and something. That's what she smells like. Lavender and vanilla and something else… Trouble. That's definitely what I'm sensing. "Good night, then," I say as I slowly swing the door shut.

She sticks her leg inside, and the rest of her quickly follows. She is quick on her toes, despite her inability to climb three flights of stairs without falling backwards. Not that I minded.

"I didn't want to bother you," she says, "but I need help…" She sighs and twists her lips to the side.

"Are you going to make me guess what you need help with?"

"I need help unzipping this dress in the back."

Now that she's standing closer, I can also smell wine on her breath. Not something I noticed when she gave me the key. Guess I drove her to drink between then and now. I could use one myself. Hell, I needed one as soon as she ran toward me on the sidewalk and dropped to her knees. Okay, so she was running to my dog—but it will take a while for me to forget that image.

"If I'm going to return it, I don't want to risk tearing it, and I can't quite reach the doodad for some reason. This thing is so tight, I'm afraid the sides will rip if I…"

"Turn around," I say. I honestly didn't mean for it to sound like a sexual command, but for some reason it came out that way.

She blinks her big hazel eyes, bites her lower lip, and then slowly turns her back to me. In one swift motion, she sweeps her long hair out of the way, over one shoulder, and then stands straight as a rod, her arms tight at her sides.

This dress.

The front is quite enchanting, or maybe it's her cleavage that had me in danger of being under a spell.

But the back of the dress, even though it covers a lot more of her, is even more enticing.

It's a long zipper, from the base of her neck all the way down to her waist. There are still a few hairs in the way, so I brush them aside, unable to avoid touching the bare skin of her long neck. I notice her shiver. She wraps her arms around herself, as if she shivered because she was cold. I'd better get this over with quick.

I unzip her, not all the way to her waist. She can do the rest herself, I imagine. I can't help but notice that there's no bra under there, which is interesting.

Her crossed arms slide up the front of her body, adeptly keeping her private parts in place and out of sight. She glances over her shoulder without turning around. "Thank you. Sorry to bother you."

"No problem."

She uses her foot to open the door. "Daisy settling in okay?"

"So far so good."

I want to talk to her about her painting, but it doesn't feel like this is the right moment, after I've basically just undressed her.

"Great. Well…"

"Hey, uh…"

"Yeah?" She shifts her body around so that she's half facing me, checks to make sure she isn't showing any side-boob, and then decides to face me full-on.

"I was just going to ask if there's a good place that delivers around here."

"Well yeah, there are tons of good places! Actually, your aunt has a great list up in the kitchen by her phone. We pretty much order from the same restaurants. She has a landline. You don't have to answer it. It goes straight to voice mail. Oh, and I forgot to tell you the thermostat is set pretty low, so you should turn it up at night. It makes a little noise when it starts up. That's normal."

"Right. I am familiar with heating system noises. But thanks."

"Okay, then." She furrows her brow at me, and I'm not sure why it feels so necessary to be such a dick to her. It just does. "Good night, Daisy!" she calls out, looking around for her.

Daisy barks a happy "yarf" greeting from inside the

guest room. She rarely barks, so it's weird that she'd respond to a new person like that.

"You know where to find me if you want to hang out with a nice human!" the new person yells out again.

"I'm nice to my dog," I growl.

"Lucky her," she snaps as she spins back toward the door. "Good night, Miss Farmer."

"Good night, your esquireship."

And then she's gone.

I get Daisy's feeding station all set up in the kitchen and then check out Dolly's impressively detailed food delivery list. I use an app, of course, so I don't have to actually speak to a human being on the phone, but I'm too hungry to do all the research necessary to make an informed decision. According to the list, the fastest delivery after 7:30 p.m. is from a bar & grill, so I find them on my app and order a burger and fries and guacamole and chips because it has been that kind of week.

It's been years since I've hung out or eaten on the Upper West Side. The last time my parents came to visit, we all met up with Dolly, who insisted on eating at a bistro just south of Columbia University. It was actually really good, but I would never make the trip out there if I didn't have to. And I guess Vanessa and I went to a fundraiser at the Museum of Natural History a couple of years ago…

Vanessa.

Fuck.

My phone buzzes with a message, and what do you know? It's from Vanessa. Three little words. ***How are you?***

Good question.

I'm kind of numb.

I'm in a weird place, emotionally, but I'd never admit that to another human being.

I'm not clear if this is really a breakup or just a break, and I'm afraid to even talk to attractive women who aren't you yet because I don't need any of that Ross and Rachel "We were on a break!" drama.

I miss you, but I'm afraid I might just be missing some glorified fantasy of you.

I miss us, but I can't remember the last time it felt like we were the Us that I loved.

I don't want to hate you, but I'm not thrilled by the way you've handled this situation so far.

I'm wondering how it's possible that you haven't even asked about Daisy, even though you've always been kind of jealous of her and I used to think it was cute but now I'm afraid it's because you might actually be a bit of a bitch.

If you really did break up with me because of another guy, I wish you'd just fucking tell me. It would kill me, but at least I'd know.

But what I type is: ***Fine. You?***

Hit Send.

Maybe if I'd already changed out of my suit I would have been able to respond with a few more words, in the way that I know she'd appreciate, but fuck it. After four days of radio silence, a lot of guys wouldn't respond at all. The animated dots tell me that she's typing a fairly long response. I stare at the phone and wonder if, given her response, Daisy and I should go back to SoHo tonight. I guess I'll wait until the food's been delivered. Gotta take care of me first, right Oprah?

Then the animated dots disappear. No response comes. I look down at Daisy, who is sitting by her water bowl staring up at me, like: *"Oh, buddy. Just let her go already. I'm the only girl you need. You'll see."*

And not a minute later, I find out from Facebook that my relationship status has changed.

Apparently I'm officially single again.

CHAPTER 3
BERNADETTE

Even though the walls between our apartments are quite soundproof, I was able to hear last night's little outburst quite clearly. Normally, if I'd heard my neighbor yell out *"What the fuck?"* I would have sent Dolly an email to ask if she way okay. While I do have Matt McGovern, Esquire's email address, it didn't seem appropriate to check on him so soon after meeting him last night.

While the walls of the building are thick and solid, due to a charming quirk of the vents and ducts, I can hear much of what goes on next door in certain spots of my apartment—mostly in my bedroom. Before Dolly's current boyfriend was her boyfriend, he was an out-of-town friend staying in her guest room, and let's just say I had the pleasure of hearing exactly what happened the night she looked in on him and asked if he needed anything, because the head of my bed is up against the other side of the wall that the headboard kept banging against. There is no other way to arrange my tiny bedroom. I did put my headphones on, once I realized that what he needed would take several hours (likely thanks to a prescription).

Last night, after hearing Matt's expletive, I waited and listened for any more signs of agitation, but there weren't any. Not another bark from Daisy or her person, but then I heard him talking to someone who I assume was his assistant, followed by loud AC/DC music and some angry grunting (which I attributed to vigorous crunches and/or pushups). A couple of hours later when they were apparently both in bed, I heard him playing guitar for a few minutes and then saying such sweet things to Daisy that I almost liked him. He really is nice to his dog. I figured it must have been some kind of momentary work-related outburst. He seems like the kind of guy who only gets passionate about work.

I didn't see or hear him leave this morning, and if my boss hadn't called to ask me to pick something up from Anita at her gallery on my way to his place, I probably would have spent at least five minutes on the floor of the fourth-floor hallway, trying to talk to Daisy through the crack under the front door. Love at first sight happens so rarely in life, it really shouldn't be ignored.

I'm here to pick up some of Sebastian's favorite Italian watercolor paper, which Anita brought back from her most recent trip to Europe, but ever since I walked into her Chelsea gallery, I've gotten an earful about the testosterone pellet she's recently had implanted in her back.

"Look at my skin!" she says, "Feel how tight it is!" She grabs my hand and places it on her neck.

"Very nice," I say. Anita is a stunning fortysomething woman who owns an amazing art gallery, knows everything about everything, knows everyone who's anyone, and has never been satisfied with her looks or energy levels for as long as I've known her. I have never been so exhausted and impressed by a woman. I can't wait to get out of here.

"At my age—at any age really, if you're a woman, getting your hormones balanced is so important. Now I look younger, I have boundless energy, and I just want to hump everything!"

"Well that is great news. So, I'll just write you a check for the paper?" I pull out Sebastian's checkbook. I love signing my name to Sebastian's checks and credit card transactions. But not in a creepy I'm-pretending-to-be-his-wife kind of way. I just like to sign for things that I don't actually have to pay for—who wouldn't?

"We live in exciting times," she says. "I like what you're doing with your hair. You seeing anyone special?"

I have no idea why I think of my new temporary neighbor all of a sudden. "No, not at all."

"Ah. Still obsessed with your boss, I see."

"I'm obsessed with my job. And thinking about my boss and his needs *is* my job. That's not the same thing. I'm just really good at my job."

"Oh, I bet you're good at your job, little miss lips like two pillows."

"Anita. You're the classiest gross lady I've ever known."

"I call it as I see it, sweetheart. You've been working for him, what? Three years now?"

"Three and a half."

"And you're what? Twenty-six?"

"Twenty-seven."

"Well fuck, honey. You should have a solo show by

now. You need to quit. You still have time to make the Thirty Under Thirty Artists in NYC lists."

"I've never cared about those lists. I make more money than everyone I went to art school with." What I don't mention, what I never mention, is that I don't just stay at this job because of my boss. I do this because I don't want my hippie artist parents to lose their farm and end up on welfare. Which reminds me, I need to call them to make sure they remembered to pay their utility bills.

"Yeah. Good for you. I'm glad he pays you so well. It's practically impossible to find someone as qualified as you who's also good at the mundane practical stuff. But you should be making art. Or love. Instead you're making google-y eyes at a middle-aged married man who will never give you what you want or deserve."

"He is divorced, and he is thirty-eight. I thought you liked him."

"Of course I like him. I literally love him. But I'd never date him."

"Too old for you?"

"Too much. Men like that—and you'd know better than anyone—are so busy being amazing they have very little left to give a woman. You need a man who can be your anchor so you can lose yourself in your work. I mean, you saw what it was like with Sebastian's most recent wife."

"His most recent *ex*-wife."

She rolls her eyes at me, but I do know what she means. I just happen to think that I'm better at dealing with him than his ex-wife was. She wasn't an artist, so she didn't understand him. I'm his work-wife. I get him.

Suddenly, I remember the crazy storm and power outage we had a couple of weeks ago, a couple of hours after I'd gotten home from work. He called me immediately, and I answered saying, "I'm fine, I'm at home!" foolishly thinking he had called to check up on me, but he was calling to ask where the flashlights and LED lanterns were.

"It's just easy for me to anticipate his needs," I say to Anita, "and he inspires me. I've learned so much from him."

"Oh, honey." She tsk-tsks. "You're worse off than I thought. Well, I have to make some calls. Lovely to see you."

I refuse to apologize for this crush I have on my boss. It makes my job more fun and bearable. Except for the times when I wish he'd grab me and kiss me and he never does that—but no job is perfect. He's a proper boss, and it just makes me like him more. I have no idea why I thought of Matt McGovern again when Anita mentioned needing an anchor. I could never really like a guy like that. I might like to do very specific things with a guy like that, but nothing more.

When I let myself into the converted loft, I can hear Miles Davis on the house speakers, which means Sebastian's in the zone, and I see my friend Tommy's shoes by the front door, which means he's here modeling for him. It means that this is going to be a great day because Sebastian will be in a good mood when he takes a break and I get to see my best friend, whom I don't see enough of anymore because he lives in Brooklyn now, and while I may love *being in* Brooklyn, I hate *going to* Brooklyn. I would sooner donate one of my kidneys to him than spend almost two hours of my precious free time commuting to and from his borough and my place. That's one of the reasons I got him this job. The other is that he's a perfect fit for this project that Sebastian is working on.

It's a series of mixed-media paintings that bring together the urban club scene of his youth and the rural landscape that moves him now (it's the landscape paintings that earned him the bonkers money). It's meant to subtly convey a disconnect between these two worlds, with the human figure in distress, fractured and slightly out of focus in the foreground, the natural landscape stunning but disappearing in the background. Visually, it works on many levels, but thematically, it seems to be slowly ripping apart Sebastian's soul for some reason. Which is why I feel so protective of him right now. He pays me for emotional support as well as administrative.

After removing my shoes and going to the office that I share with Sebastian, I check the messages on the landline to make sure there isn't anything urgent to attend to and then shuffle over to the studio to take a peek. The door is wide open, and I hold my breath as I watch my boss sketch Tommy on the 40x40-inch canvas that I stretched and primed for him yesterday. Sebastian isn't classically handsome, with his slightly crooked nose from a teenage street fight (so he says), and his thin lips that are almost always pursed in contemplation. It's the sharp steel blue eyes that grab you, take you in whole, deconstruct you, and then put you back together into something simple and beautiful in a way that only he can see. His light brown hair is just above chin length and shaggy in the way that only a two-hundred-dollar haircut can be shaggy. It's the most artsy-looking thing about him, other than his black-rimmed glasses. When he isn't working, which is rarely, he looks like a really sexy cool accountant. But more importantly, he is a genius artist who works harder than anyone I know, and I've never known anyone so inspiring.

To be in the presence of such great talent and discipline is stimulating but also humbling. I'm grateful for it. I don't remember the exact moment when I went from being a dreamer to a realist, but it was within a week of working for Sebastian Smith. And I don't mean that in a bad way. It's how I imagine it would feel when you go to the Grand Canyon. To be in awe of something so much greater than you but also grateful to be able to experience it in person. So many dreamers become realists when they meet their idols and realize they're assholes. I became one when I met my idol and realized I'm not as good as he is at painting, plain and simple. But I am a lot better than him at doing almost everything else.

I manage to turn my gaze from Sebastian to my friend, who is sitting on a tall stool, slouching, dressed in a slim-fitting gray shirt and jeans. He's posing like a sad, pensive young man. This sight is hilarious to me because while he may be brilliant, Tommy is the most physically active and naturally upbeat person I have ever known.

"If you stand there staring any longer, I'm going to have to start charging you," Tommy says without moving his head and knowing perfectly well it wasn't him I've been staring at.

I laugh and cover my mouth.

"Oh hello there," Sebastian says, smiling but without looking away from the canvas. "I was wondering when you'd get here."

"I didn't want to disrupt your flow. I got the watercolor paper from Anita. It's on your desk."

"Oh great, thank you. Hey, before you get settled in, I forgot to ask you to go to that store in Chinatown to get those bamboo calligraphy brushes I like. One of each size."

Fuck. I was so ready to hunker down at the desk. "The red sable?"

"Yeah, and the goat hair-nylon mix. To tide me over until the ones you ordered from China are delivered. I'm finding it really relaxing to play around with ink and watercolors when I need a break."

"Sure. Anything else you can think of before I leave?"

He finally glances over at me, and I swear his eyes light up for a second as he scans the length of me in my blouse and jeans. "Your hair is different."

I can see Tommy grinning like the devil and manage to ignore him as well as the humiliating flutter in my chest as I run my fingers through my hair. "I just… I just parted it on a different side today, I think."

"It makes your features look more striking. Isn't that interesting." He smiles appreciatively. "Oh, if you get the chance, maybe you can pick us up some of those steamed dumplings for lunch." He turns back to his canvas.

"I was just going to suggest that."

"That's why you're the best," he says.

"That's why you're my dumpling!" sings Tommy.

After returning from Chinatown, we had a quick early lunch break, and then I returned calls, worked on Sebastian's schedule for the summer, did some RSVPing, and worked on his expense report for the first quarter. It's almost five when Sebastian comes into the office and grandly declares that I can go home for the day, now that he's temporarily done with Tommy. His hair is really messy and his face is tense, and I can tell he wants to be alone.

"Okay. Good day?"

He sighs. "Decent day. Started out good, and then…" He collapses onto the sofa by his desk. "I need to look through the pictures I took yesterday. Tomorrow, when you get in, can you start on a list of venues for a gathering? I feel like throwing a party for my city friends. Nothing huge, maybe a hundred people? Not right away, maybe a couple of months from now."

"Yeah, definitely. That's great! Have a good night. Your updated schedule is on your iPad."

He nods and rubs his face vigorously with his hands. "Perfect. Thank you. Good night."

Normally, if Tommy weren't here, he'd probably start showing me the pictures on his camera and waxing poetic about the Hudson Valley, but he just smiles at me and then reaches for the cell phone on his desk. And so, I'm dismissed.

"Okay, he's obviously a genius," my friend says once we're outside, "and he's definitely a sexy motherfucker who is very fond of you, but I really think your vagina deserves to have way more fun than you're allowing it to have at this point in your life. I mean, let the poor thing loose on Manhattan every now and then! Like *Ferris Bueller's Day Off* for your pussy. I want to see that thing drive around in a stolen Ferrari and sing 'Twist and Shout' on a parade float!"

Tommy Blank, ladies and gentlemen. The 27-year-old gay pretty boy potty mouth who has been my best friend since we were at Bennington. He looks like Zac Efron, if

Zac Efron didn't give a shit about how he looked. Tommy has so many talents and interests that he's not capable of being truly successful at any of them, but he gets by and he is doing a lot more than me and having a lot more fun than I am. Like, a lot more.

For instance, right now we're walking down the sidewalk away from Sebastian's place, and he is talking to me while texting someone else and maintaining eye contact with me the whole time. That's one of his talents. Envisioning an extravagant life for my lady bits is another.

"I don't think my vagina is licensed to drive in the state of New York."

"I'm just saying that if Sebastian Smith won't fuck you—"

"Shhh!" I look around to make sure my boss isn't behind us, as if he'd quietly follow us around instead of calling Ethan Hawke to talk about jazz or whatever the hell they talk about.

Tommy lowers his voice a tiny bit. "If he won't have sex with you, then why aren't you having sex with someone else?"

I truly have no idea why I immediately think of my new temporary neighbor again. "I do have sex. With other people."

"When?"

"Up until several months ago."

"*Several months ago?* That's like three decades in New York time."

"It's just a phase. Sebastian's been extra busy and stressed-out lately, and I had to get all his tax stuff in order for his accountant, and it's just easier for me if I can focus on him all the time."

"Wow."

"Professionally, I mean."

"You're a professional obsessed stalker lady. So modern! So, soooo sad. Hey, what are you planning to go home and watch tonight? Because first let me invite you to my thing, which I promise you will be nine thousand times more exciting." He pauses for effect and holds a hand up, daring me to picture the evening he is about to describe.

I hold back on telling him that nothing could be more exciting to me than watching Season Two of *Sherlock* for the fifth time and starting on the list that Sebastian asked me to make. But I still want my friends to invite me to things, even though I never actually want to go them.

"First, we grab a Matcha green tea soft serve in Little Italy…"

"Damn you." I love me some green tea ice cream. But not as much as I love Benedict Cumberbatch and list-making. "Go on."

"Which we consume on the way to the Lower East Side, where we meet Portia and Damian—and whoever he's currently fucking—at Blue Ribbon for sushi because it's her birthday."

I nearly trip myself up and make a sound that's something like *NUH!* because dammit, I love Blue Ribbon sushi.

"And Damian's paying for everyone. And then we sidle on over to Garfunkel's for drinks—super chill room that you would love—"

"Okay, now I'm already tired."

"There are bookshelves lining the walls of Garfunkel's, with real books on them! You can take a nap there, and you'll need to because then we Uber to Williamsburg for a warehouse party, where two super-hot LA guys are deejaying and one of them might be straight!"

"Nope."

"Gah!" He throws his hands up in the air. "I almost had you. I should have just told you about sushi and then kidnapped you for the rest of the night."

"I just want to be mentally functional for work tomorrow. Man, I miss being an irresponsible, entitled idiot."

"You wore it well, my friend."

"I love you." I hug him and kiss him on his cheek. "Thank you for the invitation, but my bed is calling me."

"Your bed is calling you a boring loser!" he yells out to me as I skip away from him.

While I'm waiting for the train, I read the text that Tommy sent me as soon as I left him: ***FYI your ass looks hot in those jeans and also you need to get laid like yesterday but also you probably should just have a boyfriend since you're already so lame anyway, just sayin'***

He's not wrong, but he's also not exactly right. I send back an emoji of a squirrel holding a nut, just to confuse him and because my train is here.

I'm so excited to go home, not just to get into bed and watch Netflix but because I may get to see that beautiful neighbor I met yesterday. And her grumpy lawyer roommate.

CHAPTER 4
BERNADETTE

Walking up Broadway, once I'm near 85th, my stupid heart skips a beat when I see a tall man in gray step outside the corner store, holding a small paper bag. He is nodding his head and smiling, in a way that suggests he is thinking "no" and "I'm in hell." Hot on his tail is a hot lady in a business suit who's holding up her phone at him. She is either trying to take a picture of him or trying to get his number. Her eyes are intense, like she would knock him over the head and haul him into the back of a van if she could.

When he turns and sees me crossing the street toward him, he does a double-take and then waves at me. "Hey, babe!" he says.

I look behind myself, because surely I am not "babe."

"Bernadette!" he says, sounding annoyed. He waves me over and watches me impatiently as I slow my pace and approach him warily. "Finally," he says. "I was just telling Carrie here that I was getting worried about you. We were supposed to meet here fifteen minutes ago." He raises an eyebrow at me, barely perceptible, as he wraps a muscled arm around my shoulder and kisses me on the top of my head.

What. Is. Happening?

He squeezes my upper arm.

"Right! Sorry. The train was running late. I forgot to text you."

"Okay, well, it was nice meeting you, Matt. Maybe we can get that drink another time." Carrie doesn't even acknowledge me. She just backs away slowly without taking her eyes off Matt. Probably taking a series of mental pictures to store in her spank bank.

His arm is still around my shoulder as he guides me down 85th toward our building. I can feel that his muscles have relaxed. Mine have not.

What's weird is, despite the jarring effect his stupid gorgeousness had on me yesterday, I had forgotten exactly what he looked like until seeing him again today. When I thought about him, I only remembered the spazzy way I felt in the stillness of his presence, his deep voice, the way he carefully budgeted his words, and the way he swept my hair to the side before unzipping my freaking dress.

He looks back over his shoulder, decides the coast is clear, and releases me.

We say nothing as we walk another half a block beside each other.

Walking alongside him, I'm so aware of how tall he is. Now that he's unencumbered from duffel bags and guitar cases, I can see that he moves with the strength, confidence, and grace of an athlete. When he takes out his key to open the front door of our building, I can't stop staring at his hand. He notices me staring at it.

When he holds the door open for me, I ask him if he goes for manicures.

"No" is all he says.

"There's no shame in it. A lot of men in this town do, nowadays."

"I'm aware of that."

I don't bother checking my mail today. I just want to keep walking beside this strangely quiet tall man with the beautiful hand that was very recently touching my shoulder. I have been waiting for him to explain what just happened, and I don't want to have to ask.

"So, what is there to do around here that's fun and interesting?" he finally says as we round the corner to the next flight of stairs.

"I recommend ordering in and watching Netflix with headphones."

"Sounds about right."

"Being boring at home is kind of my thing."

"I'm sure you're really good at it."

"Hey. I'm really busy out and about all day. In my experience, people don't like it when I try to take a nap at a bar or ask deejays to turn the music down, so I just go home."

"You don't have to explain. It's fine."

"Really? *It's fine?* You think it's fine? This is such great news—I was hoping you'd approve, and now I know that you do! Yay!"

"Wow. You're really good at being sarcastic too."

"Thanks, I really value your opinion about that also. Who was that Carrie lady?" *Damn you for not telling me and making me ask—you're such an asshole.*

"I don't really know. She just started talking to me in the market."

"And she asked you out?"

"Yeah. Why do you look so surprised?"

"She met you just now and then asked you to drinks?"

"Yes."

"Does that happen to you often?"

He shrugs. "Sometimes. I'm usually out with my girlfriend so it doesn't matter."

And there it is.

"I mean…" He hesitates on the step for a second before proceeding. His stone-cold-fox face goes stone cold. "I mean I *was* usually out with my ex-girlfriend."

"Oh. Sorry." And now I'm realizing that's why he's moved into Dolly's place temporarily, with just his dog, some clothes, a guitar, and a really bad mood. Lord. I'm so single, it doesn't even occur to me that other people still have relationships that begin and end. "Is that why you need a new place?"

He ignores my question.

Fine. We won't talk about that.

"So what's it like having Dolly Kemp as an aunt? Must be fun."

He seems to appreciate the abrupt change of subject. "It's a nonstop party."

"I like her."

"She likes you too."

"She does?"

"She used to talk about you quite a bit. How you're an artist and you're a good, responsible, quiet neighbor who waters her plants when she's out of town. The way she talked about you, I thought you were at least seventy."

"God, I wish! I'd love to be seventy. Maybe then people would finally stop judging me for staying home at night."

He wrinkles his brow at me and then smirks. "You're pretty weird, huh?"

"Only to people who are either really straight-laced and narrow-minded or outrageously extroverted."

"I'm none of those things."

I laugh. *"Oh really?"*

"You're the one who's straight-laced and narrow-minded."

"Um no. I don't feel the need to do extracurricular things just because other people are doing them. I'm a free spirit who happens to be very practical. It's the best of both worlds, really."

I frown at him, bracing myself for a wry comment, but he just nods his head and says, "Yeah. You're right."

I'm right?

"You're lucky."

I'm lucky?

"Most of the talented people I know are a mess."

I'm talented?

"How do you know I'm talented?"

We reach our floor, and instead of answering me like a normal properly socialized human being, he says, "I'll talk to you later. I gotta walk Daisy."

Daisy is shuffling around inside the apartment, making a "yarf" noise, and sounds like she's going a little nuts. I couldn't hear her doing it a few seconds ago, so she probably heard him and got excited. Or…maybe she heard me and got excited? It's a possibility. A girl can dream.

When he opens the door, I get a glimpse of her. She jumps at Matt's legs, snorting and snuffling, but then she sees me and she looks so happy.

"Hi, Daisy!"

Matt pulls her inside, mumbling that he has to get the leash on her, and then shuts the door.

"Bye, asshole," I mutter.

"Later, weirdo," he says from just behind the door.

About forty minutes later, I'm in my sweat pants and T-shirt, about to make popcorn for dinner, when I hear a knock at my door.

"It's Daisy," says Matt. "And dessert."

"*What?*" I whisper to myself as I shuffle over to the door, barefoot. "Hang on," I say. I fiddle with the deadbolt and yank the door open. There's something going on with the door hinge, and it always takes a few seconds to open and shut my door now.

"The door sticks," I explain to him.

"You should get that fixed."

"Ya think?"

"How long has it been like that?"

"A few weeks. I don't know."

"That's really dangerous. What if there's a fire and you have to get out in a hurry?"

"I told Marco about it, but he has a knee issue right now. It's hard for him to get to our floor."

"That's ridiculous."

He walks in past me, carrying Daisy and two takeout bags.

"No, please, come in."

Daisy is licking her lips and wiggling her entire body at me.

"Hi, baby! Hello, beautiful girl!"

Matt rolls his eyes as he unleashes her and puts her on the floor. He looks surprised that she is so happy to see me. I sit down on the floor, cross-legged, so she can wiggle around on me.

"I brought you a gluten-free carrot cake. To thank you for earlier." He places the smaller brown bag on my coffee table and strolls around the living room.

"Earlier? You mean when you called me *babe* and put your arms around me instead of just being a dick to that lady?"

"Yeah. So where do you do your painting?"

"Oh, I just get into my time machine and travel back to college. I've been too busy to do any paintings of my own since I became an assistant. I mean, I do sketches and sometimes little watercolors."

"Do you paint for someone else?"

"No! I just do prep work. But it's mostly administrative stuff that keeps me busy. For my boss."

"You don't paint anymore? That's a shame."

"I will. Eventually. That was always the plan." I stand up, and Daisy immediately sits at my feet, staring up at me. So cute.

"Save money so you have time to paint?"

"Yeah. I mean, I was hoping I'd have time to paint while I was working, but…Sebastian's got a lot going on and he depends on me, so…"

"Sebastian, huh?"

"Sebastian Smith. He's the artist I work for. That's how I met Dolly. She's a big supporter of his work."

"I've heard of him."

"Yeah?"

"Sure. I've seen his work at MOMA. He had a big sale a few years back."

"Huge sale. Twenty million at Christies. That was right before I started working for him."

"That his real last name? Smith?"

"Actually, his last name is Paris, but he figured people would think *that* was a fake name."

"Uh-huh. And how long have you been in love with Sebastian Smith?" he asks without even looking at me. Like fucking Sherlock Holmes.

"What? I'm not in love with him."

"Those inflections in your voice when you say his name and talk about him tell me otherwise."

"Oh what—were you trained to read people in law school or something?"

"Yes."

"Well. You're lucky you graduated, because you're not very good at it."

"I am lucky. And you're very talented. These are all yours on the walls here?" He gestures at the paintings that line every wall in my living room.

"Yes. Well, that collage is a gift from my friend, and another friend did all the framed photos. And that watercolor is my mom's work and the acrylic is my dad. But yeah. The oil paintings are me. Thank you." I don't know why it makes me so nervous to watch as he studies my work, but it does.

"Your parents are artists too?"

"Yes."

"Interesting."

"Yeah. It's a long story that I don't really want to get into right now."

"Good. I wasn't going to ask."

"Great."

"I really like the one of yours that's in Dolly's guest room."

"You do? Thank you."

"Why do you look so surprised again?"

"Because you just complimented me again."

"And you're not used to getting compliments?"

"Not from you."

"You can't be used to anything yet. You just met me."

He sees a painting on the fireplace mantle, leaning against the mirror. A Vermont winter landscape. It's the forest's edge behind my parents' house.

"I like this. This is good." His deep voice is so quiet all of a sudden, but I still hear him very clearly.

"Thank you."

He continues to stare at it, and I wish I could take a picture of him, the way he's looking at my painting. It's like he recognizes a soul mate or something. I think I'd either cry or run away screaming if someone ever looked at *me* like that.

"I want this," he says. Spoken like a guy who knows what he wants and is used to getting it.

"It's not for sale."

"Everything's for sale."

"Not everything."

"You painted this to keep for yourself?"

"Not exactly. I painted it because I *had* to paint it."

"Maybe you had to paint it because I need to have it."

I don't know why I'm feeling such resistance to the idea of this guy owning my painting, but I do. "Explain to me why you need to have it."

He stares at it, slowly shakes his head. "I can't. I just do."

"Well. I appreciate that, but I need to know that it's going to the right home."

"You'll never make a living as an artist if you care who buys your work."

"So I've been told."

"I'll give you two hundred for it."

Two hundred for a piece of my soul. "Why?"

"Three hundred."

My face twitches. Three hundred dollars is a lot for a small oil painting by an unknown artist. No one has ever wanted to buy this one before. But it still doesn't feel right to sell it to him.

"Does it have a name?"

I stare up at him and blink, wide-eyed.

"What?"

"Nobody's ever asked me that before."

"And I've never asked anyone if their painting has a name before. Three-fifty. But only if you tell me the name."

"It has a secret name. But it's still not for sale. But thank you."

"For what?"

"For wanting it."

His gaze briefly turns from my painting to my face, scans my body, and then turns his attention back to my painting. "That was definitely the weirdest and least successful negotiation I've ever engaged in. Don't tell anyone about this."

And with that, he heads for the front door, picking up Daisy to take her with him. When he tries to open the door, of course, it sticks. "You really need to get this fixed."

Like it's my fault. Like I made the hinges uneven on purpose. "I know that. I've told Marco five times. Just lift up the doorknob while you turn it and pull."

He shakes his head, pulls the door open, and leaves without saying goodbye.

. . .

Before I've finished licking the last of the cream cheese frosting from the fork I used to attack the carrot cake, there's another knock at my front door.

"It's not Daisy," Matt says from the hallway.

I go to open the door, and Matt stands to the side, revealing Marco the super.

"Look who I found."

Marco is only slightly out of breath as he carries his toolbox in, shrugging and waving his hand at his knee. "I'm sorry—I'm sorry I didn't get around to it yet, okay? My knee, it's hard to do the stairs with this knee, okay? I'm sorry."

"It's fine. Thank you for coming now. Would you like something to drink?"

"No thanks. I'll get to work here. Should be done in no time. No big deal. I'll take care of it, okay?" He's looking at Matt, not at me.

"Good idea," he says.

"That'd be great, thank you," I say in a sing-song voice, overcompensating for Matt's gruffness but also trying to hide how terribly turned-on I am right now. After being the girl who gets things done for a man all day long, I feel like a princess right now. An appreciative, secretly horny princess in sweat pants.

I have never felt so many different things for one person in such a short period of time.

I probably have big red pulsating hearts for pupils right now, because Matt gives me a look that says, *Calm down, kid. I got a guy to come upstairs and do his job for you. This isn't a marriage proposal.*

He goes back to inspecting my artwork, crossing his arms over his chest and planting himself in front of the mixed media piece I did in my last year of school.

"You go to art school?"

"Visual Arts at Bennington."

"*Bennington?*" He spits out the word. This doesn't surprise me.

It's a relief that he's being a jerk again. It's easier to want to slap him than kiss him. "Let me guess where you went… Harvard."

"Incorrect. Didn't even apply there."

I hate being wrong. I narrow my eyes at him, like I'm turning on my psychic laser beams. He seems like a West Coast guy. I'm feeling Southern California, but he also seems like the kind of guy who doesn't want to be what you expect him to be. "Stanford." I know nothing about law schools, but I repeat it again, very self-assured. "Stanford Law."

For one second his face betrays him. He seems impressed. "Yeah. I went to SLS. Care to guess where I got my Bachelor's?"

"USC."

He blinks once and then nods.

I mentally high-five myself because I'm awesome.

Marco is mumbling to himself over by the front door, talking to his cordless screwdriver. I silently will him to take his time fixing things, because I want to continue blowing the esquire's mind over here.

"You should really be painting."

And just like that, he has me feeling defensive again. *I know this.* Do people actually think I don't know that I should be painting? Every single atom of me tells me I should be painting every second of every day. I'm not going to have that conversation with him.

"I'll definitely get back to it. One day."

"How much do you have saved?"

"A fair amount."

"How much more do you think you need to save before you can quit working for that guy?"

"It's not just the money I save. I also get full benefits."

He arches an eyebrow.

"Not *that* kind of benefits. Health, pension, holiday bonus."

"Really? How much does he pay you?"

"Plenty."

"Six figures?"

"Not quite. Almost. Last year, with my Christmas bonus, it came close."

"Well. That is good money for an assistant job."

"Executive assistant."

"That too."

Marco is muttering happily to himself, packing up his toolbox. He turns to Matt, who is ignoring him, and then tells me, "All done. Fixed. Good as new. See?" He shuts the door and then opens it again.

"Thank you, Marco."

"Yeah. Sorry about how long it took. My knee gets better when the weather's good." He sighs and looks toward the stairs that he's going to have to go down. "Okay. Bye-bye."

"Have a good night, Marco."

Marco leaves, and I wait by the door because I'm ready for this other person to leave now too.

Matt walks slowly toward me and then pauses in front of me and says, "I think I'm drawn to that painting of the edge of the forest in winter because I'm from the West Coast and I'm so used to the ocean and sunlight."

"Interesting."

"Can I buy it from you now?"

"No. But you can come over and look at it whenever you want to. Within reason."

He smirks as he walks out. "Have a good night, then."

"Thank you. For getting him."

"Sure," he says. "See you around."

I shut my door, exhausted and so ready to be alone in bed with my Netflix.

And yet…

When I check my phone and see that my parents still haven't replied to the texts and emails I sent them yesterday, I know that I'm going to have one more infuriating conversation before this night is over. I'm going to call my parents. I'm going to call them and I'm going to make sure everything's okay, and then I'm going to hang up and it's all going to last one minute, maximum.

My parents are hippie artists who live on a farm in Vermont. They can't balance a checkbook, but their chakras are always aligned. Legend has it they met in New York in the eighties when they'd both come here to party hard and sell out big-time. Almost as soon as they fell in love and married, they decided to move to the farm that he inherited, to make love and art and a tiny person who would eventually grow up to be the opposite of everything they now stand for.

Even though I can feel my chest constricting, I call their landline. My parents have a landline because the cell phone reception is so spotty out there, although there's usually only about a twenty percent chance anyone will answer it. They are stubbornly off the grid, even though their only child is vehemently on the grid, in a different state.

"Hello?" an unfamiliar man's voice answers on the third ring.

"Hi, this is Bernadette. Who's this?"

"Hi, it's Elijah. Bernadette who?"

"Bernadette Farmer. I'm Steve and Leslie's daughter. Can I talk to them? Are they around?"

"Yeah hey, I'm the artist in residence here now. I've heard a lot about you. I really dig your painting over here in the living room. It really speaks to me."

"Cool, thanks. So can I speak to my parents?"

"Yeah, hang on."

Okay, so at least they're alive and still living on the farm and the electricity is still on.

"Bernie?" My mother always yells into the phone, and yet I immediately relax when I first hear her voice.

"Hi, Mom."

"Bernie, it is so amazing that you're calling me right now, because I just visualized it five minutes ago."

"Awesome. Well, you guys didn't respond to my texts or emails, so I'm just making sure you're okay."

"Oh, honey, you have to stop sending texts and emails! It's so passive-aggressive!"

And this is why I don't like to call my parents.

"Tell her, Steve."

I hear my dad pick up the other phone. "Tell who what?"

"Hi, Dad."

"Bernie Baby? She called us? Our daughter willingly called us on the telephone?"

"Tell her, Steve. Texting is the communication equivalent of that powdered orange cheese that comes in those boxes of mac and cheese that you used to beg us to buy you. It's not real emotional food."

"Okay, well, I'm glad to hear that you guys are alive and not homeless, and I have to go now."

"No, you don't, Bernie. Just talk to us. Just sit down, take three deep breaths, visualize connecting your spine to the earth and your crown to the skies with a golden shaft of light, and open up your lungs and your heart and tell us how you feel and why you needed to call us."

"I mean, obviously it's because you visualized it five minutes ago."

"Sarcasm is the lowest form of wit," my dad says. "Oscar Wilde said that."

"Actually, the full quote is: 'Sarcasm is the lowest form of wit but the highest form of intelligence.'"

"She's right, Steve. She may be emotionally closed-off, but she has a mind like a steel trap."

"A mind and a gift that's being wasted on secretarial work. Just tell us if you're painting at all."

"I'm always doing sketches." This is true. I always have my sketchbook with me. I'm always sketching, but I just keep drawing different versions of the forest's edge, over and over. It's like I can't get past it. That painting that Matt is so taken with is the last one I did before I started working for Sebastian. The real reason it's not for sale yet is that part of me is afraid I'll never paint another one. "Don't worry about me. I just wanted to make sure everything's okay and that you remembered to pay your bills and all that."

"We made a trip to the bank yesterday to pay them, thank you."

"Can you please just let me set up automatic payments?"

"Just as soon as hell freezes over," my dad grumbles.

I swear, my parents are so cool and liberal in so many ways, but they do not trust the Internet or most forms of technology, and I don't think they ever will.

"It's just that if you keep paying your bills late, your credit rating could get really low."

"Fuck the credit rating. I'm not letting some bank tell me what I'm all about. We have all we need here, always have, always will. You would remember that if you ever came to visit."

"Do you have a boyfriend yet, angel? We need to see your face so we can have a real *converge-sation*!"

"Okay, great. I'm going to wire some money to your account. Love you. Bye!" I hang up. I hang up on my parents because I love them and I want to keep loving them. From over here.

They've been forcing me to open up and talk about my feelings for as long as I can remember, when they of all people should understand that I prefer to convey my feelings through painting. Or at least, I used to.

When I finally crawl into bed, I can hear Matt McGovern's guitar through the vent. I don't recognize the tune he's playing, but it's pretty and soothing, and even though I was so worked-up a minute ago, it calms me down immediately. For the first time in ages, I drift off to sleep without even turning on Netflix.

CHAPTER 5
MATT

My twelve o'clock meeting ran long, and it isn't until just after one that I can finally check my phone for an update from the dog daycare. It's Daisy's second day there, and the owner promised to send me a photo of her. I go straight to that text, ignoring all of the work emails and group texts from my friends, and there she is. My girl. Cavorting with a Cocker Spaniel and an Australian Shepherd on a lawn. She looks so happy to be outside, it makes my heart hurt.

I text back a quick message to thank the dog caretaker, when I hear my protégé, Lloyd, say the thing that I've just been thinking.

"That's the first time I've seen you smile in ages."

I immediately look up and frown at him. I don't like knowing that people are aware of my moods. It's not like I'm surprised—I know I've been a moody little shit this week. I just don't want people to notice. Because when people notice, they tend to ask questions. And I don't have answers. No, that's not true. I just don't like the answers I'll have to give.

"You had lunch yet?" he asks. Lloyd isn't in my department. He's in the engineering department of the leading ad tech company I work at. He and hundreds of other math and computer science geeks work to create a simple platform for corporations and individuals to market themselves on whatever channel, format, and screen they choose to. My department provides legal support for global commercial/client transactions, data and licensing agreements, internal contracts, as well as strategic legal advice and counsel for the sales teams. It's a lot of work, but being on an in-house general counsel team for one company is a sweet, cushy job compared to working at a law firm. I know because I've done both. I've come to decide that I actually prefer working with nerds than other lawyers. In particular, I've somehow formed a friendship of sorts with Lloyd because he keeps coming to me asking for dating advice.

As if I'm some kind of expert.

He's several years younger than I am, and I always wanted a younger brother. I suggest grabbing a bite outside. Our office has all the amenities we've come to expect from leading tech companies: top-notch healthy cafeteria, gym and yoga studio, ping-pong table. But seeing Daisy frolicking outside makes me want to get some fresh air too. Maybe I'm not pissed about Vanessa. Maybe I just need more oxygen.

Nope, I'm pissed about Vanessa.

Being outside and seeing New Yorkers wandering around and eating lunch on benches and steps while gazing at cherry blossoms just makes me mad, as we head toward our usual lunch spot.

"So, that girl I told you about last month, the one I was texting with for a few weeks?"

"The one from the wedding?" Good. Let's talk about Lloyd.

"Yeah. That never ended up going anywhere. We went back and forth making plans to meet up, but she kept having to reschedule, and then finally she told me she got back together with her boyfriend."

I stop walking for a second. Lloyd looks back at me. I don't know why that revelation makes me so sad and angry, but it does. We continue on. "Sorry to hear about that, man. I know you liked her."

"Yeah, well. So, you think I should just let it go?"

"Yes. Definitely. Let it go."

"Yeah." He looks over at me. "Everything okay with you?"

"I'm just hungry."

"I've noticed that you've been working out at the office gym this week instead of the one you usually go to with Vanessa..."

Hearing someone else say her name is jarring and grating on my nerves.

I grunt a noncommittal reply.

"And you've been...not happy lately. Stop me if I'm overstepping."

"You are."

"It's just if you want to talk to me, you can. I'm always blabbing to you about my love life or lack thereof, but this should be a two-way street."

"We broke up."

He exhales as he pushes his glasses up the bridge of his nose. "Wow. Sorry. That's... So you don't live with her anymore?"

"I moved out."

"Really? Wow. Where are you staying?"

"I was at a hotel in SoHo for a few days. Now I'm at my aunt's place until I find more permanent arrangements."

"Yeah? My cousin's a rental agent if you need a good one. He's not a scammer."

I have no idea why Bernadette Farmer's face pops into my head when I think about how I don't feel like dealing with real estate just yet. "I'm still deciding if I should rent or own next, actually. Thanks, though."

"Okay, let me know." He scrunches up his face. "Well, now that you're single, I feel obligated to tell you that I have a female friend from college who wants to meet you. I brought her to the Christmas party last year, but she said that seeing how gorgeous your girlfriend was just made her want to cry. She wants to marry you and have your babies, actually. I'm ninety percent certain she won't even kill me when she finds out I told you that."

I really don't appreciate that I get some phantom whiff of Bernadette's fragrance all of a sudden. Now I'm not only picturing her face but also her perky breasts. They aren't particularly large, but they seem so…friendly. And now I'm thinking about the outline of her nipples beneath the fabric of that dress she was wearing when I met her and even under that T-shirt she wore when I was in her apartment. And now my dick is getting hard while I'm talking to Lloyd on the way to lunch.

That woman needs to stay in her apartment and out of my thoughts.

I clench my fists, finally remembering to respond to Lloyd. "Thanks, but I don't think I'm ready for that yet."

"Okay, let me know. She would probably also be happy being your sex slave."

"You probably shouldn't go making offers like that on behalf of other people."

"It's just that she literally said that after seeing you at the party."

I pat Lloyd on the back. "Nice to know." We are across the street from the café, and I see an empty table outside that I want. I'm about to step out into the crosswalk, but I realize Lloyd has stopped in his tracks.

"Whoa," he says.

I follow his gaze across the street and get a weird feeling in my gut when I see what—or rather *who*—he's staring at. It has been a couple of days since I saw her in her apartment. Seeing her out in the wild is strange and exhilarating, and I fucking hate how pretty she looks with her hair up. She's wearing a long black dress with a jean jacket and carrying her huge tote bag as well as a shopping bag, standing on the sidewalk outside our destination. She looks at me hesitantly, like she doesn't know if she should walk off in the other direction or wait there to say hello.

"That girl is," Lloyd says under his breath, "my type."

She is definitely not my *type* is what I'm thinking. Although I can't really say what type she is, other than jarring and exhilarating to the point of aggravation. But I say nothing, and I am trying to will her, with my expression, to run away in the opposite direction. Instead of complying, as usual, she chooses to do the very thing that annoys me. She grins, plants her feet on the ground, crosses her arms, and waits for me to cross the street.

I just shake my head at her as we advance toward her.

Lloyd sighs audibly as he looks back at me. "She's

staring at you. Of course." He notices me frowning back at her. "Wait—do you know her?"

"Barely," I mutter.

"Well, hello there," she says, arms still crossed, as if she's been waiting for me for an hour. The black dress accentuates her creamy skin, and the sun lights up her reddish-brown hair. It makes her even more striking than usual, despite the casual outfit. I can't take my eyes off those damn rosy lips that look like they've been kissed hard, for hours. I get mad, wondering if some other guy has been kissing those lips—maybe her boss.

"Hi there," I say, clearing my throat.

"Fancy seeing *you* here. This where you work?"

"Not right on this sidewalk exactly, but yeah, a few blocks from here."

For some reason, she appears to be pleased that she's evoked a sarcastic utterance from me. "I was just running an errand for my boss." She finally notices Lloyd staring at her. "Hi," she says with a smile.

"Hi," he says, holding his hand out. "I'm Lloyd."

She shakes hands with him. "I'm Bernadette."

"Bernadette," Lloyd muses, like it's a small song. "Nice. Hi."

Christ, Lloyd, you already said that. "Lloyd and I work together," I say out loud but not to anyone in particular. "Bernadette lives in the apartment next to the one I'm currently staying in."

"Oh, you're neighbors?"

"For now," she and I both clarify at the same time.

She laughs. I don't.

There is a long, awkward pause in conversation, and all of the street noises of Manhattan can't seem to silence the voice in my head that is yelling at me to invite her to lunch.

I start to walk past her as I say, “Well, we’re going to have lunch and I have a meeting in an hour, so…”

“Right,” she says, shaking her head and laughing. “Me too. See ya.”

Lloyd stammers, “Hey, you should—we should…”

“See you around, Farmer,” I say, ignoring the looks I get from both my temporary neighbor and my work friend.

Over lunch, I make a brief and convincing case to Lloyd that Bernadette is nuts and that she is obsessed with her boss and not a good candidate for him to date for many reasons.

I list all of the reasons for his benefit, not for my own. It’s not like I need to remind myself of all the reasons why I wouldn’t and shouldn’t date her. I’d just rather talk about that than explain to Lloyd why Vanessa and I broke up.

CHAPTER 6
BERNADETTE

What. An. Asshole.

It was so sunny before I encountered him, but as soon as I decided to stop to talk to him, it clouded over.

I stomp around lower Manhattan for half an hour before finally settling on a place to eat lunch, fuming about how rude Matt McGovern is, and then stomp back to Sebastian's place and settle into his office to stare at my laptop without typing anything because I have so much anger coursing through my veins. At least, I think it's anger. It might be an infuriating cocktail of anger, confusion, and horniness. But the horniness has nothing to do with the fact that he looked so fucking great in his sleek black shirt and jeans and everything to do with the fact that I need to get laid. In general. By no one in particular. Especially not by one particular person who happens to be living next door to me, one who is a total asshole.

I briefly flip through my mental Rolodex of past and potential sexual partners. It takes all of two seconds because my past partners are either now partnered up with someone else or have moved out of state or got too clingy for comfort and I swore off seeing them again. The only potential partner I can think of is my boss, and there's barely any real potential.

Sebastian is in his studio with the door closed. Tommy is done posing for him, and I probably won't see him for a while because he just started rehearsing an off-Broadway play. But I pick up my phone, planning to text him to tell him I'm available to meet up tonight if he wants, because he is an awesome wingman and he will definitely help Mama get some.

I almost swallow my tongue when I see that I have an e-mail notification from "iammattmcgovernsemail@gmail.com."

TO: BERNADETTE FARMER <thisisbernadettefarmer@gmail.com>
FROM: MATT MCGOVERN (personal) <iammattmcgovernsemail@gmail.com>

Subject: Hi.

Sorry if I was rude earlier.

That's it. That's all it says. I scroll down to see if I'm missing something, like an explanation as to why he was rude earlier, or why he's a rude person in general, or perhaps an emoji of a sad face, but nope. That's the message.

Without hesitation, I click "Reply."

. . .

TO: MATT MCGOVERN
FROM: BERNADETTE FARMER

Subject: That's nice.

I assume that by "earlier" you are referring to every interaction we've had since we met.
I thought you said you had a meeting to get to.
I'm sorry you felt the need to lie just to get out of having lunch with me.
I would have declined the invitation anyway.

TO: BERNADETTE FARMER
FROM: MATT MCGOVERN

Subject: Nice try

Already had the meeting. On FaceTime.
FYI, my protégé thought you were hot, and I was just trying to save you the annoyance of having him ogle you while you tried to eat your lunch.

TO: MATT MCGOVERN
FROM: BERNADETTE FARMER

Subject: Thanks?

What makes you think I'm not totally used to being ogled while I eat lunch?
There's usually a circle of adoring men around me while I shove salad into my mouth, so it's not like your protégé would have made me feel uncomfortable.
Also—who refers to another person as their protégé?
Maybe he just thinks of you as an old guy who needs some company.

TO: BERNADETTE FARMER
FROM: MATT MCGOVERN

Subject: I…

Deeply regret emailing you.

TO: MATT MCGOVERN
FROM: BERNADETTE FARMER

Subject: I deeply regret not running away when I saw you

Also…maybe I would have liked to get to know your so-called protégé. He was cute. If you were really trying to protect me from him, then maybe you should have waited for a sign from me that I *needed* to be protected from him.

TO: BERNADETTE FARMER
FROM: MATT MCGOVERN

Subject: I think I'm the one who needs protection

From your emails.
If you would like Lloyd's number or would like me to pass along your email address to him, it would be my great joy to make the connection for you.
He is a very bright young computer engineer. Despite his charmingly nerdy façade, his favorite music is hardcore techno, he is an enthusiastic user and lender of Adderall, and in his free time he enjoys wearing eyeliner and going to raves. The last girl he dated broke up with him because he has screaming fits in his sleep and kept giving her hickies.
You guys would make a super-cute couple.

TO: MATT MCGOVERN
FROM: BERNADETTE FARMER

Subject: I deeply regret responding to your email

<Devil Face Emoji>

I get no response after that. I keep checking my phone every ten seconds for the next half hour while trying to itemize Sebastian's receipts. I don't know if I'm mad at him for abruptly ending our back-and-forth email conversation or at myself for being so mad at him for abruptly ending our back-and-forth email conversation.

I decide that I'm mad at him for forcing me to send him another email in response to his lack of response.

TO: MATT MCGOVERN
FROM: BERNADETTE FARMER

Subject: RUDE

<Red Frowny Face Emoji>

TO: BERNADETTE FARMER
FROM: MATT MCGOVERN

Subject: NOT RUDE

I choose to never respond to messages with emojis in them.
I don't do emojis.
I never use emojis.
I don't like emojis.

TO: MATT MCGOVERN
FROM: BERNADETTE FARMER

Subject: WHUCK?!

That's like someone refusing to use abbreviations in the twentieth century.
I like emojis.
They save time, and you can judge a lot about a person by which emoji they decide to use in a situation.

TO: BERNADETTE FARMER
FROM: MATT MCGOVERN

Subject: I have plenty of other ways to judge people

If you'll excuse me, I also have many other emails to respond to and several other people to judge.
Have a great afternoon.

Asshole.

I can't stop myself from responding with a smiling cat emoji, but then I place my phone facedown on the desk and get back to work.

I honestly didn't think about Matt McGovern at all for the rest of the day, but once I'm back in my apartment, I can hear him next door. It sounds like he's tossing a toy down the hall and Daisy's running to fetch it and return it. I swear, if I only ever heard him through the vent, I would be under the impression that he's a totally sweet man. It's not like I can always hear what he's saying—in fact, most of the time I can't. But I can hear the tone of his voice when he's in bed, talking to Daisy, and he's so unabashedly loving ("Who's my girl? Who's my sweet, beautiful girl? Yes, *you're* my girl! I love you, sweet, crazy girl.") Last night I heard him play guitar and sing to her in a high pitch to make her howl along with him. *"Daisy, Daisy, give me your answer dooooo. I'm half crazy, all for the love of yooouuuu!"* It's all very charming and endearing. And so annoying that he shows absolutely no sign of being that sweet person at any other time.

I have now removed my soaking wet shoes and clothes (thank you, surprise windy thunderstorm!) and slid into my slippers and sleep shirt before hastily towel-drying my hair. Now I am padding around the kitchen, opening the refrigerator door and staring inside. I'm opening cupboards, staring inside. I'm opening up my food delivery app and staring at it before finally opening up the thing that I have been wanting to open up ever since my encounter with Matt earlier… A bottle of Pinot Noir.

It is well after eight, and I'm hungry, but I just want to go to my bedroom and listen to nineties angry-girl anthems while sipping wine and fuming about what a dick my temporary neighbor is.

Alanis Morissette has barely started ranting about why she's here to remind her ex of the mess he left when he went away, when all of a sudden there's a loud noise and I scream and everything goes dark and silent. I screamed a few weeks ago when it happened too. My heart is racing, but my brain already understands that it's a blackout from the storm.

Within seconds, I'm screaming again because there's

banging on my front door.

"You okay in there?" It's Matt.

I don't know what's more startling—the sudden power outage, the banging on my door, or the genuine concern in Matt's voice.

I shout out, "Yes! Be right there!" and then feel my way around for the flashlight that I keep in the drawer by my bed, making sure I don't grab my vibrator instead.

I pause before opening the door. "Are you still out there?"

"Yes," he says, as if that's a ridiculous question.

I open the door and see that he's holding Daisy, as well as his keys and cell phone, which he is using as a flashlight.

"Awww, hi, Daisy!"

I shine my light in Matt's face to illuminate his frown.

"I heard you scream like a maniac," he says.

"That was not a maniacal scream. I was just surprised, that's all."

"If you say so."

"Did you come by to issue a formal noise complaint?"

"I came to make sure you're okay."

"I am fan-fucking-tastic, thanks."

"Fucking A. Do you know where my aunt keeps her flashlights and candles?" he asks.

"No. Would you like to come in?"

He sighs and enters, waiting for me to close the door before putting his dog down on the floor.

I hand him the flashlight so I can bend down and give Daisy a two-handed welcome. "Hi there! Hey, girlfriend! Were you scared, huh? Were you?"

"Dogs have night vision," Matt says.

"I know that," I snap. "But it's not as good as a cat's."

"I know that," he says, and I can tell that he's grinning.

I give Daisy an awkward kiss and then stand up and take the flashlight from him. "I've got another flashlight and some candles if you want to borrow them."

"Actually," he says, "hang on. I want to look outside. I want to see how far the blackout extends."

I shine the light in the direction of my living room windows, which look out toward the street. I turn it off when we get to the windows and look out. It's not like we're all that high up, but it's clear that it's dark for as far as we can see, save for the lights of cars. The rain is hitting the glass, and lightning flashes, illuminating everything for one weird second.

All that electricity in the air out there is not making it easy to ignore the highly charged energy between us today. I don't want to call it sexual energy. We probably both just haven't had dinner yet.

"It's so quiet," he says.

And then a bunch of asshole drivers start honking.

We both laugh.

"The blackout shouldn't last long," I say. "It didn't last month, anyway."

"I know. We lost power downtown too."

He's quiet for a while. I imagine he's thinking about his girlfriend, whom he was still living with during the last power outage. So, instead of bringing up our email exchange, I stand next to him in silence, both of us looking out the windows. I place the flashlight on the window ledge.

Daisy is very calm and still near Matt's feet.

I am suddenly aware of how close he's standing to me.

I can smell his cologne and hear him breathing.

I can definitely hear Daisy breathing through her

adorable flat nose.

But it's Matt I'm so aware of, even in the dark. It's not like he's a big burly guy, but something about him just exudes masculinity. In spite of the anger and frustration, I feel especially girly next to him. I'm not used to it. When I'm working with Sebastian, I tend to overcompensate by wearing basic, almost asexual clothes, because I want to be professional. And of course, the guys I know in the art world are all about expressing themselves all the time in every way possible. But Matt's quiet strength is magnetic. Infuriating, but also magnetic. This guy is making all my girl parts wake up with a jolt, and they're crying out, *Notice me! Touch me! Make me feel like a natural woman!*

Oh God. He can probably hear my uterus yelling at him right now.

"You don't have to stay here," I whisper. It seems wrong to speak any louder than a whisper now, in this rare and treasured quiet time.

"Do you want us to go?" he whispers.

"No."

My arm accidentally brushes against his when I reach up to push my wet noodle hair out of my face.

"Sorry," I say.

He says nothing.

I can feel him watching me.

If I looked, I would be able to see the outline of him, as my eyes are adjusting to the darkness.

I can't believe he came over.

Why can't you just be an asshole all the time so my brain doesn't have to keep readjusting to new information?

I shift my body to face him the tiniest bit.

He is there, right there, being all tall and quiet and strong and exasperatingly sexy. His arm brushes against mine as he crosses both of his across his chest. Even in the dark, he is so handsome that my eyes and almost every other part of me instinctively wants to feast upon him. After slapping him.

I can hear his breathing pattern shift, and then he holds his breath. I realize I've been holding mine too. Only Daisy is inhaling and exhaling now.

If two temporary neighbors kiss each other in the dark and nobody sees it or discusses it afterwards, is it still a kiss?

My chin is tilting upwards, lips parting. I can't stop it. I think I feel him slowly leaning down toward me, his body only a couple of inches from mine. I take in a tiny breath, and then—

I scream when the lights suddenly come back on and Alanis resumes her rant in my bedroom.

I cover my mouth and laugh. "Sorry."

Matt is standing still, his arms still crossed in front of his chest, staring down at me. I remember that I have stringy damp hair and am currently wearing a sleep shirt that says ***Nap Queen*** across the chest. Probably not what he was imagining I looked like a minute ago.

Was he even leaning down toward me, or did I imagine it?

I'll never know.

Thank you, Alanis Morissette and Thomas Edison, for being such timely cockblockers.

That could have been awkward.

"Guess we'll be going now," he says. He picks Daisy up and heads for the door.

"Okay. Thank you. For checking on me. I appreciate it."

He nods. "Your deadbolt still working properly?"

"Yes. Thank you."

Another nod. "Good night, then…Nap Queen."

And just like that, just like always, he is gone.

I go back to my bedroom to turn off the record player and fetch my phone.

Much to my surprise, there is a text message from Sebastian. All he wrote was: ***Hope you're safe at home.***

I am safe at home, I write back.

Although, my heart is still pounding in my chest.

Normally, I would attribute that to the message from Sebastian.

It really was sweet of him to think of me.

But I am fully aware that it was Matt who made my body wake up tonight, in the dark, next to his.

It feels like the power hasn't just returned to my apartment—it's back on inside me too. I may have imagined the electricity between us, but I feel a surge of desire to draw him, or at least to sketch out the images that he inspires. This is the first time I've drawn something besides trees in years. It's my appreciation of his physical landscape that demands expression now.

I sketch quickly, not wanting to lose this feeling, trying to capture the outline of him in the darkness. I flip the page and find myself frantically drawing two figures—a man and a woman about to kiss. They're standing still, but the rapidity of the strokes gives the impression of motion. That's how it felt for me for a few seconds. Like we were headed somewhere spectacular, even though we weren't moving.

Just as I don't want to stop to think about where I'd want things to go with Matt McGovern, I don't want to do any more work on this sketch. I flip the page, letting my hand tell the story without allowing my brain to get in the way, but after a few more drawings, both my brain and my body need both of my hands for something else…

CHAPTER 7
MATT

FROM: DOLLY KEMP <doloreskemp123@yahoo.com>
TO: MATT MCGOVERN (personal) <iammattmcgov-ernsemail@gmail.com>

Greetings from Vienna! Oh, what a city. You know, I never thought of myself as an elegant person, but all this grand architecture just makes me want to put on a ball gown and stop swearing so much (or at least learn how to swear in German).
So fucking happy to hear from you, Matthew. I'm so glad you and Daisy are enjoying my apartment, and yes, you may continue to do so for as long as you need to. Marty and I are not done trying out all the hotel beds in Europe yet. Speaking of beds and men and women—I do hope that your reason for staying there really is that you haven't found a new place for yourself and Daisy yet and not that you're still hoping you'll move back in with that Vanessa.

It has been ONE MONTH!
Nut up and move on, my dear boy. You're a catch, and I've always told you that you deserve better than her. Bless your sweet little boy heart, you're good at so many things, but you've never been good at choosing girlfriends. Remember that redhead you had a crush on when you were fifteen and I came to visit? You thought she was an angel, and I told you she had the fiery blood of hellhounds coursing through her veins. But you didn't listen, and it's fine. Tell me, did you keep in touch with her when she was in juvie?
Speaking of better than Vanessa—I'm glad to hear that you've made Bernadette's acquaintance. She never ceases to delight me, that one… Not that I don't trust you with my plants, but maybe you should have Bernadette over to check on them. She has a green thumb. And nine other magical fingers that I'm quite sure are capable of making other things grow and thrive as well…
But don't listen to me! I'm just your dottie old Aunt Dolly.
xx DK

S*ubtle, as always, Aunt D.*

It's Saturday, and my buddies refuse to come uptown to hang out, and I don't want to go downtown to meet up with them, because I don't want to run into Vanessa again. The last time that happened—three weeks ago—she just happened to be at the same bar where my friend had his birthday party. She accused me of stalking her, started crying and apologizing for being so awful to me, saying she missed me, grabbing me and burying her face in my chest and then telling me she can't see me because it's too hard for her, and then ran off. It was pure *telenovela*-caliber drama, and it made me want to break things. But I didn't.

Again, she didn't ask about Daisy. I don't know why that pisses me off so much, but it does. I don't know why I was so sure she needed me, but I did. I don't know why I thought I needed to love her, but I did.

I do?

I did.

But it lingers. I don't know why, but it does. That's a lie. I know why.

It's the falling in love part that I don't want to let go of, even though it let go of me so long ago. It's the first month of Us that I'm hanging on to. It's the first time I saw her, when I held the elevator door open for her. The way I felt when I found out she was the summer law clerk at my law firm. She wore no makeup, her hair pulled back into a tight bun, obviously trying to tone down her looks, to no avail. The way she laughed when I quietly gave her the low-down on every single employee, including myself, in the break room. The way she said my name the first time I kissed her when we worked late that night.

I stayed in love with the firsts. I stayed in love with the beginning and the fantasy of our future, even when it became clear that we had two completely different ideas of the future and two completely different ideas of who I was and who she was. I stayed with her even when it became clear that she had no desire to be the person I thought I'd fallen in love with. Even when it was obvious to everyone that I was blinded by her beauty, I needed so badly to believe that it was more than that, as if you can will yourself into being the right person for someone. As if you could try to will the other person into becoming the right person for you.

I hate that I can tell my brain what to think and I can tell my heart not to feel, but I haven't been able to stop my body from missing hers.

And I hate that I am so fucking horny.

And moody because of it.

It's been almost three months since I've had sex.

Things did change for me after that night when I ran into Vanessa, though. That was when I told my brain it could stop feeling obligated to think about her when I got off. And that's when my brain made it clear to me that it's a total fucking asshole.

No, Aunt Dolly, it's not because of Vanessa that I'm still in your apartment. I just haven't found a new place that would be good for Daisy and me. And also because Daisy is having this annoying love affair with your fucking hot weird neighbor.

Bernadette. I like her paintings. I don't like that it bothers me so much that she isn't painting anymore. I hate that I now despise Sebastian Smith, even though I used to like his work, because she's at his beck and call all day every day and because of the way her voice changes when she talks about him. I like her apartment. I don't like that when I was in her apartment, my dick of a brain scanned each and every surface, picturing which would be the best to fuck her on, against, over. I definitely don't like that I can hear things. I don't like that I know her nighttime habits and her weekend morning routine. I don't like that I wonder what she's doing when she's not on the other side of a wall from me. I really don't like that I wonder what she's wearing or not wearing when she is on the other side of the wall from me.

One day last week, I had forgotten to take my suit to work. I'd needed it for a dinner meeting with my company's investors, so I came home on my lunch break. When I was in the guest room getting the suit out of the closet, I'd heard moaning from the vent. I hadn't expected her to be home in the middle of the day. At first I'd been concerned. I'd honestly thought that maybe Bernadette was sick in bed with food poisoning or something. Then, when I'd gotten closer to the wall, I heard the sound of a vibrator. A loud one. Like a mini jackhammer. Soon, she'd begun groaning and gasping and swearing like she was in pain, and then finally she half-screamed, and I thought surely she was done, but she kept going.

I was so fucking hard that I knew I'd have to take care of it before going back to work. I pictured her with her head thrown back, her eyes closed tight, her pouty swollen lips forming an "O" as she caressed her tits with one hand and worked the vibrator with the other. I'd imagined opening my eyes and finding that she had snuck into my apartment to find me here and then she'd wordlessly climb on top of me for a little afternoon delight. Grabbing on to the headboard and riding me until I exploded into her. After we both came, she'd just kiss me once and then leave. I could see her doing that in real life, and that was a huge turn-on for me. I'd stayed as quiet as a mouse, but following her resounding grand finale, I heard the jackhammer turn off and a drawer slammed shut.

A few minutes later, I was out my front door, wearing my suit. Fuck my co-workers if they can't handle me in a suit at the office—I needed to wear that suit so I could feel more in control of myself. When I'd gotten down to the foyer, Bernadette was there, looking very relaxed and cheerful, talking to a lady with a poodle. The look on her face when she realized I had just been upstairs was priceless. I nodded at her and the other lady and continued on my way back to work.

I'm always startled by how beautiful she is, every time I see her. It's strange. It must be some kind of defense mechanism. Despite my asshole brain's insistence on casting her as the star in every filthy fantasy I've had in the past few weeks, when my hand isn't on my dick, when Bernadette's not around, that same brain keeps reminding me that she's not my type. And then I catch sight of her, a block away, three feet away, wherever, and my type is wavy, dark auburn hair, bright hazel eyes that observe and question and mock me, and a sassy grin that simultaneously makes me want to spar with her and slam myself against her. Yeah. I'm feeling the Bern.

I feel that Bern when I smell her as I jog down the steps to the ground floor. There she is, at her mailbox, wearing jeans, a T-shirt, and sneakers. Saturday morning clothes. I like how comfortable she seems to be in her own skin. When she turns and sees me, she smiles. And then she realizes she's smiling at me and forces herself to frown.

"Morning," I say.

"Hey there."

"You had breakfast yet?"

"No."

"Come with me."

"Now?" She shoves her mail back into the mailbox and locks it.

"You got something else going on?"

"I mean… I was supposed to clean my apartment and do laundry this morning."

"Supposed to?"

"It's on my list."

"Your To-Do list?"

"I don't like to call it that."

I hold the front door open for her, and I don't think she even realizes that she's coming with me yet, even once we're on the sidewalk.

"What do you like to call it?"

"My *Will-Do* list."

I give her a look and shake my head.

"None of your business," she says.

"What?"

"I know what you're thinking, and it's none of your business."

Oh Bernie, you have no idea what I'm thinking.

"And that's not why I am the way I am."

"Nuts?"

It's cute, how defensive she is all of a sudden. As she walks along beside me, I can't help picturing how easy it would be to pick her up. She's taller than average, but she looks…amenable. She likes to keep up with me. I like the back-and-forth. I didn't at first, but it gets me high now.

"I'm not that nuts."

"No. But you're not *not* nuts."

"Everyone in New York is a little bit nuts."

"Can't disagree with you there."

"But you'd like to."

"I get no pleasure from it, if that's what you think." *Lie. That's a lie. I get more pleasure from this than I do from most things lately.*

She laughs. She has been so focused on bantering with

me that she hasn't even noticed we've stopped walking and are now standing in line. "And what exactly *do* you get pleasure from, Esquire?"

"Kind of a personal question, don't you think?"

"You're the one who wants to know if I'm getting laid or not."

Okay, so she did know what I was thinking. "And did you hear me ask the question? You did not."

"But you're dying to know."

"I'm definitely not dying to know." I look down at her and smirk. "How do you like it?"

She blushes and pushes her hair behind one of her ears. "*Excuse* me?"

"What do you want on yours?"

She looks so confused right now, I almost feel sorry for her, but I also sort of want to hold her and kiss her.

"What do I want on my what?"

"Your hot dog."

She finally realizes that we're standing in front of a hot dog cart.

"Oh. Sauerkraut and mustard."

"Interesting. Two sauerkraut and mustard."

"So this is breakfast?" She reaches into her back pocket. "Oh shit, I don't have my wallet."

"I got this."

"Thank you. I can't remember the last time I ate a hot dog."

"You're not a vegetarian, are you?"

"I'm the kind of vegetarian who occasionally eats meat when she feels like it and briefly feels guilty while doing it."

"So you *will do* things if you feel like it."

"Why, Mr. McGovern, that is a rather personal question."

"It wasn't a question."

"Yes, it was. You're wondering if I'm lame and uptight because I haven't gotten laid in ages. But I'm lame and uptight even when I am getting laid regularly, and besides, it hasn't been that long. Not that it's any of your business."

I can tell by the way her lips tighten as soon as she stops talking that she regrets blurting out what she just said.

"Isn't it interesting how you answer questions that have never been asked?"

"Is that a real question?"

"When I have a real question for you, Bernie, you'll know it."

"Don't call me Bernie."

"Okay… So you're seeing someone?"

"No."

"But you were? Recently?"

"Not exactly."

"Is that a real answer?"

"When I have a real answer for you, Esquire, you'll know it."

"Fair enough."

"If you must know, I had a…buddy. But he moved to Miami."

Very interesting. "A *will-do* buddy?"

"A friend with benefits. He did do quite nicely, actually. As did the buddies who came before him, but something always ends it."

"Yeah. Something always ends everything."

"Yeah, but you know. At least when you have an arrangement like that, the endings aren't messy."

"How do you know it wasn't messy for them?"

She shrugs and takes a big bite of her hot dog as we step back from the vendor and lean against the side of a building. Gotta like a girl who likes to eat. The only time I ever saw Vanessa really enjoy consuming anything other than grilled salmon salads or smoothies was when she would inhale a red velvet cupcake once a month.

Bernadette's free hand sweeps the length of her torso. "I'm sure it's difficult to believe that any guy could have sex with *this* and not fall crazy in love, but you'd be surprised what a few well-defined parameters can do for two people who don't want to get involved with each other in a serious way."

Intriguing. Intriguing that she feels this way, and intriguing that she's sharing this information with me. I want to read into it, but I'm too busy staring at her mouth as she chows down on that sausage.

"So, you don't let things get messy, is what you're saying?"

She makes some kind of noise as she takes another big bite of hot dog. Once she has lowered the thing from her face, I slowly reach my hand up. She stops chewing, holds still but keeps her eyes on me as I barely lean in and wipe the huge gob of mustard from the corner of her mouth with my thumb and then hold it up for her to see. Her whole body relaxes when she realizes that's all I was doing, and she resumes smiling and chewing. When I suck the mustard off my thumb, I hear her gulp so loudly it's comical.

Her eyelids flutter. She has a very confused expression on her face. It's kind of sweet. And now it's gone. She clears her throat.

"Should we head back?"

"Sure."

We polish off our breakfast as we stroll. I take the waste from her and toss it in a bin when we pass by one. It's a beautiful spring day, and it's the first time I've gone for a stroll around here without Daisy, and even then I'm usually looking at my phone. I'm actually starting to like it up here. I'd like to suggest we head over to Central Park, but my strolling companion seems hesitant now.

"Don't you have someone more interesting to hang out with today? I seem to recall Dolly saying you were always out and about."

"All my interesting friends live downtown, and they refuse to come up here unless it's for an event of some kind."

She gasps. "Are you telling me that hanging out with *you* doesn't qualify as an event of some kind?"

"Not for my guy friends."

"Ooohhh. Enticing."

"Don't get too excited."

"Oh, but I am! I'm so excited to be walking up Broadway with you! Those downtown people don't know what they're missing! I mean, we just ate a hot dog for breakfast—we are crushing it!"

She holds up her hand for me to high-five her. I oblige, but the sarcasm isn't lost on me. Her earlier revelation isn't lost on me either. I am about to bring it up again when I notice a striking woman who's staring at me as we cross the street. It takes me a second to recognize her, which is weird. That stunning face that I saw every day for years, in every possible hairstyle, every possible expression. Vanessa is standing on the sidewalk outside of Zabar's, holding a big Zabar's bag, watching Bernadette and me as we unwittingly walk toward her. And she's holding hands with some douchebag in a suit.

"Hello, Matthew," she says. Her tone accuses me of following her here, once again. "Small world."

"Vanessa. What are you doing up here?"

"We're going to meet Todd's parents for brunch at their place. We were just picking up a few things for them first. Oh—this is Todd. I don't think you've met. This is Matthew and…"

She arches a perfectly groomed eyebrow at Bernadette, who is wiping her lips, making sure there's no residual mustard.

"Bernadette. She lives next door to me. She lives next door to my aunt. We're staying at my aunt's apartment until I find a place."

"Hey. I'm Vanessa," Vanessa says, looking at Bernadette as though she should know exactly who Vanessa is.

Bernadette waves at both her and the douchebag. He makes a big show of the fact that he can't shake our hands because both of his are busy holding on to Vanessa and a Zabar's bag.

"Hi there."

Douchebag smiles and nods and gives Bernadette the once-over.

"So you live around here, then? How is Daisy doing?"

That's when Bernadette puts her arm around my waist and rests her head against my bicep. "Daisy's amazing. We're all one happy little family here on the Upper West Side. We should probably get back to her, huh, babe?"

I'm so numb that it takes me a few seconds to realize she's doing the pretend-girlfriend thing. I don't know what she's thinking, but I do appreciate what she's doing.

I finally put my arm around Bernadette's shoulder, but I can't look Vanessa in the eye.

"Yeah, we should get back. Nice to, uh… Have a good brunch."

"Bye, Matthew."

"Nice meeting you," says the douchebag in a suit.

Bernadette is pulling me away. It's not that I don't want to get away from them. I just seem to have forgotten how to walk for a second. That whole encounter lasted less than two minutes, but I suddenly feel like I've had the shit kicked out of me every day for years. How do you go from living with someone and saying "I love you" to running into them on a street corner with someone else and talking like we're strangers?

"Are you okay?" Without the sassy tone in her voice, I barely recognize it.

"Huh?"

My arm is still around her shoulder, but Bernadette has let go of me now that we've turned onto a side street.

"Are you okay? You seem…"

"No, yeah."

"So that was…"

"Hmm?"

"Was that your ex-girlfriend?"

"Yeah."

"She uhh… I like her bangs. She has good hair. She seems nice? She's ridiculously gorgeous. That Todd guy looks like a total douchebag though…"

I have nothing to say to that, although I certainly appreciate her assessment. I realize I should probably remove my arm from her shoulder finally. She clears her throat.

After half a block, she finally says, "Sooo, did you know she was with someone else, or…"

I shake my head. At least I think I do. I do not want to talk about this.

"I'm sorry, Matt. That really sucks."

I clear my throat. "I'm not that surprised."

"Oh good, well… How long were you guys together?"

I glance down at her.

She blinks when she sees the look on my face. "Right. Not important. We don't have to talk about it. You just go ahead and process your feelings in your own quiet, masculine way."

"Sounds good."

She really does let me stay quiet and masculine, all the way back to our building. I appreciate that a lot. It used to drive Vanessa crazy when I wouldn't talk to her about my feelings. Like feelings are such a fascinating thing to talk about.

When we get to our floor, Bernadette says softly, "Matt, if you want someone to talk to…I'll be here all day. I have a thing tonight, but…"

I nod and say, "Thanks for having breakfast with me," and then go inside to snuggle with Daisy in the bedroom and wonder what kind of "thing" Bernadette has tonight and who she's having a "thing" with.

CHAPTER 8
BERNADETTE

That. Poor. Guy.

That poor, poor guy.

I can't stop thinking about how sad and confused and vulnerable he looked as soon as he saw his ex-girlfriend with another man. Those sad eyes. All that time, I'd been thinking he was a dick, but he was just protecting his heart because he's sad. I can't stop thinking about those sad, sad eyes.

I also can't stop thinking about how insanely beautiful that Vanessa was. I mean, what's the story there? They must have just stared at themselves in the mirror all the time and congratulated themselves on how gorgeous they were. A couple of years ago, I briefly dated a guy who was into football, and I went to a Super Bowl party with him. I am quite certain that Vanessa was in a Super Bowl commercial eating a burger in a bikini on the beach. I swore off burgers and bikinis then and there.

I just wish I hadn't seen Matt looking so sad. It's no fun hating him when I know that he has actual human feelings. I don't want to pester him with questions and push him to share his feelings with me. I just want to make him feel better. I want to put my arms around him and sing him Adele songs and bake him brownies. Well, I want to *order* brownies to be delivered to him. I could actually feel my own heart breaking when I looked at his face. It was not a good feeling. It was terrible.

I touch the side of my mouth, where his thumb pressed against me for one second and it felt like his whole body was touching my whole body, and gosh darnit that was the best damn hot dog I've ever had.

I need to stay away from him.

Or…

Or!

Or maybe we can be friends.

I can do that.

"You can do what?"

Tommy's voice startles me out of my interior monologue.

"Huh?"

"You just said 'I can do that.'"

"I did? I said that out loud?"

"Girl—I sent you to the bar to get us a bottle ten minutes ago, and I find you here polishing off a glass of wine and talking to yourself. You need to get out more."

I am out. I am out on a Saturday night. I came out to see my best friend in an Off-Broadway play, and now we're celebrating with drinks at the bar in the Public Theater, and I'm sitting here thinking about my neighbor. I was thinking about him so much all afternoon, I didn't even get around to doing laundry because I wanted to be home in case he felt like talking. Apparently, he did not feel like talking, but he did feel like blaring Led Zeppelin while doing Lord knows what (but probably push-ups and crunches), and then he calmly played some pretty guitar songs for his dog.

So now my apartment is really clean, my delicate unmentionables are hand-washed, but I don't have my usual going-out outfits to wear. This is why I am currently wearing a ridiculously tight cardigan over a camisole and the skinny jeans that I usually only wear to fancy parties because they cost over two hundred dollars. And I'm still thinking about my neighbor, instead of my wonderful best friend, whose talent I am here to celebrate.

That is why I need to stay away from Matt McGovern, Esq.

"Yes," I say to Tommy. "Thank you for getting me out. Did I mention how brilliant you were and how handsome you are and how proud of you I am?"

"Yes. Did I mention we're all waiting for that bottle of wine?"

"I ordered it and paid for it. Someone's supposed to bring it out."

"So why aren't you back at the table with us? If you're sitting here thinking about Sebastian Smith, I swear to God—"

"I'm not! Shhh! Don't say his name so loud! I'm not thinking about him. If you must know, I was thinking about my neighbor."

He screws up his face. "The sexed-up retired lady?"

"No. Her nephew. He's been staying there for the past month. She's in Europe. He's only there until he finds a new place for him and his dog, and I love his dog, but he's a total asshole lawyer who sometimes turns out to be kind of nice…"

"Oh my God. What's his name?"

"Matt McGovern."

Tommy sucks in his breath. "You like him. I can tell by the way you said his name."

"*What?* No." What is it with these guys who think they can tell how I feel about someone by the way I say their name? "I mean, I don't *not* like him."

"On Opposite Day."

"What? Don't confuse me." I cover my face. "Why is it so hot in here? I'm confused."

"Yeah you are! You are one hot, confused, enamored little girl who wants to bang her neighbor!"

"I do not."

"Yoooouuuu like him!" Tommy is more excited right now than he was when he told me he got the part in this play. Bless his heart. Too bad he's so mistaken.

"I like his dog. I care about his well-being insofar as it affects the well-being of his dog… Don't look at me." I polish off what was left of my wine. "Stop it. Let's talk about you."

"Yeah! Let's talk about how happy I am to see you liking someone other than your boss!"

"I don't like him. I just seem to have a weird physical reaction to his handsomeness."

"Okay, now I must demand visual proof of this alleged lawyerly handsomeness."

I whip out my phone and open up my photo app. "There," I say, holding my phone up in front of his face. "Isn't she perfect?"

"That's a dog. You're showing me a picture of a dog."

"That's Daisy! His dog. She's a Boston Terrier. Look, that's Matt's lower pant leg in the corner there. He's holding the leash. He has…big feet. And nice shoes."

Tommy glances up at me, not even wasting his considerable performer energy on raising an eyebrow or rolling his eyes.

"*What?* Why would I take a picture of him? He already thought I was crazy for taking a picture of his dog."

"Okay, well, she's a beautiful canine, and that's a totally humpable lower pant leg. Congratulations. Enjoy."

Tommy's friends call out to us from the table when the waitress delivers the bottle of Malbec to them. Tommy jumps up and waves to them. "Let's go sit down."

I give him a look, silently apologizing and pleading with him.

"You want to go home, don't you?"

"Am I a terrible friend? And before you answer that—consider the fact that I have already paid for everything that's been ordered at the table."

He pulls me in for a hug. "I love you. Thanks for coming to the show."

"I love you, I loved the show, and I really loved seeing you in it."

"I really love that you're going to bang your hot neighbor."

I am so tipsy that I barely even remember hailing a cab or walking up the stairs to my apartment. I vaguely remember the driver saying, "You're not going to bang *who*?" so I guess I was thinking out loud again. But I'm definitely not going to bang him.

Now it's eleven on a Saturday night, and my heels are making a lot of noise as I stomp lady-like toward my front door and take my time fiddling around with the lock, jangling my keys. Gosh, I hope I'm not bothering anyone with all the noise I'm making as I return home alone…and it certainly seems like I'm *not* bothering anyone. Which is fine.

He probably went out, and that's good. He should. Maybe he went to see Vanessa. If so, good for him. That would make him a total idiot and I'd feel a little sick about it, but good for him!

I restlessly wander around my tiny apartment, picking random things up and then putting them back down. I don't want to go out again, but I have too much energy to just get into bed. I have to do something. I check my phone to see if Sebastian sent me any messages. He's been in such a weird funk the past few days. I barely see him when I'm at his office because he's holed up in his studio, and when I do see him, he just moans a lot and needs emotional support.

He has not sent any messages.

I realize that I am staring at an overflowing laundry basket, and now I can cross one more thing off of my Will-Do list for today. Get back on track with my weekend plans. The plans that don't involve thinking about or banging my hot neighbor.

Again, I barely remember walking down four flights of stairs while carrying my laundry basket and detergent, which is a tad alarming. But not as alarming as walking into the laundry room while thinking about Matt McGovern and then seeing Matt McGovern leaning against one of the washing machines, arms crossed, facing the door like he's waiting for me. I don't scream, but I do stand frozen in the doorway. Because he is looking at me in a way that he has never looked at me before. The way a man looks at a woman in a nightclub. His eyes move so slowly down the front of me to the cement floor.

"Nice boots."

"Nice *what?*"

"Boots. On your feet."

"Oh! Thank you." It's weird that I forgot to take off my high-heeled boots before coming down here. Normally I'd be in my Ugg boots. Normally, I wouldn't be trying to make so much noise while walking around the building. I finally remember how to move and place my laundry basket on the floor in front of the other washing machine, the one against the opposite wall from the one he's using. "You doing laundry?"

"No, I just like to come down here to think." He's grinning at me. Well, at least he's not frowning. "Are *you* doing laundry?"

"Yes. I'm doing laundry."

"You really shouldn't be doing laundry down here by yourself at night."

"Good thing I'm not by myself, then."

He blows air out of his nostrils, which I am counting as a little laugh. I made Matt McGovern laugh a little. What a magical night. I think we can be friends.

"You have fun at your thing?"

"Yes, I did." *Even though I was thinking about you the whole time.*

"Great."

"Did you have a good evening?"

"Fantastic."

"Great."

I don't think the laundry room has ever smelled this good, like clean clothes and dirty man and dear Lord—how can anyone look so attractive in sweat pants and a T-shirt? It's just not right. Maybe if I don't look at or smell him, it will be easier to be friends. If I were smart, I'd keep my eyes shut and hold my breath until I can get away from him.

As I bend down to place all of my clothes into the washing machine, I am suddenly very conscious of how unbearably amazing my ass probably looks in these jeans and decide to squat instead. I don't want him to think I'm bending over to flaunt my amazing ass in his face. But I can't squat. Because my jeans are too tight. So, my soon-to-be-friend Matt McGovern is getting a sweet eyeful of premium Bernadette Butt. I know this, because I peek over my shoulder and catch him staring. Instead of quickly looking away, his gaze slowly rises to meet mine.

"Nice jeans," he says. "They look expensive."

I clear my throat. "They weren't cheap."

"Guess that's one of the benefits of working for Sebastian Smith."

"And one of the benefits of living in this building," I say coyly. I wait for him to smirk before turning back to face the washing machine.

"You're mixing your lights and darks?" He just can't stop judging me.

"It's a big machine and I don't practice segregation. So far, in my whole life, I've only ruined two white shirts." I shrug. "They're just clothes."

"You're as serious about laundry as you are about being a vegetarian."

"Except I don't even feel guilty about turning white shirts pale blue. You having any luck with the apartment hunting?"

"I'm not having any luck finding the time to apartment hunt."

"Oh really? I would have thought you had plenty of free time, given that your cool downtown friends refuse to hang out with you up here and apparently you don't like to hang out down there anymore."

"Oh, I like to hang out down there," he says in a tone of voice that makes me wonder which "down there" he's referring to. "I've just been avoiding going down there lately."

I don't turn around to look at him because I don't think I could handle it if he's staring back at me and also because my eyes are bulging out of their sockets. "Umm… you mean because of your girlfriend?"

"Ex-girlfriend."

"Did she get in touch with you at all? After this morning?" He doesn't respond while I'm pouring the detergent into the detergent drawer, while I close the detergent drawer, or while I check my pockets for the quarters that I forgot to bring. I swear under my breath.

When I turn to ask him if I can borrow some from him, he is right there, two inches from me. There are four quarters in the palm of his large, capable, open hand.

"Thank you." I watch him as he reaches around me to drop the quarters into the slots. He notices me shivering.

"Cold?"

No, I just had another orgasm zap while watching you insert things into slots. "Yeah. It's chilly down here."

"Cold water? You have to choose your settings."

"I do know how to operate a washing machine."

"Proceed."

He steps back to the other washing machine and recrosses his arms. He's never going to answer that question I asked about his ex-girlfriend, so I'll ask another one.

"How'd you meet her? Vanessa. If you don't mind my asking."

He looks down at his feet and scratches his head. "At work."

"Really?" That's surprising. "Isn't she a model?"

"She is now. I mean, she was doing some modeling when we first met but just to pay for law school."

"Oh. So she's a lawyer? A model slash lawyer?" *A unicorn. Your ex-girlfriend is a fucking unicorn with perfect bangs, and you're here in a laundry room with me on a Saturday night?*

"She never ended up becoming a lawyer. She didn't finish law school because the modeling jobs became so lucrative. So now she's just a model."

She's just a model. I finally start the load and turn to face him. He's still staring at his feet. Still having feelings about his ex-girlfriend. Mixed feelings, I'm sure, but feelings nonetheless.

"She must miss Daisy."

He snorts. "I'm sure she must."

"Have you been seeing other people?"

"*Other* people?"

"Anyone?"

He shakes his head, almost imperceptibly.

"Fooling around?"

"Is that a request?" He smirks, big-time, revealing a dimple.

Where the hell did you come from, dimple?

"When I request something from you, Esquire, you'll know it."

Dimple's staying put, and I will take that as a "no" to my question.

"Surely you've gotten hammered at strip clubs with your bros."

"Not since I was in my early twenties. Your concern is touching."

"Awww. Were you afraid of getting into a Ross and Rachel 'we were on a break' situation?"

There goes the dimple. "I am a thirty-two-year-old man—I don't make life decisions based on episodes of nineties sitcoms."

"Except for this time."

He sighs. "Except for this one time."

I lean against my washing machine and cross my arms over my chest, mirroring him. "I think that's sweet." I need to stop asking questions about his ex-girlfriend. I need to stop wondering why they broke up. He needs to stop staring at me because it's cold down here in the basement and my nipples are pointing right at him, like *hey you, yeah you, over here!* "So, why'd you guys break up?" I can't believe I asked that. I don't usually ask guys this many personal questions. I don't usually ask *anyone* this many personal questions.

He takes three slow steps toward me, arms still crossed, brow furrowed. "I think we're done talking about my ex-girlfriend."

"What do you want to talk about?"

I drop my arms to the side and push back against the washing machine just as his arms reach out on either side of me. He presses his hands down on top of the laundry machine and lowers his mouth to my ear. "I want to talk about you, Bernie."

"Don't call me Bernie," I whisper.

And then my butt starts vibrating against the metal of the machine. It's the phone in my back pocket. I am staring at Matt McGovern's mouth as it hovers, inches away from mine, but instead of doing what every single cell in my body wants me to do, I reach for the phone and look down to check the Caller ID.

It's Sebastian. If he's calling me this late on a Saturday night, it's because he's really stressed-out and needs to talk.

"I have to take this," I say, watching his jaw clench. "It's work."

CHAPTER 9
MATT

"It's work," she says.

Fucking millionaire artists and their Saturday night work calls.

The cell phone reception down here is terrible, of course, so I back away from her and she runs out of the laundry room in her sexy black boots, leaving me with the heavenly scent of her shampoo and a dick that's about to start doing jumping jacks in these sweat pants.

I'm glad she left.

This would have been a bad idea anyway.

Coming down here to do my laundry was a dumb idea. Normally I'd have my laundry picked up and delivered, like my aunt does. Instead, I decided to hang out in a basement on a Saturday night in the off-chance I'd run into my neighbor.

There's about twenty minutes left on my dryer cycle and half an hour for the load in the washing machine. No point waiting around.

I count to twenty and then go up to my apartment. Bernadette left a scent trail along the stairwell and in the hall outside our units. I can hear her talking just inside her door, in a calm soothing voice. Her boss is probably having one of those "it's so hard to be a rich, famous painter that people expect brilliant things from" kind of breakdowns, and it's her job to remind him that he's a genius and everything's fine.

He just better not ask her to do any actual work for him now.

Daisy doesn't even run to the door when I come in. She's all curled up on the dog bed on the living room floor with her chew toy. I am not having much luck with the ladies tonight. Some days the magic works, and some days it doesn't.

I go to the guest room to change into a pair of jeans. Jeans that are better at keeping my body's secrets from beautiful, fragrant, sassy young women who happen to be doing laundry within a few feet of me in revealing little sweaters and tight jeans and sexy black boots. I can hear her through the vent now, still talking in that soothing voice. I don't like that she's talking to him while she's in her bedroom, but at least she's still at home.

I also don't like that I care so much that she's talking to her boss, when she could be talking to me…when she could be *not* talking to me.

I pull my phone out of the pocket of my sweat pants and toss it onto the bed while I change. There's another unread text from Vanessa on there that I'm going to have to look at eventually. I didn't hear from her at all after running into her a few weeks ago, but two hours after seeing her and that Todd guy this morning, I got a "Great to see you!" text. I didn't respond to it because what would I say? *"Not very great seeing you with your new boyfriend, and oh, by the way, since when do you have a new boyfriend?"*

Then I got another text from her that said: ***You look like you're doing great. That girl seems nice…***

I didn't reply to that one either.

That girl *is* nice.

But I'm not going to get into a text conversation with Vanessa about what kind of relationship I have with her because I don't have a relationship with her.

I can hear Bernadette laughing in her bedroom. Sounds pretty fake to me. There is no way that Sebastian Smith is funny. I've seen pictures of him. He looks like an interesting guy, he looks like a charismatic guy, but there's no way he makes her laugh for real. I could make her laugh. I could make her feel all kinds of good things.

I zip up my jeans and pick up my phone to open the message from Vanessa, the one she sent four hours ago: ***Glad you're happy, Matthew. You deserve it.***

Well, isn't that swell of her to say so. What a great ex-girlfriend she is. I don't even care if she's trying to alleviate her own guilt about moving on so quickly or if she's trying to leave the door open a crack for me to tell her I'm not happy. I just know that when Bernadette Farmer put her arm around me this morning and rested her head on my arm in front of Vanessa and her Todd guy, all I could think about was how sad it is that I spent so many months of my life trying to convince myself that I had to make things work with Vanessa when she never once did anything like that for me. It was a small thing, but it was an act of kindness. And I'd been trying to keep that wall between us for a month.

Fuck that wall.

Fuck our differences.

Fuck Sebastian Smith.

I do deserve to be happy.

It doesn't have to be complicated.

It doesn't have to be messy.

I'm tired of wondering what Bernadette Farmer is like in bed.

I'm going to find out.

I don't hear her talking or fake-laughing anymore. It doesn't feel right to just knock on her door, and it doesn't seem cool to just open my door right when she happens to be going back down to the laundry room, and it definitely wouldn't be cool for me to just go down and wait around for her to show up. I pick up my laptop and open up iMessages, type in her email address. Let's see if Miss Farmer is still busy with work...

Me: If there's an art emergency, I just want you to know that I'd be happy to wake up one of the other neighbors to get them to finish doing your laundry for you.

BF: Art crisis averted. You may continue being a surly neighbor.

Me: Surly?! Surely you don't mean that. Would a surly neighbor buy you a hot dog from a street vendor when you were planning to do something else?

BF: ...I really am sorry about...you know...what happened earlier...<sad face emoji>

Me: We're done talking about that.

BF: Surly!

Me: I didn't mean that in a surly way.

BF: How would I know that if you don't include an emoji? <winking smiley face emoji>

Me: I deeply regret texting you.

BF: <three dancing lady emojis> Hey neighbor, how'd you like to accompany me back down to the laundry room so I don't have to go all by my little girl self this late at night?

Me: How do you know I'm not still in the laundry room?

BF: How do you know I'M not still in the laundry room?

Me: Because you just asked me to accompany you back down there. Are you drinking MORE wine?

BF: ...Shut up, McGovern.

I give Daisy a kiss on the head before grabbing more quarters and heading out the door. I'm willing to bet that Miss Farmer forgot to bring her own again. True to form, just as she steps out into the hallway and locks her door, she curses under her breath and starts to unlock it again.

"I got quarters," I say. "Hot dogs are on you next time."

She smiles as she holds out her hand. "My hero."

"Once again, let's not get too excited." When my fingers graze the palm of her hand as I place the coins in it, I swear I notice her shiver again. She does look like she has magical fingers. Aunt Dolly was right about that.

She has changed out of her sexy black boots and into a pair of furry slipper boots, but it does nothing to dampen her appeal. We say absolutely nothing, all the way down to the basement. The overhead basement lights are on all the time, and while it's far from romantic, I think it's safe to say that we're both acutely aware of how sexy it feels to be the only two people down here in the middle of the night. To be honest, it feels sexy to be the only two people living on the top floor of this building as well. It almost feels like we're roommates more than neighbors.

But we aren't.

We are two steps away from being something other than friendly neighbors, and I am so ready to take those steps.

I put my wet dark clothes into the dryer and start folding the dry light-colored ones on the table along the back wall of the room, while Bernadette hastily shoves all of her wet clothes into the dryer. It's kind of refreshing, this lack of reverence for her clothes. The two women I've lived with—my mother and Vanessa—gave their wardrobes the same careful consideration and attention as their skin and hair, which meant that any tear, stain, split-end, wrinkle, or pimple signaled the end of the world.

My back is to Bernadette, but when I hear her exhale loudly as her feet land on the floor, I know without a doubt that she has just tried to jump up on top of the dryer but her tight jeans limit her ability to move.

I walk over to her. She turns to face me, and before she says a word, I've lifted her up by her waist and set her down on top of the machine. I go back to the folding table before she can clear her throat and say thank you.

"So you're on call twenty-four seven, huh?"

"Yeah. I mean, within reason. You probably think it's silly to be at his beck and call, but a lot of people are relying on him to complete this series of paintings he's working on, and if I can prevent him from having a meltdown, it's no small feat."

"I don't think it's silly. I think your job is important, and it's adorable that you have a crush on your boss."

I look over my shoulder at her. She wrinkles her nose at my use of the word "adorable." Too bad she looks so adorable when she wrinkles her nose.

"Do not call me that."

"Sorry. I think it's sweet that you have a crush on your boss, Bernie."

"Don't call me Bernie."

"Okay." I place my last piece of laundry in my basket and turn to face her. She seems pensive.

"I have had a crush on him. Maybe it's dumb. I guess I need to get over it."

"I agree. How do you plan to do that?"

"I can't say that I've formulated an actual plan yet. How do you plan to get over your ex-girlfriend?"

"I have some ideas." My eyelids feel heavy. I might have bedroom eyes. Whatever my face is doing right now, it's making Bernadette uncomfortable.

She wrinkles her brow. "What is with you? You're behaving so…differently toward me all of a sudden."

"Yes, I am. *That* was me trying to stay away from you." I walk over to her. "*This* is me wanting to get closer to you."

Her legs and knees are welded together. I see how her body tenses up. I place my hands, one on each of her knees, and then slowly move each of my hands up the sides of her thighs. She sucks in her breath. Her shoulders lower a little. When my hands reach her hips, I look straight at her. Our eyes are about the same level now. Her lashes flutter, and then her eyelids remain half-closed. She wets her lower lip with her tongue—barely perceptible, but I see it. I feel it. I wait for her body to give me another sign as I grip on to her hips a little tighter.

When she arches her back a tiny bit, raising her breasts, I feel her knees relax apart. I pull her toward me and step between her parted legs. Her hands are on either side of my face as mine reach for her waist. I wait for her to lower her lips to mine, but she doesn't. She's studying my face, her fingertips caressing my facial hair, probably deconstructing my features—light and shadow, straight lines and curves.

Fuck that.

I don't want to be deconstructed by this woman.

I want to disappear into her face and curves and dark, wet places.

I lean in and kiss her. Quickly, decisively, startling her out of her little artist's reverie. I squeeze her waist. My face is still so close to hers. She shifts around on her ass, lets out a sigh, and my mouth finds hers again. She's with me now, not just responding but with hungry, little gasps and quiet moans as her soft lips and tongue move in response to mine but also with their own clear intentions. I like the way she kisses, with her whole body, like it's the beginning of a really interesting conversation that I want to keep having. Something shifts, and she goes in deeper, grabbing my shirt to pull me closer. She's groaning into my mouth and biting my bottom lip, and her tongue is a caged wild animal that's been set free, and I don't know if I want to tame it with my mouth or let it roam all over, but I have never had such a sensual fucking kiss in my life and I don't ever want this to stop.

Then she jerks back like she's been slapped awake.

"What are you doing?" Her voice is breathy and it's not really a question, but I have answers for her.

"Behaving differently toward you." My voice is deeper than it's ever been, and I may be the king of controlling my emotions, but managing this raging hard-on just might kill me.

"You certainly are."

"I think we should have an arrangement."

"An arrangement?"

"The kind you've had with other guys."

"Oh. *That* kind of arrangement."

She slides back farther onto the top of the washing machine, squeezing her thighs back together and shutting me out.

"Either that, or we can both listen to each other get it on with other people through the vent."

She bites her lower lip and stares at my mouth. "Did you hear me that afternoon when I…"

"When you were pleasuring yourself? Yes, I did. Thank you for that, by the way."

She covers her face and groans.

"Oh—are you giving me a repeat performance?"

She punches my bicep. "No. And what makes you think I listen to *you* through the vent?"

"You obviously listen to me when I'm in the bedroom, or else you would have told me about this acoustic situation when I moved in."

She grins. "First of all, I don't listen to you so much as I happen to be able to hear you. And secondly, it's very cute when you sing with Daisy. Thirdly…you aren't half as smart as you think you are."

"Maybe not. But you like me twice as much as you think you do."

"Oh yeah? How much do you like me?"

"Exactly as much as I think I do. Despite everything, I think I'm attracted to you and I think you're attracted to me, and I propose that you and I engage in casual relations with each other. For now and until it is no longer convenient or fun for either or both of us. This way I don't have to be away from Daisy for too long, so she won't pee on my aunt's hardwood floors, and your walk of shame will only take five seconds. Everybody wins."

"I don't spend the night with guys I…do that with."

"Even better. Daisy doesn't like to share."

"You mean she doesn't like to share *me*."

"Now let's get one thing straight, Bernie."

"Don't call me Bernie."

"This arrangement would be between you and me. Daisy is off the table."

"Okay, but that whole conversation we just had earlier, about your girlfriend…"

"Ex-girlfriend."

"Ex-girlfriend. We wouldn't be able to have that kind of talk anymore. I don't want to hear about her."

"I'm the one who didn't want to talk to you about her."

"This isn't about being right or wrong here, Esquire."

"You're right."

She seems to be equal parts exasperated, flustered and turned-on. I do have that effect on women, but it looks good on her. There's a lot of energy to be tapped into, and I am beyond ready to tap that.

Just when it feels like she's about to lean in and let that energy loose again, the phone in her back pocket starts vibrating again.

We both lower our heads and exhale.

"Sorry, I have to…"

"Go ahead." I step away from her.

She looks at her phone. "Shit, it's his agent. That means he called his agent in a panic and now his agent is panicking."

"Take it. It's fine."

It's pretty clear that it's not at all fine. She looks down and covers her mouth when she notices the astonishing bulge in my pants.

"Oh God. Sorry! So sorry!" she whispers as she runs out of the room and up the stairs.

I wait three minutes before taking my laundry back upstairs.

The no-strings concept is still quietly floating around in the air out there, somewhere between us, like a paper airplane. It may never land, could very well get crumpled up in her smooth, capable hands or burst into flames if she decides to light a match and toss a few incendiary words at me. As much as I enjoy the back-and-forth, I'm not sure how much more of it I can take. One more kiss like that, and my life is ruined.

I've decided it's probably best to treat my disillusioned body to an ice-cold shower and call it a night, when I hear a quiet knock at the front door. When I open it, no one is there, but I find a folded piece of paper taped to it. On the outer fold of the paper, she has scrawled the words: ***Didn't want to slide this under the door in case Daisy gets to it before you do…***

I unfold the note, impressed by the controlled but swirly handwriting and even more impressed by the words.

• • •

Dear grouchy neighbor: I'm considering your offer and need clarification before proceeding. Despite being an artist, I think you know that as a busy New Yorker, I am also practical and straightforward.

That said, I need to make sure you know that this could never turn into anything serious. I don't care if you're trying to get over your ex-girlfriend or hoping she'll eventually want to get back together with you—just don't project your messy feelings about her onto me.

Because, despite your resemblance to an underwear model, I won't be falling for you. Ever.

Yours, with clear boundaries,

Bernadette

P.S. I'd like to be very clear that regardless of whether or not we do this, nothing will change my feelings for your dog (and we both know she loves me too).

CHAPTER 10
BERNADETTE

Now that I've gotten that out of the way, all I want to do is get into bed. By myself. Because I should sleep on this and see how I feel tomorrow, when I'm fully sober. Truthfully, it's not even the wine that's been making me feel light-headed all night, it's Matt. I just need to sleep. I'm not even going to stay up long enough to get my laundry once it has dried. I'm just going to get into my pajamas and call it a night. My friendly neighborhood pajamas. Because that is what I wear when I get in bed by myself with my glass of wine and my Netflix.

But before I get really comfortable, it seems wise to check my phone five times and then tiptoe to the front door, just in case there's a note…

There's a note!

On the floor by the door.

I've never been so happy that there's a slight gap between the bottom of the door and the hardwood floors.

• • •

Dear nutty neighbor: As a lawyer, I must clarify that I never made an offer. It was a suggestion regarding the possibility of a nonpermanent, no-strings-attached arrangement between two consenting adults whose beds are separated by a wall.

As a man who shares your disdain for messy feelings, I applaud your confidence in your ability to not fall for me. Hold on to that. I'd also like to make it clear that I don't care if you want to get over your crush on your boss or if you still hope he'll realize you're the woman of his dreams. That said, I definitely wasn't thinking about my ex-girlfriend when I kissed you in the laundry room, and I'm quite sure you weren't thinking about your boss.

As a dog daddy, I'm glad you're so taken with my girl. But if you try to steal her, I will get all Liam Neeson up in your pretty face.

As a busy New Yorker, I think clear boundaries are hot. I have one hour free to blow your mind tonight. So turn off Netflix, put down that glass of wine, and let's do this.

Yours for now,

Matt

Freaking know-it-all big-talking lawyer neighbors with their panty-vaporizing letter writing skills.

Thinks he knows exactly what I'm thinking and what I'm up to at all times. I haven't turned on Netflix yet—so there! And he should know better than to promise an hour of mind-blowing sex to someone he hasn't had sex with yet. What is he—a novice?

I put down my glass of wine so I can text to let him know that I'm coming over to discuss this matter further. I grab my keys, check myself in the mirror, and leave my apartment before changing my outfit or my mind.

Matt slowly opens his door and watches me shuffle over, barefoot. He backs up against the door, allowing me to step inside. When he shuts the door, he says, "Nice pajamas."

"Nice note."

"Right back atcha."

"I've never done this with a neighbor before—for good reasons."

"What reasons?"

Because I've never had a neighbor as hot as you before.

"Because it's too close for comfort. But also convenient, yes. I get that."

"Good. Any other concerns?"

"I just want to be clear about this..."

"Go on."

"Whether I get it on with someone or not has nothing to do with Sebastian. Well, it does, but not in the way you think. It's just that I spend every day talking to him about him and doing things for him, and I don't have the bandwidth to be in another thing where I have to talk to a guy about his life and his feelings. And I don't want to have to compromise or figure out his needs or any of that crap that you have to do when you're dating someone."

"That does sound like crap."

"I just want a guy I can have orgasms with."

"I'm the guy. You talk an awful lot for someone who says she doesn't want to talk about stuff."

"I just want to be clear."

"We're clear. Take your clothes off."

"You first."

We have a staring contest for a few seconds before

lunging and reaching for each other's clothes. I grab his shirt as he grabs my pajama top. Before he can remove mine, I pull his off over his head, and when I get a look at his bare chest and abs, I actually gasp and cover my mouth.

"Oh my God!"

"What?" He looks down at his stomach, probably expecting to see an alien baby emerging from it based on my reaction.

I place my hand flat on one of his pecs and push him back, laughing. "What is your problem?! Why do you have to look this good? You're a freaking lawyer. Are you also a model?"

"No. I was." His hands are slowly roaming my curves.

"I knew it."

"In college. To pay for law school. Is this a problem for you?"

"I don't know." I allow him to pull my pajama top over my head. "Maybe. I've never had physical contact with this many abs at the same time before. Was there a sale at Abs R Us? Buy six get two bonus abs free?"

He stands still, holding my pajama top and staring down at my chest, but he isn't laughing and he also probably isn't wondering if I was Photoshopped.

"Do you always wear a pink and black lace bra under your pajamas?"

The truth is, I've never worn this before, and *hot damn La Perla bra*—you just paid for yourself! The way Matt McGovern is looking at me right now, I might just spend all my savings on lingerie. I feel like a goddess. A goddess in a really expensive bra and cotton Target pajama pants.

"No. I usually wear the white lace one, but it's still wet."

He grunts as his hand reaches behind my head to fist my hair, tugging my head back so he can kiss my neck. My knees nearly give out. I swear, I can hear my whole body chanting "Get it, Girl!" but when my eyes partially open, I see a sweet little black and white head tilting in the living room, staring.

"Daisy's watching us," I whisper.

"What?"

"She's looking at us. I don't want to do this in front of her."

"Oh for Christ's sake."

He hands me my pajama top, picks me up, and carries me to the guest room, shutting the door behind us. I am determined not to think about how I've overheard Dolly and Marty have sex in this bed. I am determined not to think about anything for the next hour, except how easy it is for him to lift me up and how I would probably let him move me around in pretty much any way he wants to.

He places me down on the bed so my head can rest on a pillow. He raises my hips up, carefully pulls my pajama pants down in one swift motion, and stares at my matching pink and black bra and panties. There's just so much to take in. My eyes don't know what to focus on—the way he's looking at me, the pecs, the abs, the sculpted biceps and veiny forearms, the colossal protrusion in his jeans… He continues staring at my body while he removes those jeans, and now there is only one thing I can pay attention to—the magnificent erection that's straining to be released from his black boxer briefs.

My knees are bent and I'm squeezing my thighs together, writhing around alone on the bed, because there is so much agonizing tension in my clit and it's just so slippery down there. He moves my legs apart and kneels between them. He's stroking my hips as he seems to be carefully considering what he wants to do to me first.

I glance down at my bra and panties. "Be careful taking these off," I say in a husky voice that I don't even recognize as my own. "I know I said I don't care about clothes, but these are special."

"I'm gonna take these off so slowly you'll be begging me to rip them from your body."

I'm about to scoff, but he lowers himself to kiss my mouth before any more sass can escape from my lips. My hands go to his back and then travel all over, everywhere I can reach. I like that his muscles aren't too bulky, and I'm surprised by how smooth his skin is and how good it feels to touch it. I try to concentrate on how his muscles move beneath my hands, but when he pulls one bra strap off my shoulder and kisses my neck and then just beneath my shoulder blade, I shudder. Since when is that spot beneath my shoulder blade an erogenous zone?

I make a guttural sound and drag my fingernails down his back, ever so lightly. His breath catches, and I feel his body clench up. I reach down inside the front of his boxer briefs and whisper, "oh fuck," because my fingers barely touch as they clasp around below the head. The skin of his hard cock is so hot and tight. He groans and I lick my lips, but he pulls away from my grasp before he kisses me between my legs, over my panties, lifts the lacey elastic of them, and lets it snap back against my skin. He kisses me all the way up the center of my torso, grabbing my wrists and holding them up over my head.

I squeeze my eyes shut as he kisses me behind my ear and then pulls back. I can feel him watching me as I shiver and writhe around beneath him. My back is arched and my breasts are straining upwards, begging to be touched.

He releases my wrists and squeezes both breasts, licking and gently tugging at the left nipple through my bra. I moan, and he slowly peppers kisses along the top of the bra then pulls down the other bra strap and bites my upper arm. It doesn't hurt, but it takes me by surprise and I fucking love it.

I start to reach behind my back to unhook my bra, quietly swearing and cursing him because I just want his hands and mouth on my bare skin already. I glance up at him briefly because I know he's got a cocky grin on his fiendishly handsome face. But I'm wrong. He looks so serious. His hooded eyes are cloudy, and he isn't hiding his desire for me, and it's fucking beautiful and I've never felt so wanted by a man. I toss my bra to the floor, grab the back of his neck, and pull him down to my breast. He swirls his tongue around my nipple, sucking and licking and moaning until I am so close to orgasm, I cry out, "Oh my God…just fuck me already…please just do it!"

"Not yet," he groans, lowering himself to kiss around my lower abdomen. My fingers are raking through his short hair until he pulls down my panties so slowly that I have to cover my mouth with both hands to keep from begging him to rip them off. "Fuck, you're so wet, Bernadette." He pulls my panties down over my feet. I hear his own feet pad on the floor, and then he yanks me down toward the foot of the bed, kneels on the ground, wraps his arms around my bent legs to brace me, and buries his face between them.

I whimper and quiver when I feel the tip of his tongue on my clit, and then he proceeds to do so many wonderful things to my vagina that I fear I might black out. The concentrated tremors quickly become full-body quakes, and while I'm in the middle of what feels like an eternal orgasm, I barely notice when he pulls away from me to put on a condom, and then he's pushed me up to the center of the bed and inside me when I'm mid-shockwave. He slides in quite easily, despite his size, and the mild burning sensation makes me sharply suck in my breath, but the heat of it melts away the pain quickly. The way he moves in and out so smoothly—not too quick and not too slow—feels the way I've always wanted sex to feel. It's like we're made for each other, if only in our nether regions.

I clench around him, relishing the hissing sound he makes as he arches up and drops his head back. His hands are around my head, tugging on my hair, while his abs are doing all the work here, and now I get exactly why an eight-pack is so useful. I'm not even self-conscious about all the crazy sounds that are coming out of my mouth, because Matt McGovern is panting and moaning too. My feet are gripping the mattress by his thighs as I move my hips with him, and I squeal as he suddenly grabs one of my ankles and brings my leg around so that I'm on my elbows and knees and he is so deep inside me, hands on my hips. I cry out because it's such an unfamiliar feeling of dull pleasure that spreads from inside my abdomen, radiating all over. I haven't said "oh God" so many times in a row in my life, but somehow it feels like if I say Matt's name out loud it would be too intimate. He has complete control over my body, but I still feel like he's totally *with* me and not just trying to gratify some primal need for release, although it's definitely that too.

Despite his patience and skill, I can tell he hasn't done this in a while. My body can recognize that sense of urgency, because surely it's not just about being with me. When he flips me over onto my back again, he places both of my legs straight up on either side of his head and plows into me. I'm so tight around him, and I want to tell him it's okay for him to come now, but I am overtaken by a tidal wave of bliss, over and over, until I am so unaware of where I end and he begins that it doesn't feel necessary to talk anymore.

It's the place I've always wanted to get to with my art, and somehow this person I barely know has managed to take me there, right here in this bed.

An hour later, I'm on my back and I have to raise my head to check to see if my body not only feels but actually *looks* like jelly. My mind really is blown, but my entire skeleton may also have dissolved. That's some pretty gross imagery, considering how good and beautiful I feel. I stare back up at the ceiling and then turn my head to look at Matt, who lies beside me. He seems happy but annoyingly unshaken. I guess he's better at hiding it when his world has been rocked. He places his hands behind his head and grins, aware that I'm watching him.

"That was not at all disappointing," he says.

Understatement of the century.

"I have no complaints," I say casually. "It's like there was a whole army of you down there at one point."

"I'm good at multi-tasking. You're not so bad yourself. I think you might be the best neighbor I've ever had."

"You have definitely rocketed to a solid spot on my Top Ten list… It's kind of an aphrodisiac, actually."

"What is?"

"Knowing it can't go anywhere. It's freeing."

"I'm glad you brought up this arrangement."

"Uh, *you* were the one who brought it up."

"I mean, you gave me the idea."

I hike myself up on one elbow. "Matt McGovern! Are you telling me you've never had a no-strings arrangement like this before?"

"I'm not telling you anything."

"Oh, come on. You haven't. I can tell. I mean, you clearly have very little sexual experience, because you barely managed to pull off whatever you want to call that stuff you did just now…" I wish I could have said that with a straight face. We both laugh, because obviously it was a joke. When the laughing subsides, I get up and put my underthings and pajamas back on while Matt lies back and watches. I don't need to know about his relationship history. It's irrelevant in this situation. Totally irrelevant.

Which is why I'm not going to ask.

"Okay, but are you just like, Mr. Boyfriend Guy or what? I need to know what I'm dealing with here."

He smiles. "I've had one-nighters, I've dated girls for a short period of time, I've dated multiple women at the same time, and I've had monogamous relationships. I've lived with one woman, once. But yeah, this will be a first for me."

"Well. I'll be gentle."

"No thanks. You go right on being whatever you want to call what you were tonight."

"Earth-shatteringly hot?"

"If that's what you want to call it."

I sit back down at the edge of the bed and place my hands in my lap. "If this is your first no-strings thing, then I should familiarize you with some ground rules."

He fluffs up a pillow, places it behind his back so he can sit up and rest against it, and then rests his chin on his knuckles like an eager student. "Go on."

"No sleepovers. No I love yous, even if you don't mean it. No 'where is this going' conversations. No conversations about feelings. No obligations regarding texting the day after sex. No dates, obviously. With each other, I mean. We don't make plans to have sex; we just get together when it's convenient for both of us. No public displays of affection. No blabbing about our arrangement to anyone else. If you start dating someone else, I won't want to do this with you anymore. For the other person's sake. And vice versa—if I happen to start seeing someone. Because that's when things can get messy. So, if you even go on a first date with someone, I want you to tell me, or if you decide you want to start seeing Vanessa again, you have to tell me first and we will end this immediately. As soon as it stops being fun and convenient, it's over. Got it?"

"Got it. These are very negative rules."

"If you don't like rules, then we shouldn't do this again."

"That's not what I meant. I don't know if you know this, but lawyers uphold the law, and laws are rules. I'll have no problem abiding by those rules. I'd just like to add a more positive one to the mix, if I may."

"Go on."

"If you're here in this apartment and I make you come so hard that you pass out, I will allow you to stay here until you regain consciousness, even if it requires sleeping here overnight."

Although it is in my nature to guffaw at that kind of statement, I don't. Because I now know that it is completely within the realm of possibility that he could make me come so hard that I pass out. "That is…bold and generous of you, and right back atcha. Okay, Esquire." I reach over to pat his leg. "Thanks for the sex, neighbor. I'm gonna begin my five-second walk of shame now."

He starts to get out of bed.

"Don't get up. I can see myself out."

"Oh, I'm going to see you out. I want to make sure you don't take Daisy with you." He smirks as he steps into his underpants, and I really wish he hadn't gotten up, because now I can't look away from his beautiful exposed body. Seeing all of it like this, while he's standing, in the amber glow of the bedside lamp is just so damned awe-inspiring.

He crosses his arms in front of his bare chest, silently daring me to continue on out the door, but I can see that he too is having second thoughts about my departure.

I play with the bottom of my pajama top, cross one leg in front of the other. "I mean…I'm not tired yet, are you?"

"I don't have to get up early."

I am back in his bed and naked again in three seconds.

I'm back in my apartment before the sun comes up, but I still feel wide awake.

Looking at myself in the mirror again, this time the woman staring back at me has tousled hair, flushed cheeks, swollen red lips that are pulled into a huge smile, and the skin on my chin is pink from scraping against my neighbor's stubble.

When not in the throes of ecstasy, I've been trying to keep my cool with Matt. He is well aware of all the orgasms I had, but I didn't exactly weep or squeal with glee in his presence. Now that I'm alone, I drop the act and quietly leap and twirl around my living room. I may even fist-pump a few times, because that's what you do when something awesome has happened.

That was so much more than what I usually got from my friends with benefits! What I usually get is the sexual equivalent of a cold pizza midnight snack. What that was is the sexual equivalent of the tasting menu at Le Bernardin.

I run into my bedroom, jump onto my bed, and do a quiet little jig, because *damn* that was the best sex I've ever had!

But also.

Damn.

That was the best sex I've ever had.

CHAPTER 11
MATT

A week has gone by, and I'm not a guy who's easily freaked out by anything, but I've been a little freaked out by how great the sex was with Bernadette.

I'd forgotten what it was like to have a sex partner, as opposed to being with a gorgeous woman who allowed me to pleasure her and worship at the temple of her body.

We haven't really seen each other since we slept together. After Bernadette left my apartment, I went back down to the basement to get her laundry out of the dryer and then placed the basket of clothes in the hallway outside her door and texted her that I had. I mean, I didn't fold it for her or anything—I'm not her maid. I just didn't want her going down there by herself at like three in the morning.

I've been busy with work, but she doesn't seem to have been home much either. A couple of days ago I saw her coming toward me down the block when I was walking Daisy, but I looked away because a dog started barking. When I looked up again, Bernadette had vanished. She was probably hiding in the corner store. I don't know why she'd feel the need to hide from me. I can only assume that she was equally freaked out by the awesomeness.

She was right, though. I do have to be careful not to get my thoughts and feelings about Vanessa confused with whatever it is that I've got going on with her. Maybe I'm just getting caught up in the firsts again. Maybe the only way to know for sure is if we have sex a few more times. If we're lucky, it will fall short of our expectations following the initial encounter, which will make it easier for both of us to find someone more appropriate.

I have never been so eager to have disappointing sex with someone that I'm really attracted to. She may have broken my brain. This is what I'm thinking when I'm heading down to the laundry room on a Friday night, instead of hanging out with my buddies at a bar in the West Village. One of my friends was intent on setting me up with an ex of his who's in town for the week, but I just didn't feel up to it.

If I don't run into Bernadette, I'll text her to see if she's available later on, as per the arrangement. But I don't run into Bernadette. I run into Mrs. Benson and her poodle. Mrs. Benson is probably in her sixties, and I'm guessing her poodle is around two hundred years old. I remember what Bernadette had said about Mrs. Benson's dinner parties, so at first when she invites me to her dinner party tomorrow night, I politely decline. When she insists that I come to meet an interesting young lady she thinks I would like, I reconsider.

When she says, "Oh wait—you must know Bernadette from the building! She'll be there!" I finally accept her invitation.

"Okay. Thank you, Mrs. Benson, I would love to come to your dinner party."

"Hooray!" she squeals. "Now, I wish I could invite you to bring your dog, but Alessandro doesn't like other animals."

"Not to worry." Although, now I'm very worried about entering the home of a woman who named her poodle Alessandro.

When she asks me to show up early to help her with a few things, I have to wonder if the interesting young lady she thinks I would like is *her*.

But if she tries to set me up with Bernadette Farmer, Bernie and I may never stop laughing.

I've been in Mrs. Benson's apartment for ten minutes and I'm considering faking a migraine or accidentally falling out the window to get out of the dinner. After setting up the dining table extension, she had me bring out the fine china from the cabinets and set the table, constantly directing me and reminding me that fine china is fragile—meanwhile I could smell something burning on the stove. She's wearing an old black Chanel dress and slippers and keeps going back to her bedroom to check on her poodle, who will be kept in there all night. Apparently Alessandro not only dislikes other animals, he also doesn't care much for people.

Now I'm in the kitchen, opening the three jars of pickles she has set out on the counter. She isn't going to be serving them to us. She just wanted me to open them for her. I take the liberty of opening up the bottle of wine that I brought, to let it breathe. Thankfully, I hear music coming from the living room now. The silence was so awkward. Unfortunately, the music that Mrs. Benson has selected is Barry White. Don't get me wrong, I love me some Barry White, but that is a seriously weird choice for an Upper West Side dinner party. My whole body tenses up, as I wonder for a second if the dinner party is all a ruse to get me to her apartment and Mrs. Benson is going to walk back in here in a chiffon nightgown.

All of this awkwardness is made up for as soon as I turn around and see Bernadette walk into the kitchen, carrying a bunch of flowers. She is shocked to see me. She's blushing so hard. I'm pretty sure she'd walk right back out again, except Mrs. Benson is right behind her, an impish grin on her face.

"Surprise, Bernadette! You've already met our new neighbor, haven't you?"

"Um. Yeah. Hi."

"Hello." I put my hand on my chest. "Matt."

"Yes, I remember. Nice to see you." She widens her eyes at me.

"Oh, Matt, can you get the vase down from the top shelf in that cabinet right behind you?"

"Certainly."

The front door intercom buzzes, and Mrs. Benson leaves us alone together in the kitchen. Suddenly, it's hilarious that "Can't Get Enough of Your Love, Babe" is playing in the other room. I hand Bernadette the vase. She takes it to the sink to fill it with water and proceeds to focus all of her attention on arranging and fluffing up the flowers in their new home.

I clear my throat. "How've you been?"

"Excellent. Fine. Super busy. You?"

"Same."

"Excellent."

What follows is a pause that's so long and quiet, I find myself wistfully remembering how fun it was when Mrs. Benson was telling me how to set her table.

She gives me a look. It's the look that I recall, from my earlier years as a single man, as the look that women give you when they're pissed at you for not calling after sex.

But she's the one who told me not to call.

That was supposed to be the point.

"I was going to text you last night," I whisper. "But then I was invited to this thing, and I figured it would be fun to surprise you."

"Oh yeah? And is it fun for you? Because I am definitely surprised to see you here."

"I'm having the time of my life."

"So happy to hear it."

After five more seconds of her scowling at me, I say in a hushed voice, "You told me not to text you the day after."

"I know that!" she hisses. "I'm not mad about that."

"Then what are you mad about?" And now I'm trying to navigate the minefield that is a woman's feelings after I've had sex with her. We might as well be dating.

"I'm not mad at all! I'm totally cool—you're the one being weird about everything!"

"Yeah. That seems like an adequate assessment of the situation."

"You know what—fine. I'm not going to do this." She huffs and then lowers her voice so much that I can barely hear her. I have to lean down to make out what she's saying. "I *was* annoyed that you didn't send the obligatory text the day after, and I *know* I told you that you weren't obligated to do that. But apparently when you blew my mind last week, my brain cells accidentally got reorganized into the brain cells of a woman who needs a little reassurance after being intimate with someone for the first time."

She takes a deep breath, and I don't even pretend not to watch her breasts rise and fall. However, the thing that's really knocking me on my ass and turning me on right now isn't those gorgeous mounds. It's her straightforward honesty. Now there's a trait I've never looked for in a woman, but now that I've seen it in action, I can't get enough.

She continues, "But I've recovered now. The brain cells are back in place. I am not mad at you for not texting me the day after we had intercourse, and I am still grateful that you brought my laundry up. And to be really honest, I probably just wanted to be mad at you because it was easier than thinking about how…"

"How what?"

She bites her lower lip and shakes her head. "Nothing. Anyway. We're good."

"Good." I lean in a little more to whisper in her ear. "Because I haven't been able to stop thinking about how great it was and how hot you were, and I want you back in my bed tonight."

I stand back from her just as Mrs. Benson returns to the kitchen, oblivious to the fact that Bernadette's giving me a hot look and I was about one second away from throwing Miss Farmer over my shoulder and charging up to my apartment. This is going to be a long night. My only consolation is knowing that it's going to be just as long for Bernadette as it is for me.

• • •

Most of the other guests have arrived, and they do nothing to make me think that Bernadette may have been exaggerating when she warned me about Mrs. Benson's dinner parties. I know why I agreed to come tonight, but I have no idea why she's here. Except that she's a nice person who seems to like retired ladies. We're introduced to Pearl, a fiftysomething woman who used to work in a human resources department with Mrs. Benson. She calls our hostess Regina, and I'm pretty sure that Pearl and Regina either hate each other or have had a secret lesbian affair that ended badly. There's a married couple (whose names I didn't get and will never remember) who seem to have agreed to come tonight because they were looking for a sublet in this neighborhood last month. Mrs. Benson invited them up to see her apartment, and they've kept in touch because one day she "might" sublet this place and move to a smaller one that doesn't have so many memories of her dearly departed husband. And there's Mrs. Benson's accountant—Carl. Carl is a little older than me, significantly shorter, not bad-looking, and he walks in wearing a vest and a fedora. He doesn't remove the hat until he's made sure everyone has seen him in it, and then he carefully places it on top of the coat rack by the door. I want to punch him in the face as soon as I meet him because it is obvious that he was invited tonight so he could be introduced to Bernadette.

He puts one hand on her elbow when they shake hands, and then he goes in for a hug. It's nauseating. "The lovely Bernadette. I hear you're a painter," this Carl guy says to her with a smirk. "What restaurant do you wait tables at?"

Oh come on. I hate him. I can tell she does too. I can't wait for her to unleash the sass on this poor unsuspecting idiot. But she just smiles politely and tells him that she works full-time as an executive assistant to a famous painter and doesn't have time to do any painting herself currently. A standard answer.

Great—now he's going to ask who she works for and I'm going to have to hear her say his name like she's twelve and he's a boyband.

But again, she surprises me by saying, "His name is Sebastian Smith," in a very casual way before excusing herself to go visit the poodle in the bedroom.

Is it weird that I feel a slight twinge of jealousy because she cares about another dog besides Daisy?

"Matt!" I turn to face our hostess, who is yelling at me enthusiastically. "Last but not least—come meet my niece, Liza!"

As Mrs. Benson drags her niece toward me, I can confirm that Bernadette was not the one she intended to introduce me to. Liza appears to be in her early twenties, has dyed jet-black hair, is perfectly pretty despite wearing far too much make-up, probably has an eating disorder, and gets tears in her eyes as soon as she sees me.

"Oh Jesus," she mumbles. "Seriously, Regina? *In what world?*"

In my peripheral vision, I can see that Bernadette has returned from the bedroom and is leaning against the wall, arms crossed, watching in amusement.

"Liza's parents are in Chicago for the weekend, and I wanted to make sure she eats something."

"Because obviously I'm an infant."

"And I wanted her to meet you! Liza, this is Matt McGill from upstairs! I don't know why she's crying—Liza, why are you crying?"

"Matt *McGovern*. Hi. Nice to meet you." I hold out my hand to shake Liza's.

"Oh yeah, I'm sure you're thrilled to meet me," Liza mutters. She turns to her aunt. "Was Bradley Cooper not available? Because there's just as good a chance of *him* wanting to date me." She turns back to me. "I'm so sorry you got dragged into this. Feel free to leave now and go to…your *GQ* photo shoot or whatever."

Bernadette is covering her mouth to keep from laughing out loud.

Regina Benson tries to loosen up her niece's tight shoulders. "Don't listen to her! Liza, you've been drinking, haven't you?"

"Not nearly enough."

"I'm uh—I'm happy to stay for dinner."

"I just love being surrounded by youthful energy! Now that Liza's finally here, we can sit for dinner and you two can start getting to know each other."

"Seriously. You don't have to talk to me. As you can see, I'm not living my best life right now. You can go ahead and talk to the hot one over there." She gestures toward Bernadette.

Trust me, Liza. I would very much like to.

Mrs. Benson has Bernadette and me help her bring out all five dishes at once, and they're all lukewarm, even the salad.

"Let's all go around the table and say our favorite book and why it's our favorite! It's a great conversation starter! I'll go first! *Eat, Pray, Love*! Because it gave me the courage to open myself to love again after losing my Marty."

"And how's that working out for you, Reggie?" snipes Pearl from the other side of the table.

"Better than the Bumble app has been working for you, my dear. Bernadette, you next! Favorite book and why!"

Bernadette seems to have her answer ready, probably because she's been to a dinner party here before. "My favorite book is called *Just Kids* by Patti Smith. It's about her friendship with Robert Mapplethorpe, and it's beautifully written, and I loved reading about two passionate young people in love with their art and New York and each other."

"Wasn't Mapplethorpe gay?" asks Carl.

"You'll have to read the book," she says, raising her shoulder to her chin, but I can tell she wants to punch this guy in the face.

"I'll take your word for it. My favorite book is everything Stephen King has ever written because I like to read them, and screw you to anyone who thinks he's a hack."

"I love all of his early work," Liza practically yells out. "Up until *Bag of Bones*."

"Well then, half-screw you."

"I do find Stephen King's work interesting from a pop culture standpoint," says Pearl, as if giving a seminar, "but it's hardly literature."

"Nobody said it was!" both Carl and Liza blurt out at the same time.

"I have a long list of books that I'd call my favorite, but if I had to choose one, I'd say it's Tolstoy's *War and Peace*."

"As opposed to Danielle Steele's War and Peace," Mrs. Benson quips. She might be holding an imaginary cigarette.

Pearl ignores her and continues. "Of the hundreds of

books I've read, it's the most brilliant, profound, unpredictable, and all-consuming."

"Next!"

I'm not sure why Mrs. Benson invited Pearl, because they seem to hate each other, but she referred to her as the only friend she keeps in touch with from work. Also, I don't really care about anything besides Bernadette right now. I just hope no one can tell that I'm currently picturing her sliding off her chair under the table and crawling toward me on her hands and knees…

The married couple talk over each other for five minutes, criticizing their spouse's taste in absolutely everything, and Bernadette and I keep exchanging furtive glances while hiding our smirks behind wineglasses. When it's time for me to proclaim my favorite book, the truth is that *New York Contract Law* is my favorite book to refer to on a regular basis, but that usually leads to more questions about me being a lawyer, and I don't want to get into it with this crowd. This is the most awkward combination of dinner party guests I've ever seen.

"My favorite is whatever recipe book you used to cook this delicious meal, Mrs. Benson," I say without a hint of irony—really.

Bernadette rolls her eyes at me, Mrs. Benson totally falls for it, and everyone else scoffs.

"Where are you from, Matt?" asks Mrs. Benson without giving Liza a chance to tell everyone what her favorite book is.

"Your crazy wet dream," Liza mumbles. "And my favorite book is *A Discovery of Witches* because I like it—thanks for asking!"

I notice Bernadette waiting for my answer, even though

Carl is going on and on to her about the pros and cons of the various dating apps he's been abusing.

"I grew up in Santa Barbara," I say to Mrs. Benson. "California."

"Oh, lovely! Liza's always wanted to go there, haven't you, Liza?" Before Liza can answer, she continues, "Oprah lives there, doesn't she?"

"I think she's in Montecito, yes, which is in Santa Barbara County."

"Do you have siblings? Liza is an only child."

"I can speak for myself, you know," she grumbles to her aunt.

"Well then, why don't you do that instead of mumbling *to* yourself?"

Liza rolls her eyes and then angles her body toward me slightly, without actually looking directly at me. "Um…do you have siblings?"

Again, I catch Bernadette's gaze darting over to me, but she quickly looks away when she realizes I'm looking at her. "I'm an only child too, actually."

"Oh yeah—me too!"

"Look at that," declares Mrs. Benson. "Something in common!"

Liza guffaws. She is exasperated. "Are you really even single?" she asks, still barely turning her head to look at me.

"I am. I just got out of a long-term relationship."

"Why'd you break up?" Carl stops midsentence in his conversation with Pearl and Bernadette to ask me this with a challenging tone. I'm not a big fan of this guy. If Mrs. Benson actually thought that he and Bernadette would hit it off, she may be kookier than I thought.

Bernadette doesn't look up at me, but her body has gone still, and I can tell she's waiting for my answer.

"We grew apart," I finally say. It has become my standard response, and it's the simplest way to convey the truth of the matter. It's certainly all that Carl needs to know about the situation.

"Yeah," he says, nodding. "Been there. Can't live with 'em, can't live without 'em."

"I heard that," the married guy says. I can hear his wife punch his leg under the table. I'm not sure if they'll be married much longer.

After staring at me, for what feels like an eternity, Pearl blurts out, "I'm only saying this because I'm slightly intoxicated, not because I'm a bitch, but I don't think you're all that handsome, Mr. McGovern."

Everyone else in the room but Pearl and I burst into fits of laughter.

"I agree," I say.

"Right? But I don't mean it as an insult. You guys—stop laughing! He's got magnetism. I mean, yes, he has a perfectly symmetrical face and a perfect body from what I can tell, and it's hard not to stare at him, but it's because of his magnetic personality."

"Thank you," I say as earnestly as possible, because how the fuck else am I supposed to respond to that.

"Bullshit!" Mrs. Benson yells out! "Bull! Shit! You are such a phony, Pearl Wexler. Why can't you just admit you're lusting after him? You think that makes you an intellectual? You think you're better than us if you aren't drooling over a man? Look at Bernadette! She couldn't care less about him, but she's not flaunting it like an asshole!"

"There it is! Here we go! It's not a party until Regina

starts yelling at me." Pearl raises her wineglass in Mrs. Benson's direction, spilling it a bit. "Doesn't matter if it's coffee and donuts in the break room or a birthday dinner at the Algonquin—the grand tradition continues!"

"Oh yes, as always, let's make this all about *you*!"

Finally, Bernadette's eyes meet mine. We both struggle to suppress our smiles. We both inadvertently stare at each other's lips before looking away.

I get a second wind, knowing that within a couple of hours, we will be one floor up and those lips will be touching mine.

CHAPTER 12
MATT

Bernadette and I are the last to leave, but it's not even nine thirty yet.

Needless to say, the dinner never got any better. At one point, Liza leaned in to smell my shoulder with her eyes closed, sighed, and then she just ignored me for the rest of the night. No one stuck around to chat over coffee in the living room once we'd finished dessert. I've never seen people leave a dinner party so quickly and never wanted so badly to be one of those rude and hasty people. Mrs. Benson requested that I help her return the dining table to its original four-seater state, which also meant clearing the table first. Bernadette offered to help with that. Mrs. Benson ran to her bedroom to check on Alessandro, declared that she needed to take him for a quick walk, and she would do the dishes as soon as she was back.

It's a strange combination of torture and relief to be left alone with Bernadette in this apartment, knowing that our hostess could return at any moment.

We don't say a word to each other the entire time she's

gone, and that's how I know for certain that she is as eager and conflicted about getting into bed again as I am.

No one seems to have noticed our many furtive looks and stolen glances all evening, which is surprising because it felt so obvious to me that my attention was entirely focused on her. Now, Bernadette basically only makes eye contact with my crotch and my hands while we are piling dirty dishes into the sink.

When she reaches out for me to pass her the empty wine decanter, I place it in her hands and then let my fingers lightly graze up the inside of her bare arm. I push her hair out of her face. She shivers in exactly the way I wanted her to, but she still refuses to look up at me. I am about to lean in to kiss her. When I hear the front door open, we quickly back away from each other like school kids who are afraid of getting caught.

"You would not believe what we just saw!" Mrs. Benson calls out as she lets the poodle off the leash. "Carl and my niece sucking face, right there on the sidewalk on Broadway! I'm so sorry things didn't work out for you two," she says, but she doesn't look like she feels sorry for us at all. "I'll have to have a good think about who I can invite for you both next time." Her eyes get that impish glint in them again when she says, "Unless you're both spoken for by then, of course." She attempts a slow wink, I think, but just kind of closes her eyes while opening her mouth wide for a second.

"Great!" we both say at the same time, a little too loudly, a little too quick to respond.

We both give her a hug as we leave, thanking her so much for a fun evening, overcompensating without guilt as we speed-walk toward the front door.

• • •

All in all, it wasn't the worst two and a half hours of my life, and I feel like it was all worth it as soon as we walk out into the hallway and I hear Bernadette take in a long. deep breath, preparing herself for the night that's about to begin. To be honest, it feels like this has all been building up to so much more than just this next encounter. But, first things first.

As soon as we turn the corner of the stairwell, I pull her to me and kiss her. When I pull away from her, her eyes are still closed, her lips still mid-kiss. I run up ahead of her, feeling like an adolescent boy once again, as if it's the running that's making my heart race.

Oh wait—I forgot that I was rooting for the sex to be worse this time so I wouldn't get hooked. Oh well. Maybe next time.

When we get to the top of the stairs, she grabs on to my shirt and pushes me against the wall. Her eyes are practically glowing with desire. All of the glowing desire that she's been successfully hiding until now. She raises her face up to kiss me and then retreats back, teasing me, as she starts unbuttoning my shirt.

"Tell me—is that the first time a woman has cried the first time she looked at you?" Her voice is hushed and husky, and every word out of her mouth just sounds like "sex sex sex" to me.

"It was, and I hope it's the last. At least she didn't laugh."

She pauses for a moment, fumbling with one of the buttons. "I don't believe I'm the only one who's done that."

"You are."

She pulls me toward her and kisses me hard, probably

trying to make me forget that she laughed when she first saw me. I never will.

"What's your favorite book, really?" she asks in between kisses.

"It's a legal reference book."

The kissing comes to an abrupt halt. She frowns. "Why am I not surprised. That's your *favorite* book? Really? Like, if you could only read one book over and over for the rest of your life—that's what you'd pick?"

"I couldn't do my job without it."

She shakes her head, genuinely disappointed. "We are very different."

"We agree on that. Don't let it stop you from coming over."

"My place this time," she whispers. She takes my hand and leads me to her door. My hands are massaging her hips while she comically struggles to get her key in the lock. She's trembling, and I can't stop touching her. If knowing that it can't go anywhere is an aphrodisiac, then not seeing her for a week, followed by hours of seeing her without being able to touch her, is a fucking Viagra bomb.

It's entirely possible that I'd feel this way about anyone I'd have sex with now, but one whiff of her neck and I find myself holding in a sigh. It's not cool. It's not good. But damn, this woman is doing something new to me and I like it.

As soon as she gets the door open, she pulls me in, shuts the door, and shoves me up against it. She's really pushing and pulling me tonight, and I'm fine with that. She doesn't turn on the lights, and that's fine too. Her lips find mine. She tugs on my lower lip with her teeth and sucks my tongue in a way that tells me she is just as fired up as I am. Her hand finds the strong-willed bulge in my pants, and I hear her catch her breath.

My neighbor takes my hand, leading me farther into her apartment. It's still dark but not as dark as when there was a blackout. I'd come so close to kissing her that night. I would have, if the lights hadn't suddenly come back on and Alanis Morissette hadn't started shrieking from the other room. Talk about a mood killer.

She stops in front of her sofa and pushes me down onto it. Still no lights. I know she isn't shy about her body. Maybe she's trying to make this more impersonal. That's probably it.

Also fine with me.

She feels as good as she looks. Her hands are smooth and deliberate, exploratory and unwavering. All my other sense are heightened.

She removes my shirt, leans down, and presses herself lightly against my chest while unzipping my pants. She has taken her top and bra off, teasing me by brushing her erect nipples against my bare skin. When I reach for them, she pushes me away. When I try to bring her closer, she moves my hands and places them behind my head. Somebody wants to be in control tonight…

I lean back and lift my ass up so she can tug my pants and boxers down. Now she's removing my shoes so she can take my pants off completely. She is nothing if not thorough, and I'm not sure how much more of this I can take. This might be retaliation for when I took my time with her last weekend. No good deed goes unpunished.

Her hands move up my legs to my thighs. She pushes my knees apart, and I feel her settle herself down in between them. I have to grip the back of the sofa to keep from rocketing to the ceiling when her warm tongue meets the tip of my cock. I groan out her name, just once, before I lose the ability to form words. An asteroid could hit Manhattan, and I wouldn't notice anything besides this feeling of Bernadette's mouth and hands on me and the sweet sounds she's making as if she's genuinely enjoying it as much as I am. Every inch of my dick and balls are enthusiastically being attended to. My hands are in her hair, and I can't think of anything that has ever felt this good. She is an artist in so many ways.

I'm not sure how much time has passed—somewhere between thirty seconds and infinity—but as much as I'm loving what she's doing to me, I need to do something before I detonate. As if she can read my filthy thoughts, I can hear her reach for my pants. She hands them to me, and I pull out the condom I just happened to have in my wallet.

I clasp my hands onto the sides of her waist as she lowers herself down onto me, oh so slowly, and I savor her tight, wet hold on me before asking, "You want to keep taking this slow?"

"Oh hell no."

Thank God.

She bears down on me, and we find a rhythm for a while, and then I get to work rocking my hips up and down, one hand on her shoulder and one on the back of the sofa in an attempt to anchor it. I really hope there are felt pads on the bottom of this sofa, because it's not staying still tonight.

"You…are…such…a…show-off!" she manages to exclaim between breathless gasps.

"You ain't seen nothin' yet."

She laughs, briefly, until I ramp things up. I'm thrusting like my life depends on it and then carefully raise her up and flip her around so I can squeeze her breasts from behind while she's bouncing up and down on my cock. I reach down to apply pressure to her clit. I wait until she's done with her chorus of "Oh God! Oh yes! Oh fuck! Oh my God—Matt!" before maneuvering her so her knees are bent on the sofa and making sure her hands are holding on to the back of it. And now that I'm standing, I grip her hips as I slam into her with so much drive to connect with this woman it overwhelms me. When I come, it's such a release, I am louder than usual. When we're done, we are both drenched in sweat. She's collapsed on top of me, breathing heavily into my neck. I'm exhausted and I probably pulled a muscle in my lower back, but I still can't stop touching her.

"Well, that was fun," she says, and I'm treated to another throaty laugh, and then she falls quiet and still.

I grunt in agreement. There's nothing I can say that would match how I feel right now, and there certainly isn't an emoji for it. I'm high on the scent of her, and she'll need to come up with a really valid reason for me to remove my hands from her perfect peach of an ass.

A few minutes later, once our heartbeats and breaths have slowed, she pulls away from me, and I feel the cool air rush in between us when she comes up with a very valid reason.

"Well…you should probably go check on Daisy…right?"

"Right," I say, feeling around for my pants. "I'll let you get to your binge-watching."

I give her a quick kiss before finding my way to the door in the dark.

"Good night," she says. "Thanks."

I can't help but laugh. "My pleasure." I know most of

my buddies would put up a statue in Bernadette's honor if they knew how cool she is about this kind of situation. I have no complaints.

We don't want to get too attached. I'll have to move to a new place eventually, maybe even soon, and this arrangement probably won't work if it isn't as convenient as it is now. She's probably still obsessed with her boss, and surely one day he'll realize what a catch she is and snatch her up. How could he not?

When I open the door to my aunt's apartment, Daisy is waiting for me in the hallway, shaking her bum, jumping and twirling around, ready to lick my face off and then go outside for a quick late-night walk.

Maybe this is the perfect situation for me.

Maybe this is all I need—an interesting woman to have amazing casual sex with and a dog that I can love with all my heart.

Daisy tilts her head at me, blinks, and snorts, as if to say, "That's basically what I've been telling you all along, dummy."

CHAPTER 13
BERNADETTE

After that somewhat awkward transitional period, Matt McGovern and I have eased into the perfect neighbors with benefits arrangement, and I am determined to enjoy every no-strings kiss and beneficial thrust while it lasts. We've had a week of nightly sex and one more intense make-out session in the laundry room. I've even started separating my lights and darks so I can spend more time hanging out in the basement with him—and I left my phone upstairs so we wouldn't get interrupted.

Get pounded by ridiculously hot neighbor while doing laundry all morning is now at the top of my Will-Do list for this Saturday.

If there were a security camera in the hallway outside our apartments, someone could edit together a pretty fun montage. I come home from work, shut my front door, open the door again, and then enter the neighboring apartment. Then I come out again with a blissed-out smile on my face and my hair all messed up. Matt knocks on my door; I open it and grab him by the shirt collar to pull him inside. He walks back out the door with his shirt unbuttoned and my lipstick all over his face. With some upbeat nineties tune playing, to signify to everyone that this is not serious.

We tease each other and chat, and I have absolutely no idea if he's looking at other apartments or when Dolly will be coming home, but it actually feels like we're doing this right. It's fun. We're respecting boundaries. Nobody's asking where this is going or trying to share their feelings. But…orgasms, orgasms, tra-la-la-laaaaaahhhh orgasms!

It's still new, so we seem to be going for the gold every time, but I find it difficult to imagine that sex with Matt could ever get boring. He's so generous and passionate and responsive. So different from what he's like the rest of the time.

I get home from work relatively early on Friday, at around five thirty. Sebastian has been fairly complacent and undemanding this past week, it seems, or it may just be that I'm not as keyed into his every mood and whim as I used to be. My plan is to give my vagina a rest tonight, in preparation for laundry day—my fingers are itching to do some sketching—and there's a new Netflix series I want to plow through. To be honest, I also need to prove to myself that I'm still capable of getting through one night alone, without a particular person's penis inside me.

As I reach my building, I find an Uber car double-parked out front. I recognize the guy who's holding his hand out to someone in the back seat—it's Lloyd the protégé. He's holding a pair of crutches in one hand and helping Matt out of the car with the other. Seeing that man accept help from another human does strange things to my heart. The tip of my nose starts tingling. When I see that he's wearing sweat pants and an ankle brace on his left leg, I get that same feeling I had after I witnessed him with Vanessa and her new boyfriend. I just want to make him feel better.

Matt doesn't lean against Lloyd for long. He takes the crutches, and the closer I get, the more obvious it is that he has the sweet hazy demeanor of someone who's stoned on painkillers.

"Hi there." I try to sound casual and not overly concerned. "What happened to you?"

"*You* happened," Matt grumbles with just a hint of a smile on his lips. He is bleary-eyed, and his face looks so different without the usual tension in his jaw. His features are slightly less defined and much less intimidating.

"Really? *I* did this to you? Seriously, what happened?"

"I have to get Daisy from daycare," he drawls to no one in particular.

Lloyd scratches his head and checks his phone. "I can go pick her up, I guess."

"No, I can get her," I say. "Hi, I'm Bernadette. I live next door to Matt. Lloyd, right?"

"Yeah hi, hey, I'm Lloyd, yeah. Hi." Lloyd reaches out, and I shake his hand while Matt dreamily stares around at the air in front of him.

"What happened?" I ask Lloyd. "Is he on painkillers?"

"Yeah, the doctor said he should only need over-the-counter, but one of the other lawyers gave him a Percocet before we left the office just now. He sprained his ankle playing basketball at lunch. I took him to a clinic. It's a grade-one sprain, but the doctor said he'd heal faster if he stays off that foot for a few days."

"I'm fine," Matt declares as he heads for the door to the wrong building.

"Hey!" I whistle. "Over here, champ." I wave at him and jerk my head toward our building.

He adjusts the direction he's heading in, as if he was just taking the scenic route. Even on crutches, he moves with grace and confidence. It almost makes me want to trip him.

"So, Lloyd," I say as I open the front door to the foyer. "I hear you're into raves and house music and all that stuff."

He laughs. "What? That's hilarious. Where'd you hear that?"

I narrow my eyes at Matt, who is oblivious.

"Guess I'm thinking of someone else."

We look up at the stairs.

Lloyd groans. "What floor is he on?"

"Fourth."

"I can go up myself," Matt insists. "I can hop on one leg."

"Don't even think about it, mister," I say. "Maybe you should get a hotel room for a couple of nights? So you can use an elevator?"

"No," he says stubbornly. "Here." He doesn't say it, but from the way he looks at me, I'd like to think that he wants to be here so he can stay close to me.

Honestly, surprisingly, it's what I want too.

Sprained ankle be damned.

It takes him less than two minutes to reach the second floor, both Lloyd and me hanging back behind Matt as he eventually gets the hang of ascending the stairs with both crutches. Good thing he has such impressive ab strength.

The only thing slowing him down at this point is probably the Percocet.

"Have to get Daisy," Matt mumbles as we reach the door to 4B.

"I'll get her," I tell Lloyd. "I know where the daycare is. Can you stay with him until I get back? Make sure he stays off his feet?"

"Yeah, sure. I have a dinner date in an hour, though."

"I'll definitely be back within half an hour."

"My keys are in my pants," Matt says to me, grinning like a naughty boy. "Wanna get them for me?"

"Oh yes, may I?" I roll my eyes as I reach into the front pocket of his sweat pants.

Lloyd quietly clears his throat and looks away.

Matt's head is tilting down toward me as I pull the keyring out. I lean back because we're not supposed to kiss in front of other people, but he probably doesn't remember that in this state. I open the front door and place the keys on the console table as Matt and Lloyd enter.

"I guess you should text or call the daycare to let them know I'm picking her up, right?"

Matt grins at me. "My phone's in the other pocket."

Lloyd is watching us curiously and looking at Matt like he doesn't even recognize him.

"Okay, well, why don't you sit down on the sofa so you can get off the crutches and get it yourself? Lloyd, why don't you help him with the texting? I'll head out to pick Daisy up now."

"Yeah, no problem."

"You better bring Daisy back," Matt warns me.

"Please," I say. "What do you think I'm going to do—take her on a bus to my parents' farm in Vermont?" Although, as I say it, I mentally picture how wonderful it would be to see Daisy running around on my parents' vast property. It makes me sad and happy at the same time, as most thoughts of the farm do. Or maybe it's my thoughts of Daisy that are bittersweet lately. Having a connection with someone who isn't mine should be freeing—because I don't have to take responsibility for her. But knowing that each time I see her could be the last is beginning to weigh on me.

It doesn't help that Daisy is so happy to see me when I get to the doggy daycare. She scampers toward me, carrying her leash in her mouth, and stands up on her hind legs in front of me. I only briefly consider buying us two bus tickets to Vermont… Walking her home is fun. I regularly consider adopting a pet for myself, but it just doesn't seem like a good idea, given that I live in a walk-up and have little control over how much time I can spend at home. As always—no-strings is the best possible scenario, and I just have to keep my feelings in check and enjoy what's happening now.

I suppose there are worse places to be living than the fourth floor of walk-up when you have a sprained ankle. Like, the fifth floor of a walk-up. Or a treehouse. But I don't really want Matt to stay anywhere else, and I really don't want to think about why he doesn't want to stay in a hotel either.

When Daisy and I get back to 4B, Matt is sprawled out on the sofa with his left leg resting on the back of it and the other foot on the floor. I'm pretty sure I was in that exact same position on that sofa on Tuesday night, with his face up in my lady business. If Dolly knew what her nephew and I have been up to on her furniture, she might double my rent. Or, more realistically, she would ask for details.

I relieve Lloyd of his duties so he can get to his dinner date. I order groceries and deli meals for Matt and go downstairs to get them when they're delivered. I put everything away in the kitchen, make sure there's toilet paper in the bathroom, make an ice pack, make more ice. I find a serving tray and load it up with a bottle of water, box of tissues, an apple, and a pack of oatmeal raisin cookies. I take it all to the guest room before insisting that Matt trade the couch for the bed.

"Why?" he asks because he's a stubborn boy.

"Because you need to sleep. For a long time. And you need to get to bed before the drug really kicks in." I hold up the crutches in front of me. "Come on. Let's go."

"Yes, sir." All eight of his abs get him up off the sofa without him having to put any weight on his left foot, and he leans into the crutches toward me. His face stops two inches from mine. "Hi," he whispers.

"Hi."

"Thank you."

"You're welcome."

"You aren't gonna go yet, are you?"

"I'm going to make sure you get into bed, and I'm going to make sure your feet are elevated, and I'm going to make sure Daisy's fed and walked again before the end of the night."

He pouts, a little bit, for a second. Now there's an expression I never in a million years expected to see on that face.

"Thank you."

"You're welcome."

When we get to the guest room, I take the crutches from him and he carefully lowers himself into bed.

When I lean the crutches against the bedside table, I notice the copy of *Just Kids* by Patti Smith.

He's reading my favorite book.

"I was thinking about you," he whispers.

"What? When?"

"When I sprained my ankle. I was dunking the ball and thinking I wish you could see this, and I landed wrong. You're ruining my life." He smiles when he says it, but he really seems to mean it.

"I know what you mean. You should lie back and put your foot up on pillows."

He lies back, and I run to the living room to grab a couple of pillows and then place them under the sheets and prop his foot up on them. He watches me, still smiling. It's a drugged-out smile, but my heart still skips a beat every time I catch him doing anything other than Sexy Hot Guy Face.

"You're really beautiful. I think. Do *you* think you're beautiful? I can't tell." His eyes are mostly shut as he attempts to lift his head up.

"Um. Sure."

"C'mere."

"Okay." I stay where I am, at the foot of the bed.

"Are you moving toward me?"

I'm not. "Uh-huh. Very slowly."

"Don't mess with me," he says, his voice getting less dreamy, more stern. "Get in bed with me."

"I have things to do."

"You have to get in bed with me."

"Okay. Five minutes."

"Five-teen minutes."

"Okay."

"Okay. You're nice."

"Yeah."

"You're sweet."

"Don't tell anyone."

"I know your secret… I like being with you…"

I hold my breath. This kindness and openness is alarming.

He looks over at me. "Did I say that out loud just now?"

"Nope. You're asleep."

"I'm not."

I sigh and shift around. "I like being with you too."

He nuzzles his face against my belly and wraps his arm around my waist.

My throat is starting to constrict. My heart is racing, and not in the good way. He is being so sweet, it's stupid that it makes me nervous and uncomfortable, but it does.

I shouldn't read anything into this. For all I know, he's so loopy right now he doesn't realize that it's me here with him and not his ex-girlfriend. There is still a really good chance that he'll go back to her, the second she shows any interest.

Don't ask, don't ask, don't ask.

"Hey, Matt? Have you been in touch with Vanessa?"

He'll never remember that I asked.

He furrows his brow. "No. Don't say her name." He covers my mouth with his fingers. "I don't like you saying her name."

"Why?"

"Because. No mixing feelings, remember?"

"Okay. You need to stay on your back so you can raise your foot up."

"Mmmm no." He nuzzles me. "What do you smell like?"

"What?"

"You always smell good. Vanilla. Lavender. Not like a candle. Like it's coming off your skin." His face is now pressed against my neck. He inhales loudly and then exhales with a resounding "aaaahhhhhh!" His arms are wrapped tight around my waist, pulling me into him. "What's the other thing?"

"What other thing?"

"The smell?"

"Amber and coconut."

"Whaaaaaaat?" He buries his face in my chest. "Soooo goooood." His voice is still deep and masculine, but he's being so boyish right now, it actually hurts my heart. "Nobody else smells like you."

"I made it myself. When I was at my parents' place. My mom makes perfume oils and candles."

He groans. I can feel his erection against my thigh, but I'm pretty sure he'd try to hump a body pillow right now, and I am not about to let this go any further. His fingers gently caress my nipple, over my top. All I'm thinking about is that I don't know if he meant "No, I haven't been in touch with Vanessa" or "No, don't say her name." But I guess I don't really care. Because Matt McGovern is caressing my nipple over my top. My eyes close and my head drops back just as his hand falls away and his head hits the pillow.

I watch him sleep, studying and memorizing his face. I would die of embarrassment if he ever saw the work in my current sketchbook. He'd be so creeped out. It's all quite abstract, as much of my work is. Most people wouldn't recognize him or me. But I know it's us.

It feels like I'm moving into some new phase of my artistic development, and that excites me. I've always looked through Sebastian's extensive art book collection during my breaks, and lately I've been browsing the erotic works of Gustav Klimt, Egon Schiele, and Toulouse-Lautrec. Even if he goes back to his girlfriend tomorrow, the impact that Matt McGovern has had on my life in this relatively short period of time has been huge.

All because of what he does to me in bed.

Okay, that might not be the whole truth.

Obviously, he brought Daisy into my life too. And whatever it is that he does to me in bed, it started long before we got here. But we're here, and I'm grateful.

I lean down to kiss him on his forehead. He doesn't move at all. He's out like a light, expressionless as always, but I see so much more than a handsome face when I look at him now. Despite how cozy it is in bed with him, this is outside my comfort zone. I am determined to stay here as long as possible, while trying not to get lost.

CHAPTER 14
MATT

It's dark when I wake up, but the hallway light is on.

I smell vanilla and lavender and something, so I reach around for Bernadette.

"You here?" I whisper.

No response.

"Anyone? Daisy?"

I can hear Daisy snoring in her doggy bed on the floor by the foot of my bed.

"Text me if you need anything," I remember her saying.

I have no idea what time it was when she left, but it's eleven thirty now, and I feel like I'm waking up after a year-long nap. My ankle's fine. There's a dull ache, nothing I can't handle. I'm thirsty and awake…and exceptionally horny. I'm feeling that dull ache all over. I switch on the bedside lamp. There's a big bottle of water on the table, right next to the book I've been reading. Shit, I would have hidden that if I'd known she was coming over. It's dumb to want to hide that I'm reading her favorite book, but I have a feeling it would make her uncomfortable.

She has written on the top Post-it note of the stack I keep on the table.

Don't get up unless you use your crutches! Promise me. I just walked Daisy, she's been fed, and I'll be back in the morning to take her to daycare on my way to work. Get some rest.

P.S. I bought prune juice (in kitchen) in case the Percocet makes you constipated. xx

Well, *that's* sexy.

She's thoughtful, though.

I have vague memories of saying things that I never would have said to her if I weren't under the influence of a controlled substance. Perhaps I'm still under the influence, because I don't regret it. I just wish I could remember exactly what I said and how she responded.

There's a lot that I wish I could say to her right now, things I wouldn't say or write to her.

I sit up and look around.

I remove the pencil that I was using to hold my place in the book and start writing down what I'm feeling, in a secret place.

I may never be able to say these things out loud to her, but I want to get them out while I'm feeling them.

Thank you.

You're so fucking hot.
You're good in bed.
You're good out of bed.
I think about you all the time.
I like thinking about you.
I'm glad I met you.
I don't know if it would have been better if we'd met years earlier, or months later, but I'm glad I know you now.
I want to know more about you.
I want you to know more about me.
I want a lot when it comes to you, Bernadette. It surprises me. You surprise me.
I wish you were here in bed with me now.

And on and on, I write until my thumb starts to cramp up, and even when I'm done I'm not ready to face the rest of the night alone without her.

She needs her space, I know that. I don't want her to come over and take care of me again. I just have to know that she's there. I reach for my laptop, which is on the floor by the bed. I double-click on iMessages and re-read our past conversations while eating a cookie. We've got chemistry, there's no doubt about that. I wipe the cookie dust from my fingers and get ready to make contact.

Me: You awake?

BF: Did you sleep?

. . .

Me: Yes. I feel great.

BF: Do you need anything?

Me: Yes. Are you on your bed?

BF: Yes.

Me: Good. Stay there.

Me: Are you naked?

BF: No.

Me: Unacceptable. Take off your clothes.

BF: Bossy.

Me: Just getting started. Do it, or I'll come over and take them off for you.

BF: Stay right where you are, mister.

. . .

BF: Okay. I'm naked. Happy now?

Me: Are you thinking about me?

BF: <rooster emoji>

Me: I want you to touch yourself. Be loud so I can hear you.

BF: <surprise face emoji>

Me: Don't be shy. Don't hold back. Don't think about anything but me touching you. It's all I can think about.

Me: I want you to gently circle your breast with the fingers of one hand. Reach down to stroke your clit with the other. Imagine me doing this to you. Then picture me cupping your breasts as I kiss those perky nipples. I kiss them hard and hungry because I've been craving them and then soft and slow because I'm getting exactly what I need and I like it. I like the way you taste, and I like the way you smell. I like the way you sound when you're licking and sucking, and I love the way you sound when I make you come. Now imagine me kissing a trail down between your legs, still cupping your tits, and I lightly blow on your clit before I French kiss your sweet lower lips until you scream and swear like a marine.

• • •

She doesn't write back, and I take that as a good sign.

That should get her in the mood, if she wasn't already in it.

I turn my head toward the vent.

I can't hear anything. She's taking her time, and that's good.

A few seconds later, I hear a draw slam shut and that little jackhammer's getting to work.

Well now, Miss Bernadette.

Whatever floats her boat.

The moaning and groaning begins in no time.

I push the laptop away.

Daisy creeps out of the room.

"Ahhh! Matt!" my neighbor calls out. "Oh God, Matt! Oh yes! Fuck! Yes! Ohhhhh!"

Yup. That's what it sounds like when she's on the way to a climax, and I am right there with her. I can picture her writhing around, her toes pointing as her head jerks up off the pillow, her angry O-face. It's all happening so much faster than when we're together, but it's fine with me.

Now she sounds like she's actually in pain, but I know that's not what it is, and I disappear into myself for a little while.

I'm going to have to have new sheets delivered tomorrow because I don't think I'll be getting down to the basement to wash these any time soon and I'm sure as hell not going to let Bernadette clean them for me. The evidence of my enjoyment of her is all over.

I'll definitely be buying my aunt some fresh new bed sheets when I leave here.

Meanwhile, I wish I could hear the sighs and watch Bernadette's chest heave as she catches her breath.

My laptop dings with a notification.

BF: twyuieopyrwiub1ajkfsdluiqowar;eup;uzjklgf-dapoireuwhstdfgj

BF: Just kidding. I'm done.

BF: Hope you enjoyed the show.

BF: Sorry it was such a quick one. There will be no repeat performances tonight, as the star is about to fall asleep with a smile on her face.

Me: Wham bam thank you ma'am.

Me: Good night. And thank you. Not just for that but for helping out earlier.

BF: I'll see you in the morning when I walk Daisy.

BF: Here if you need me. Good night.

. . .

Me: Good night.

I guess that no matter what I say or what I don't say, what I mean is this: *I don't need anyone, Bernadette, but I'm here if you want me too.*

CHAPTER 15
MATT

FROM: DOLLY KEMP <doloreskemp123@yahoo.com>
TO: MATT MCGOVERN (personal) <iammattmcgov-
ernsemail@gmail.com>

Ciao from Roma! My spy tells me you have taken a lover. This is excellent news, and needless to say, I do approve. Hope you enjoyed the dinner party. *Wink* (I know you disapprove of emojis).
Have fun. If you do anything stupid, like hurt her, you will feel my wrath and the tip of my pointy shoe from across the Atlantic. So be smart and watch your ass.
I wish I could travel Europe forever, believe me, but Marty is beginning to miss his home in Miami. We haven't bought a return flight yet. In fact—as you may know—we will be meeting up with your parents when they visit this fair continent. Thank you for checking in again, but please feel free to stay in my apartment until I let you know that you must leave it.

And no, I will not accept any rent from you. Save it for a down payment or some treats for Daisy.
xx Your favorite aunt (who's infinitely cooler than your mom)

P.S. I am aware that our dear neighbor has certain arrangements with certain men, and I'm sure she has convinced you that it's all she wants with you. She is a very capable, independent woman, but she is not like the towering ice queens you usually go for. She will either bend or break. Don't let her break.

P.P.S. FYI, I care very much about your feelings too, and no, I have not been in communication with her about you. Also, in case it wasn't clear—when I said she could bend or break, I wasn't talking about sex positions… I may be a little bit drunk right now.

Two weeks have passed since I sprained my ankle, and I've been walking without crutches for a week. It's healing nicely, and I just have a bit of a limp. For a few days, Bernadette insisted that I use the wooden cane that she bought in Chinatown. I did. But only around the neighborhood and only because she did a ridiculous little Charlie Chaplin walk when she presented it to me. Also, because I would do pretty much anything for her at this point, although she has no idea.

It was really starting to feel like we live together, especially since she kept coming over for Daisy. But then once I was able to take Daisy for walks, she suddenly got really busy again. It could be work, or she could be pulling away from me. I've been busy catching up with work too, so it's not like I'm going to confront her about it. Regardless of what my aunt wrote, I'm not sure which of us is more likely to break.

I take a long way home from doggy daycare Wednesday evening because it's really nice out after a week of shitty weather. Daisy and I are getting back into the swing of things. She looks back at me and snorts. I know what she's thinking: "*You're just trying to avoid seeing Bernadette because you want to tell her something that you think she doesn't want to hear. I know Chihuahuas with bigger balls than you.*"

Women.

Can't live with 'em, can't live next door to them.

"Actually, I made plans to meet up with the guys tonight," I tell her. "I'm just making sure you get everything out of your system now. So there."

When we get to the foyer, Daisy gets really excited, and I realize it's because she sees Bernadette. Bernadette is sitting on the floor in front of the mailboxes, inhaling a candle. She's wearing sweats, her hair is up in a ponytail, and there's an open package between her splayed legs. She looks like she's stoned.

"Hello."

"I got a care package," she says, grinning. Her eyes are droopy and her voice is low. "Hello, crazy Daisy!"

"From your parents?"

She reaches into the box and holds up a piece of soap. "Smell this. My mom made it."

It does smell good. It smells like Bernadette. "Did she make this stuff?"

"Yes. Everything's from the farm." She shows me a couple of jars of jam and pickled things, tiny bouquets of dried herbs, and little watercolor paintings on thick paper. She hugs the paintings to her chest. "I love my mom and dad."

"Are you okay? Can I help you up?"

She nods her head and puts everything back in the box and then manages to stand up on her own. "Carry the box up for me," she orders.

I pick up the box. "Seriously. What's wrong with you?"

She sighs. "Nothing! I don't get sick. Sebastian sent me home in a cab because I was having chills and body ache things. I took a Theraflu, and I'm gonna sleep all night and be fine tomorrow. I just need to sleep. Should I take Daisy for a walk?" She wanders in a zigzag, vaguely in the direction of the stairs.

"What? I just walked her home, and no you can't leave this building. Get up to your apartment."

"Bossy."

"Go up the stairs. Now."

She opens her mouth to yell at me and then has a coughing fit. It makes her mad, and her expression tells me she blames me for the fact that she's coughing. I feel bad for her, but it's really cute. I stay right behind her so she doesn't fall backwards. I notice that she wobbles as she reaches for the handrail.

"Are you sure all you took was Theraflu? Because you smell like red wine."

"*You* smell like red wine."

"You should not have come downstairs in this state."

"What state? Vermont? The Theraflu hasn't kicked in yet. I'm fine. Look!"

She runs up to the landing, but when she gets there, she grabs on to the wall. "Whoa."

"Don't do that."

"I'm fine."

"You're not. How much wine did you drink?"

"Not wine." She holds up an index finger to lecture me. "Medicine. Old family recipe. You heat up a cup of red wine with honey and cinnamon and lemon. All better."

"You mean mulled wine? Keep walking. Slowly."

"It's for the flu," she snaps. "Do you have the box from my mom?"

"I'm holding on to it right here, see?"

She doesn't look back, just stomps up the stairs and refuses to talk to me until we get to the fourth floor.

She tries to open her door but can't get the key in the lock.

"I'll do it."

"I got it."

"Hold on to the leash."

She happily takes Daisy's leash and frowns at me as she hands me the keys. I open the door and place the box on the coffee table in the living room.

"Thank you," she says begrudgingly. "I'm going to bed now."

"Okay." I take the leash from her.

"Can you do me a favor and make sure I'm up by eight tomorrow?"

"No, but I can do you a bigger favor and make sure you stay in bed all day tomorrow."

"*Pffft.* I'll be fine. I'm gonna take another Theraflu now."

"You can't take two doses of Theraflu in one night."

"Don't be such a bossy prude."

"You can wreck your liver by taking too much acetaminophen at once." She's infuriating.

She stomps her feet again and crosses her arms in front

of her chest. "I feel fine. Go live your life. I feel awesome. Stop moving your face."

"I'm not moving my face."

"It's jumping around too fast."

"You need to drink *a lot* of water. Like a gallon of water."

She blows raspberries at me.

I pretend to wipe spit from my face. "Now you're even more dehydrated."

"Haaaahhhhaaa." She laughs like a little girl and then practically falls asleep standing up. She is a mess.

I remove the leash from Daisy's collar and drop my messenger bag to the floor. Then I pick Bernadette up and carry her to her bed.

She keeps her eyes shut. "Are you carrying me?"

"Yes."

She grunts, and then shivers, and then holds her head. "Ow."

"Headache?"

"Everything ache," she pouts.

I lower her to the unmade bed and watch her collapse into it.

"Do you want to wear those sweats or something lighter?"

She starts to pull her top off. "Nothing. I'm hot!"

"I think you need to wear something."

She stops moving when the sweatshirt is covering her face. "Ahhhh! No!" She pulls it back on. "Everything's prickly!" She groans. "I hate this. I'm dying."

"You're not dying. I won't let you."

She waves her arm in the air and lets it flop down. "Just let me die."

"Do you feel nauseated?"

"No." She squeezes her eyes shut and then starts to say something again but then has another dry coughing fit and makes a strained, agonized wail. "If I die, tell my parents I love them and I'm sorry."

I pull her fuzzy boots off her feet. "What are you sorry for?"

"For not converge-sating with them."

"Mmmhmmm." I'm not gonna ask. I see that she already has a big bottle of water by her bed. "Okay. When was the last time you ate? Do you have food here? I'll order something."

She covers her face and whimpers. "I can't eat… Wait. I'm hungry."

I call Daisy over and bring her up on the bed. "Stay here with Daisy. I'll order something. I'll be right back. Don't go anywhere."

"Daisy!" she whispers and holds her arms out, eyes closed. Daisy licks her face and stretches out alongside her. I watch them for a few seconds before forcing myself to look away.

My two favorite girls are in bed together.

I go into the living room to order chicken noodle soup and orange juice from the deli and then send a group text to my friends to tell them I'm not going to make it to the bar tonight because I have to help out my neighbor. I ignore the "Yeah. Help her have more orgasms" and eggplant emoji responses from them. I may have mentioned to them, the one time I met them for a beer last week, that I have a nonserious thing going on with my temporary neighbor. They pressed me for more information, but I didn't give it to them. If I told them I was having the best sex of my life with an artist I have nothing in common with besides a wall and a love for my dog, they'd never shut up about it.

When the food is delivered, I look around Bernadette's apartment for a serving tray. It seems like the kind of thing she'd have. She has three of them. She must spend a lot of time in bed without me.

I carry a tray with two bowls of chicken noodle soup into her bedroom and find her doing some weird dance, jumping around with her eyes closed and flapping her arms around. It's hard not to laugh. I should be irrevocably turned-off by this, but I'm not.

"What are you doing?"

Her eyes remain closed. "My skin is prickly!"

"Get back in bed."

"*You* get in bed."

"Okay. I'll get into bed with you if you promise to eat. Come on."

"No—you can't get sick!"

"I won't get sick. I got a flu shot."

"Oh. You shouldn't get those—but good. I'm glad. But don't get those."

"Get back into bed."

She groans and opens her eyes a bit, squinting at me. "It's moving too fast!"

"What is?" I brace myself because I'm afraid she's going to say "Us. We are."

"The bed!"

I exhale. Right. The bed is moving too fast. "You need to lie down."

She wags her finger at me, her other hand on her cocked hip. "You need to stop being so loud to me!"

"I'm not being loud."

"Your face is screaming rainbows!"

I place the tray at the foot of the bed. "Okay. Down you get."

She slowly lowers herself back under the covers, gritting her teeth as if she's getting into a tub of ice water.

"Sit up. You have to eat this soup."

She sits up. I fluff up the pillows for her to lean against.

"Stop being so nice to me," she whispers. "It hurts."

"I'm not going to stop being nice to you."

"Okay."

I place the tray on her lap and hand her a spoon, wondering if she's having some kind of allergic reaction to the Theraflu or if this is just how she is once she's spent a certain amount of time with a guy. Either way, I'm staying for the entertainment value. She holds the spoon and stares at it, like she's not sure how to use it.

"Do I need to spoon-feed you?"

She frowns at me. "No. It was bending."

I shake my head. "Eat your soup."

We both eat our soup on the bed in silence. When she's done, I wipe her chin with a paper towel. Her lower lip quivers.

I place the tray on the floor and move beside her, staying on top of the covers. I take her hand in mine. "Now you're starting to act more like the eighty-year-old Bernadette I expected you to be. Soup in bed."

She rests her head against my shoulder. "Matt McGovern. I know your secret."

"What's that?"

"You're even more handsome on the inside."

I don't know what to say to that.

She sneezes into her hands. I grab an antibacterial wipe

from the packet she has by the bed and wipe her hands for her. She pushes her lower lip out, pouting.

"So sweet… I'm sorry I wanted to slap you. I don't anymore."

"Thanks. You wanted to slap me?"

When I touch her face to see how warm her skin is, she puts her hand over mine. "Why are you here?"

"To make sure you don't have any weird side effects."

"But why are *you* here with me?"

"Because I like you."

She sighs. "I like you too," she whispers. Like that's a secret we're keeping from the world. Although, I suppose it is. We've been keeping it from each other too. "This is where everything makes sense. In bed. With you."

I know exactly what she means, but it makes me sad. I've come to love the time we spend together in our apartments, but there's an awesome city out there, and I have a feeling it would feel even more awesome to be out there with her.

I stay with her until she's fast asleep, write a bunch of work emails, and then watch a movie on my laptop in the living room with the volume turned way down. I take Bernadette's keys with me when I walk Daisy and then bring a dog bed and chew toy as well as my own toiletries and a change of clothes back to Bernadette's for the night.

I'll sleep on the sofa.

I set up Daisy in her dog bed on the bed with Bernadette.

I lie back on the sofa and stare at the painting on the fireplace mantle, the one of the forest's edge.

I don't usually look at a piece of art and say "I want

that," but I just want it. If I hadn't known that she was the one who painted it, would I still have such a strong impulse? Maybe not. But she did. She had the impulse to make it, and she made it beautiful, and I want it.

Maybe I just want a piece of her because I know I can't have all of her.

I don't know.

I just want it.

I get up and look around. I'm never going to be able to fall asleep this early. I can smell the candles and soaps and dried herbs from the care package her mother sent. I'm so curious about her parents. She hardly ever talks about them. I'm so curious why Bernadette is so hesitant to leave her executive assistant job and yet her favorite book is about two young artists who live to make art in New York.

I see a sketchbook on top of the coffee table and pull it to my lap. Surely this isn't a journal. Surely she wouldn't mind if I looked through it.

Or maybe she would mind it. A lot.

On each page, I see drawings of a man and of a man and a woman together. It's not obvious, but I recognize myself in those hasty sketches. I recognize us and how it feels when we're together. I get a full-body chill. Maybe I'm coming down with something too. Or maybe I can't believe she was able to capture what it's like for us to be together with lines and shadows, when neither of us seems to be able to say it with words.

When I wake up, Bernadette is standing over me, staring at me with pink-rimmed glassy eyes.

"Hey." I sit up. "You okay?"

She starts to say something and then has a phlegmy coughing fit. When she's done, she sneezes and then curses. At least she's moving through the symptoms fairly quickly. She touches her throat and pouts, and I can tell she means it's sore.

"Don't talk. I'll make tea. Do you have eggs? Should I order breakfast?"

She blinks and then goes to the kitchen and gets a carton of eggs out of the fridge as well as the leftover carton of orange juice from last night. She opens a cupboard, takes out a box of teabags, and places it on the counter. She opens another cupboard and reaches for two coffee mugs, placing them on the counter. She gathers a frying pan, olive oil, salt and pepper, a mixing bowl, a whisk, and then pats me on the arm and goes back to bed.

While the pan is heating up, I call my assistant to tell him that I'll be working from home today. He laughs because I've never done this before, even when I had a sprained ankle. I tell him to reschedule my lunch and forward only the important calls. I don't have any meetings scheduled, so it's not that big of a deal. When he asks if I'm okay, I tell him I'm just looking after a friend who's sick.

I take Bernadette her breakfast and then take Daisy for her morning walk. When I'm back, Bernadette has finished her eggs and orange juice and is trying to focus on her phone. She holds the phone up to me. "Can you read this text from Sebastian to me?"

I take the phone from her and only glance down at it, because if I look too hard I might try to read every single text they've sent to each other. "He's just asking if you feel better."

"Type that I'll come in this afternoon. I can do email stuff here. There's things I need to get for him later."

"You are not going to work at all today."

She sneezes and then blows her nose five times in a row, filling up five Kleenex tissues. "I'm fine," she says. "Tell him I'll be there in the afternoon. I'll take a daytime Theraflu."

"I think you should just drink tea and rest."

She glares at me. "Theraflu."

"Yes, ma'am."

She doesn't notice that I take her phone with me when I go to the kitchen to make her a mug of daytime Theraflu.

When her phone vibrates and I see that it's Sebastian Smith calling, I answer on the second ring. "Hi, this is Bernadette's neighbor. Listen, she's got the flu. I don't think it's a good idea for her to leave her apartment today. She's sneezing and coughing, and she's got a fever and she can barely speak."

After a moment, a deep voice asks, "What's your name?"

"It's Matt McGovern. I live in the apartment next door."

"Dolly Kemp lives in the apartment next door to her."

"Yes, but she's in Europe with her boyfriend. I'm her nephew, I've been staying there for a couple of months. You can email Dolly to confirm this if you know her—I appreciate that you're being protective of Bernadette. But I'm being protective of her too. So, is there anything urgent that she needs to get done for you today?"

"Not urgent, no." I hear him sigh. "Okay. I'll send her an email, but tell her… Tell her I hope she gets well soon, but no rush."

"Okay. Bye."

I hang up before he has the chance to say anything else.

It's not even possessiveness that I'm feeling toward this woman. With Vanessa, I would always go out to parties and bars and restaurants with her, even though I would rather we'd stayed at home together—because I wanted to make sure other guys kept their dirty hands off her. Right now, I just want to make sure Bernadette is taken care of. And I feel lucky to be the guy who gets to take care of her.

It's different.

Everything's different.

And also, strangely normal.

After Bernadette has slept for a few more hours and then taken a bath, she whispers that we should play Scrabble. I move the care package from the coffee table, and she doesn't seem to notice that her sketchbook was on the floor by the sofa where I left it last night. I let her sit on the sofa with Daisy, and I sit on the floor on the other side of the table, facing her.

She keeps coughing every time she tries to yell at me when I throw down 78-point words, so I bring her laptop over and tell her to message me instead.

The first time she makes up a word, I let her have it because she's sick and because her definition of *cryonetrics* as software that measures sad data actually makes sense to me.

But I refuse to accept that *merdls* is a Yiddish word that means "the plural of a happily single woman."

She sticks her tongue out at me and then rearranges the tiles and takes one away.

"*Slerd* is not a word!" I yell out. "No more making up words."

"A slutty nerd is a slerd," she whispers, totally straight-faced.

"Stop talking and stop making up words, you *slerd*."

I don't think I've had this much fun in years.

She frowns, takes away the "r" tile, and I accept *sled*.

"Have you ever been in a serious relationship?" It's only the question I've been dying to ask for over a month.

Her eyes get shifty, her lips lock up, and she falls back. She's pretending to be asleep.

"You don't have to answer."

She sits back up and types: ***Not serious.***

BF: You're trying to change the subject because I'm winning.

I have over two hundred points more than her.

"So you've always been a happy *merdl*, is what you're saying?"

She laughs until she coughs and then wipes a tear from her eyes.

BF: I want to tell you the name of my painting. The one over the fireplace.

"You mean *my* painting?"

BF: No.

"One day. Okay, tell me the name."

She types slowly and carefully. My eyes are glued to my phone.

BF: It's called 'Into the Woods.'

"I like that. Why?"

BF: It's the view of the woods along the edge of the farm where I grew up… I've been staying on the edge of the woods, looking in. One day, I'll go into the woods.

"One day." I move over to the sofa to sit beside her and brush the hair out of her face. "There's really nothing to be afraid of, you know."

She looks up at me and blinks.

Her phone, which is on the sofa next to her, vibrates.

"Let it go to voice mail."

She doesn't even look down at it to see who's calling.

BF: I'm going back to sleep, okay?

"Okay."

BF: No more words today.

"Okay."

She kisses Daisy on the top of her head and goes to her bedroom.

No more words today, Bernadette. I'll just go back to looking at your pictures.

CHAPTER 16
BERNADETTE

It has been a month and a half since we started no-stringsing (yes, it's a verb), and we're not doing it right. I mean, we're doing the sex part right, by golly. We are A-plus world champions at the sex part. But boundaries have been blurred and crossed. Invisible strings are being tripped over, and so far no one has gotten hurt because we keep falling back into bed and that makes everything fine again.

But now, he has invited himself to Sebastian's party. The party I've been planning forever, the one that is so important to my boss for some reason. Matt McGovern wants to come to this party, and because he was so sweet and thoughtful when he took care of me last week, I couldn't say no.

"You taking a date to this party?" he asked as I left his apartment last night.

"No. I'll be working, basically. I'm kind of the hostess."

"Sounds like fun. I'd love to go, thanks."

I laughed and didn't look back at him because I thought for sure he was kidding. But he texted me this morning to ask if I'd be coming home first or if he should meet me there. I had to come home, and he's home now, so there's no avoiding him. If he were anyone else, I would have ended things by now. But he's like no one else. He's Matt McGovern, Esq. It's real. It's happening. And no amount of antiperspirant or sarcasm can hide how much I'm panicking.

We should end this. I should tell him so, tonight. Maybe when we get back from the party. Or before? On the way? So he can feel free to leave with someone else if he meets someone at the party.

Or maybe after we get home so things aren't awkward for either of us at the party.

But we should stop seeing each other like this, or maybe start seeing other people. It's getting too real, too intense. Too saturated. We need to dilute things with a complimentary color. Add some green to this red-hot mess of feelings.

No, that's not right.

Add white, to make it pink? But pink is too romantic. This isn't a romance. We aren't dating.

That's not right either. It's not one color. It's all of them.

That's the problem.

Somehow, this thing with Matt has developed into a monster-sized canvas covered with drips and splashes of all the vivid colors—swirling, heavy, but dizzying, abstract, and hitting me on a gut level in a way that my brain can't understand. We're redefining what it means to have a no-strings relationship the way Jackson Pollock led the abstract expressionist movement.

Maybe I should apply my favorite Jackson Pollock quote to this situation with Matt: "The painting has a life of its own. I try to let it come through."

Maybe whatever we have between us shouldn't be defined or restricted.

Or…maybe if that man gives me one more orgasm, my brain will short-circuit and I won't be able to think about anything anymore, and that will be great.

These are deep thoughts to be having while eating a flax muffin over the bathroom sink and blow-drying my hair.

I need to respond to twenty-four messages about the party.

I need to get dressed and get back into executive assistant mode.

I need to calm the fuck down and let my handsome neighbor accompany me to this party, because that's all that's happening.

I pull on my special dress, the maroon-colored one I was wearing when I first met Matt. The one I had bought with the intention of wearing to some future event, to get Sebastian to see me in a new way. The future is now, and I don't even know if I care whether or not my boss thinks I look hot in it.

There's a knock at my door, and he's here exactly when I need him to finish zipping me up.

I sprint barefoot to the kitchen to dab at my armpits with paper towels for one final time tonight, cover my mouth and release one last squeal, flip my hair, and then saunter over to the door like a fucking supermodel.

One look at Matt in a dark blazer, and I'm a goner.

What an asshole.

Why should anyone look that good in a blazer?

He stands in the doorway, eyeing my dress.

"You didn't return it."

"Never got around to it."

"Been keeping busy, have you?"

"No more than I can handle."

I turn my back to him, and he brushes my loose hair over one shoulder. He zips me up slowly. So slowly that my stupid knees nearly give out. When he's done, he doesn't move away from me. I can still feel his breath on my neck. I shake my hair out because I'm doing the big sexy hair thing tonight and because I need to not feel naked when I'm with the only man on earth who has seen every inch of my adult body *and* thrown my snot-filled Kleenexes into the waste bin.

I take a deep breath. "To be clear…"

"This isn't a date. I know. I'm just curious about this party."

"Awesome," I say, holding my hand up. I point to the palm of my hand with my two middle fingers in a V. "Here's the same page. Here's both of us on it. High five." I remove my fingers from the center of my palm. "Don't leave a neighbor hangin'."

He wrinkles his brow at me but indulges me by slapping my hand.

I am determined for that to be the lamest thing I say and do all night.

Turns out tonight's the night I exclusively say and do lame things that make me cringe. For instance, when the Lyft driver tells us to "have a good night, you guys," I immediately explain to him that Matt and I are just neighbors who aren't dating.

"I'm here because I'm working. I mean, I don't work at the restaurant. I mean, I'm not an escort. He's not paying me to come here with him. My boss is. I mean, my boss is hosting the party here, which I organized, and Matt's just here because he's curious. Not bi-curious. I mean, maybe he is. I can't speak for him."

"You want to get out of the car now and let this guy get on with his night?" Matt's standing on the curb, patiently holding the door open and holding his hand out to help me out of the car. Or maybe to strangle me.

I take his hand, and Matt shuts the door just as the driver speeds off.

I see two of Sebastian's colleagues walking into the restaurant and immediately let go of Matt's hand to wave to them. They pause at the door to say "hi" to me and wait for me to introduce them to Matt, because they're gay and apparently they also think he looks exceptionally hot in a blazer. Matt is polite and friendly and casually introduces himself as my neighbor before I get a chance to.

When I walk into this chic but cozy NoHo bistro and realize there are already over a hundred people here, I am stunned because normally I would be the first to arrive. We bought out the ground floor dining area as well as the downstairs lounge for this event, and I've been in such close contact with the manager all week that she invited me to her birthday drinks next month. But I was so consumed with thoughts of Matt that I didn't even notice it's 8:25.

Some breezy contemporary French pop song is playing, and people are seated at the small tables and at the bar that extends all along one side of the room. Many stand around chatting. It's festive and unpretentious, which is the vibe that we strive to maintain at all of the parties Sebastian has hosted. Somehow, people seem to have figured out how to show up and have a good time at a party without me. So that's reassuring. Now I just have to try not to ruin anything.

Normally, I'd approach Sebastian to make sure he's calm and has everything he needs. Tonight, I see him watch me walk in. He's near the front of the room, talking to his agent and several of his biggest supporters, but suddenly I have all of his attention. First, he scans the full length of my body in this dress. Next, he takes note of Matt. While Matt is a master of controlling his facial expressions, Sebastian's face shows every single thought and emotion when he has them. He likes me in this dress. He doesn't like that Matt's hand is touching the small of my back. But while it has been my job to know what he wants even before he knows he wants it, I am currently at a loss as to whether or not I should go over to talk to him now or let him process his feelings.

Fortunately, I don't have to make a decision. Unfortunately, I'm the one who doesn't know how to process her feelings. Sebastian excuses himself from his friends and walks toward me, smiling. He approaches me and pulls me in for a hug. This is the kind of thing that has happened exactly zero times before.

"At last, Bernadette," he says in my ear. "I was beginning to worry about you."

"I'm so sorry I'm late—traffic was…"

"I'm glad you made it," he says, cutting me off, but looks directly at Matt. "Hello, I'm Sebastian."

This is also something that doesn't usually happen.

Sebastian Smith waits for other people to introduce themselves to him.

"So nice to meet you," Matt says, offering a firm hand shake. "Matt McGovern. I'm Bernadette's neighbor. We spoke on the phone."

They spoke on the phone?

"Ah yes, Dolly Kemp's nephew. Good to meet you. Thanks for taking care of my girl here." He puts his arm around my shoulder.

His girl?

"It was my pleasure."

As soon as I register how these two men are staring each other down, my brain automatically switches to business mode. "Is everything okay here, Sebastian? Do you need me to do anything?"

He blinks and loses the staring contest. "I need for you to enjoy yourself tonight." He squeezes my arm, winks at me, and walks off to greet the art critic who has just entered.

I didn't even know Sebastian knew how to wink.

"Why don't I get us drinks," Matt says. "Malbec or Pinot Noir?"

"Whichever has a higher alcohol content."

"I'll see if they have red Zinfandel."

I watch him go. Heads turn. Some heads do double-takes. Mouths subtly drop open. Matt seems genuinely oblivious to the way people stare at him, or maybe he's just used to it.

While he's ordering drinks, I say hi to a few people and make sure everyone is more comfortable here tonight than I am.

When Matt leans against the bar and makes eye contact with me, smiling just a little bit, I suddenly feel really good. I don't know what I was so afraid of. Just because we've had intercourse and taken care of each other in each other's homes and we're in the same restaurant at the same time, that doesn't mean we're anything more than fuck buddies who happen to live next door to each other.

I finally look away from Matt when I feel a hand slap my ass.

"I've been texting you for fifty minutes, you nerd!" Tommy says as he hugs me.

"Oh my God, I'm so glad you're here!"

"I have like nine other places to be tonight, but I wanted to see you."

I pull away from him and grab his cutie pie face. "It's been ages. So your show's over but you're going on tour with it? This is amazing, right?"

Tommy takes one look at me, ignores my question, and says, "Girl. You've interacted with sperm since I last saw you."

"Shh! This is a work function!"

"Your little Ferris Bueller finally got her day off, didn't she?"

I giggle. "She's gotten off a lot more than once, if you must know."

"I must know everything!" he stage whispers. "Who's been making your vagina twist and shout?"

I burst out laughing and cover my mouth. "Shh! Please stop talking."

Tommy watches me as I look around for Matt. When I catch sight of him at the bar and realize he has been watching us even though some woman is trying to talk to him, I feel my cheeks flush and everything tingles.

Tommy grabs my arm. "Please tell me Sexy Face Magee over there is your guy."

"He's not my guy. But yes, he's my neighbor."

He gasps. "You banged your neighbor!"

"Lower your voice!"

He speaks in a deeper voice. "You're banging your neighbor."

I have to cover my face. "It's not serious. I mean, it's hot and it's really great, and he's great and everything's cool, and I love his dog, but it's not serious."

"Uh-huh."

Matt locks eyes with me as he makes his way toward us holding two wineglasses. The expression on his face is serious, as it usually is, but that doesn't mean that what he feels for me is serious. Just because I'm more aware of him than anyone else in the room or anyone else in the city for that matter, that doesn't mean that what I feel for him is serious.

"I'm only staring at you because you're gorgeous," Tommy says as soon as Matt's within earshot. "You're too good-looking to be straight."

"You're not the first person to tell me this." He hands me my red Zinfandel. "I'm Matt. You're definitely too good-looking to be straight," he says as he offers his hand to shake. He somehow manages to not make that sound flirtatious.

"You are absolutely right. I'm Tommy. Bern and I go way back."

"Tommy's my best friend," I say.

"Very nice to know she's friends with people other than retired ladies who live in her building."

"And dogs. I'm friends with a lot of dogs."

"Right. And Netflix." Tommy pats me on the back. "You're friends with Netflix. I'm already bored of this conversation, so I'm gonna go talk to that hot gay guy over there."

"You do that," I say.

"Take good care of our girl's vagina," he says to Matt as he squeezes past him.

"I'm doing my best."

I give Tommy the stink eye, and he blows me a kiss. I am horrified that Matt knows I discussed my vagina's activities with Tommy. "Sorry. I didn't mean to tell him. He dragged it out of me."

"I don't mind."

"No, but we're not supposed to—"

"Bernadette. I don't mind." He raises his chin at someone at the back of the room. "What the hell. That's my buddy Rufus over there. Come meet him. He's cool."

"Oh, um, I'll come over in a minute. You go ahead."

"Okay."

He walks away just as Anita approaches. She gives him a predatory look, which he meets with a quick nod. I get an uneasy feeling in my gut. Why didn't he just ignore her? I mean, she's a stunning woman in a skin-tight black dress and bright red lipstick, sure, but did he have to acknowledge her existence?

"Bernadette! Baby doll!" She flings her arms around me.

I can't not like this woman. Besides the fact that she's one of my boss's best friends and owns one of my favorite art galleries, she has always been kind and frank with me. So I will forgive her for eye-fucking my fuck-buddy-with-friend-benefits.

"Hi, Anita."

"You look hot! I don't think I've ever seen you in a dress before."

"Really? I just…"

"Was that your boyfriend you were talking to just now?"

"Matt? No—he's my neighbor. My temporary neighbor. He's Dolly Kemp's nephew."

"Interesting. Are you two dating?"

"No."

She eyes me. "Oh really? Are you sure about that?"

My cheeks are on fire. I lower my voice. "We aren't dating. We have…a no-strings arrangement." Why did I tell her that? *Why did I tell Anita that?*

She nudges me with her hip. "Well, honey, you need to wrap some strings around that man and tie him down before someone else does."

"No, we're not… We're different."

"Different from what?"

"Each other."

"Oh, come on. You're not still hung up on the boss man, are you?"

"Shhhh!" I look around to make sure Sebastian isn't anywhere near us. He's not. But I still don't want anyone here to hear this conversation. "No. It's not that. We're just friends. I guess. We have nothing in common, but we have great sex and we hang out at home, and I mean, I helped him out when he sprained his ankle, and then he looked after me when I had the flu last week. But it's just a no-strings thing like I always do, you know."

She lowers her chin and flutters her eyelashes at me. "Bernadette. By what ridiculous standard is that *not* considered a relationship? I've had husbands I was less intimate with than that." She swats this silly idea of mine away with her hand.

"No, really. That's how it is." I finish most of my wine in one big gulp.

She shakes her head and looks back at Matt and the guy he's talking to. "You kids today and your super chill non-relationships."

"Yup, that's me. Super chill."

"You sure you're not serious about him?" She studies

my face, the way an adult looks at a child they suspect is lying to them.

"I'm sure."

"You sure?"

"Yeah, trust me. It's totally casual."

"Mind if I have a go, then?"

"Um. What?" Why did I not see that this is where she was heading. "No! I mean no, I don't mind. Of course, yeah. You should definitely…have a go. He's single and great and nice and completely unattached. Except for a recent ex-girlfriend he lived with for a few years. He probably isn't in touch with her, though."

"Uh-huh. What is he—a lawyer? Corporate?"

"Yeah. You can tell that by looking at him?"

"Honey, I can tell *a lot* by looking at him." She licks her lip. "Early thirties?"

"Yeah. Thirty-two, I think?" Okay, now I feel like his pimp.

"Good," she says. "The twentysomethings always want a mommy who'll fuck them, but once they're in their thirties they know how to handle me."

Eww.

"Great!"

"Okay, I'm going in. Last chance to stop me." She fluffs up her hair.

I try to say the words *I'm not stopping you,* but my upper lip just sticks to my teeth as I fake a huge smile. I salute her and turn away to look for someone else to talk to, like Tommy or a shrink perhaps. I settle on the manager of this restaurant, who smiles and waves at me.

"Hi!" I say, going over to where she's hanging out at the hostess stand, giving her a grateful hug. "Everything seems to be going great tonight!"

"Yup," she says, pushing her ironed-straight hair behind one ear. "It's a fun crowd. I was expecting a bunch of uptight gallery people, but everyone's cool." She leans in. "Who's the guy you came with?"

Oh my God. Is there really nothing else to talk about tonight? Are we not educated New Yorkers? Are there no Broadway shows or political scandals we can dish about?

I sigh. "That's my neighbor, Matt."

"Are you dating him?"

I look back and see Anita give him her card. I see Matt thank her politely and put her card in his blazer pocket. I see him nod at her politely as she touches his arm and then his friend's and then walks away.

"Nope. Not dating him. Just friends."

"Is he gay?"

"He certainly doesn't fuck me like a gay guy, but how can you be sure?" *Who said that?*

She laughs. "I need more friends like that."

"Yeah," I say. "Me too."

I make my way over to the bar to place my empty wineglass on top of it. I wonder if it would be weird for me to just go home now. Alone. It feels like I've been here for a month already.

"You ready for another drink?"

I feel Matt's body right behind me, barely touching me but there. So very, very *there*.

I look up at the illuminated mirror opposite me, behind the bar. Matt's looking at my reflection too. He just stands there, waiting for me to turn to face him and ask the question that I'm dying to ask.

I refuse to give him the satisfaction.

Oh, who am I kidding.

Why not get it over with?

I turn to face him, resting my elbows against the bar. "So, I see you met Anita."

"She had a lot of great things to say about you."

"Oh yeah? Is that why she gave you her card? So you can call her to discuss me further sometime at your convenience?"

"No, she seemed pretty clear about wanting to meet me for a drink."

"Seriously? She offered to take you out for a drink? Women just do that?"

"Not all of them."

"Wow. Must be nice to be you, huh?"

"Not right at this very moment, no."

"Why not?" I punch his bicep. "You got a hot lady's number! Anita's great. You'll love her! Her skin is tight, she has bionic hormones, and I hear she just wants to hump everything. So have fun with that."

"If you don't want me to call her, just say so."

"Hey, man—I am easy like Sunday morning over here. You know the deal. It's none of my business who you call or don't call. Just let me know if it's time for us to put a pin in this thing we've been doing." *Yup. Super chill.*

"Bernadette. Tell me if you want me to call her or not."

"Not." I can't stop myself from reaching for his hand and squeezing it, just for a second. He squeezes back.

"Okay. I won't. I'll give her card to Rufus. He seemed pretty into her."

"Okay. But I mean—did you actually *want* to call her?"

"Not really."

I try not to smile when I shake my head. "That's too bad, because she's a really cool lady."

"Yeah, it's too bad. Been a while since I met one of those. I'm gonna go use the men's room. You continue being easy like Sunday morning over here until I get back."

"Cool. Awesome. Use that men's room. God speed." I reach for my empty wineglass and toast him with it.

"Right."

I try to empty a few last drops into my very dry mouth.

"You having a good night?"

I slam the glass back down on the bar. Sebastian is standing so much closer to me than he ever has before. Even when we rode the subway together once at rush hour, he's always maintained a reasonable distance. I can actually smell the vodka on his breath.

"Hi. Are *you*? I mean, sure, yes. People seem to be having fun, right? Is everything good? Is there anyone you need me to call?"

"All is well, Bernadette."

"Okay. Good."

"You look very nice tonight."

"Oh." I straighten myself up. "Thank you. So do you."

He laughs to himself. "Is Matt your boyfriend?"

"Who—*that* Matt? Matt McGovern? No, that's just Matt." Saying the words "just Matt" makes me hate myself a little. *Oh, it's just an original Picasso from his Blue Period. Oh that? That's just a first-edition copy of* The Catcher in the Rye *signed by the author.* Why do I feel the need to shield Sebastian from the truth? Or is it myself that I'm lying to? "My neighbor. He's my temporary neighbor."

"Yes, Matt the neighbor."

"He invited himself tonight—I hope you don't mind."

"No, of course I don't mind. I'm grateful to him for looking out for you when you were sick."

"Oh, right. That was…yeah. He's a good friend."

Sebastian puts his hand on my shoulder and squeezes

meaningfully. I'm not exactly sure what he means, but it's definitely a meaningful squeeze. He shakes his head.

"Sometimes I wish there was more I could do for you…"

His hand still on my shoulder, his thumb strokes me there in tiny upward movements.

What. Is. Happening?

I'm staring up at him like an idiot. "What do you mean?"

He sighs. "Bernadette. Do you really not know what I mean? Do you really not know what you mean to me?"

My eyes lower for a second, and it's enough to make him hesitate and take his hand away.

"Forgive me. It's that dress. It's the hair. It's this warm June night. It's the vodka. It's the neighbor."

Bingo. It's the neighbor.

I look around and freeze when I see Matt the neighbor watching us from across the room by the door. He doesn't look sad, or mad, or confused. He just looks like he's leaving. He gives me a little nod, a little salute, before walking out.

"I don't know why," Sebastian continues, totally unaware that all my focus has shifted to the front door and the sudden chill in the air now that Matt has actually left without me. "I really don't know why, but this year has been weighing on me. The divorce, sure, but the work just seems so labored lately, and New York feels so…"

I snap my attention back to him. "Your work is as wonderful as it always is, Sebastian. Maybe you need a vacation."

"Yes," he says. "Exactly. You get me. I need to get away."

"Sebastian, my good man," says Anita from behind me.

"If you need to get away, you should go to the luxury hot spring spa I went to in Japan. It's in a darling village in the Ishikawa Prefecture. I swear, it's so beautiful you'd just shit yourself."

Sebastian laughs and slaps his forehead.

Anita widens her eyes at me, like: *Girl, this is your chance to escape, why are you still here?*

I do like this woman. Even though she wants to hump my neighbor.

I sneak away to send Matt a text: ***You left? Are you going home?***

A few seconds later, he sends back an emoji of a high heel shoe.

I have no idea what that means. Other than the fact that he said he never uses emojis and he just used one. I keep staring at the door, as if he's going to walk back through it, but he doesn't.

"I saw him leave," Tommy says as he wraps his arm around my waist. "Did you blow it?"

I shrug my shoulders. I wish I could run after him. I wish I could call him and tell him…what? Tell him that I wish he hadn't left? That I'd like to swing by his apartment and bang him when I get back if he's up for that? That I might not be as easy like Sunday morning as I thought?

"Come sit with me for a second before I go." Tommy ushers me over to a booth and huddles with me.

"You're leaving?" I ask. "We haven't hung out yet."

"That's what we're doing right now, kid. This is it."

"Did you meet any nice hot gay guys?"

He adjusts his collar. "You know I don't like 'em nice."

I nod. "I miss you." I rest my head on his shoulder. "Sorry I suck at having a social life."

"I miss you too. I'm sorry you suck at pretending you're not in love with your neighbor."

I try to scoff at that, but it comes out like a sad squeak.

In a rare moment of seriousness, my best friend leans his head against mine and places both hands on top of my hands. He speaks just loud enough so that I can hear him.

"I just happened to see Matt's face when he came out of the men's room and saw the S-word fondling you."

"He wasn't fondling me!" I hiss.

"He may as well have been. Sexy Face Magee wants to be your guy. I saw it in his eyes. The fact that he left tells me that he still thinks you're obsessed with your boss and he's giving you space."

"Shit."

"You're always wanting your space."

I nod.

"I've been thinking… Maybe it's not your boss that you were so enamored with. Maybe it's being a work-wife. You know, all that relationship-y stuff you do for him, that feels safe to you because it's just work. Because it's not a real relationship. But maybe what you actually want, or I don't know—dare I say *need*—is to actually be in a real relationship. Not like the one your parents have but the kind you want. With a guy who wants you. Not because he wants you to be a buffer between him and the world but because he likes the world better with you in it."

I turn my head to check to see if Tommy is trying not to laugh. He is. He's such a shit. He bursts out laughing and holds up his hands when I start pummeling him. "Okay, but I actually meant what I said, I swear!"

"Get out of here. Go to your ten other parties and say hi to all the cool people for me." I kiss him on the cheek. He does get me, even if he is a turd. "Be safe."

"Be bold and live with love," he says as h
the booth. "And bang your hot neighbor, ha
until you're no longer afraid to be his girl
pounds his chest twice, flashes me a peace sign
he's out the door.

Those just might be words to live by. If I can just make it through the rest of the night.

CHAPTER 17
MATT

I guess I'm Emoji Guy now.

I didn't want to say what I have to say to Bernadette in a text, and I didn't want to *not* respond. So I literally just played emoji roulette, and when I saw that I'd sent her a fucking red high heeled shoe I thought, *Well, at least it wasn't anything cute.*

And then I spent half an hour mentally kicking myself because I'm a fucking stud and I just sent the woman I've been having sex with an emoji of a shoe.

The next half hour was spent walking Daisy and explaining to her that we'd probably have to go back to living in a hotel for a while.

And now that I've opened up my laptop to check out some housing options, I get a text from Bernadette: ***Are you home? Are you up? Can I come over?***

I think about it for a few seconds before replying with a zombi emoji.

Because she's created a monster.

She responds with a hot dog emoji.

I guess this is fun.

I can see through the crack under the front door that she's lurking outside and doesn't want to knock.

I've completely unbuttoned my shirt, and I'm not doing it up again. If she wants to talk to me, she's going to have to deal with my thoughts and my feelings and my abs. All of them.

I open the door and rest one hand against the frame, one on the doorknob. Thankful that she's still wearing that dress but probably not revealing it in my expression. "Good evening."

She stares directly at my pecs, blinks twice, and then says, "Hello." She clears her throat. "Do you have time to talk?"

I allow her to step inside but stay near the door instead of leading her to the living room. "What's up?" I cross my arms in front of my chest.

"I'm sorry if you…if you didn't have a good time at the party. I wish I could have left with you, but you know. I had to stay a bit longer. Work."

"I know."

"Nothing… I mean, in case you were wondering, nothing happened with Sebastian. He was just in a weird mood. He isn't usually like that with me. At all."

"A dress like that can do that to a man."

She frowns at me as she places her fists on her hips. "I think…things have gotten weird between us."

"I agree. I actually felt jealous when I saw you laughing with that good-looking guy friend of yours tonight. Not a good sign."

She smirks. "Who—Tommy? He's gay."

"Well, I know that now."

She searches my face for clues as to how I feel, but she's not going to find anything. People rarely do. But I like to watch her study me. She's really looking. She sees more than most.

I take a deep breath before saying, "This situation of ours isn't working anymore."

She appears to be completely crestfallen. I'm glad.

"Yeah. I don't think so either." Her voice trembles. "We should end it now."

"What I mean is," I say, as I reach out for her hand, "we should stop pretending this isn't a real thing between us. I can't tell you that I'm not going to fall for you anymore, because I have, and you're falling for me too, and I say we just fucking go for it."

I pull her in toward me and wrap my arms around her.

She goes limp and buries her face in my chest. "Go for what?" she asks, her voice muffled.

"I'm sick of holding back with you."

She looks up at me. "You've been holding back?"

I cup her sweet, confused face in my hands. "Darlin', you have no idea."

"What have you been holding back?"

"Letting you know that I can't stop thinking about you. I can't stop thinking about you, and I don't *want* to stop thinking about you. I want to see you every chance I get. I like you, and I don't want to hide it. You can tell your friend Tommy that I want to take care of more than just your vagina."

She jerks her head back and arches her eyebrows.

"I'm not talking about the other hole, dirty bird. I'm talking about your heart."

"Oh."

I'm not sure which part of her anatomy she's more afraid of me penetrating.

"Is this…a good idea?"

"We wouldn't exactly be the first people in history to start with what we have in bed and work outwards from there. But if I'm being honest, I think there was something more between us even before we started sleeping together."

She nods, shutting her eyes tight like we're about to go upside-down on a roller coaster.

"I just want you to know that I'm really nervous. Scared, even. But it has nothing to do with you." She places both of her hands over my heart, like she's protecting it.

"I know." I kiss her forehead.

"You know I'm nervous and scared or that it has nothing to do with you?"

"Both." I kiss her right cheek.

"You are infuriating."

I kiss her left cheek. "I know. I don't know exactly why you're so nervous about being in a relationship. But I promise I won't push you into anything you aren't ready for."

Her head tilts back, eyes still closed. "Just promise me you won't make me *converge-sate.*"

"I don't know what that means."

"Good."

This woman is a little bit nuts, and I'm a little bit nuts about her.

I finally do what I wanted to do the first time I saw her in this dress. I move her against the wall, slowly turn her to face away from me, and slide the fingers of one hand just inside that deep V opening, my fingertips grazing her nipple. With the other hand, I reach down to pull up the hem of her dress. She places her hands flat against the wall, shuddering.

I whisper, tickling the skin on her neck with my warm breath, "Brace yourself, Bernadette. You're about to be pursued by an esquire."

This morning, we took Daisy to Central Park to play frisbee at seven a.m. When we got back, Bernadette joined us for a folksy sing-along session in the living room. For our Saturday night date, I told Bernadette to dress up but didn't tell her where we'd be going. She didn't curse at me for nearly as long as I expected her to.

I know she's at home, but she has been strangely quiet for the past hour. I thought she'd be running around, trying on different outfits or something, but maybe she decided not to listen to my wardrobe directions.

I put on my suit jacket and straighten my tie. "Be a good girl," I tell Daisy. "See you soon."

At exactly seven o'clock, I knock on the door to 4A. Two seconds later, I'm ready to drop to my knees. Bernadette Farmer stands before me in a formal black floor-length gown with a sleeveless top and flouncy lacy skirt, like it's no big deal. Her hair is up in a messy bun, and I just know that perfectly-applied red lipstick will be all over our faces before the night is over.

She gives me a long, slow once-over. "Hot damn, you do look good in a suit, you bastard."

"You're slightly overdressed for the rave," I say with a straight face.

She laughs. "Fuck you. Let's get this date over with."

I clutch at my heart. "The eight words every man dreams of hearing at the beginning of the night."

"Do I need a jacket? Are these shoes okay?" She hikes

up her skirt to expose a pair of strappy heels and painted toenails to match her lips.

"Those shoes are more than okay, and I don't think you'll need a jacket."

She wrinkles her nose. "I better not, buster."

I hold her arm as we walk down the stairs. She uses both hands to hold up the hem of her dress.

"Is this dress the result of one of your drunken online shopping sprees?"

"Yes. You like it?"

"Did I not mention that I fucking love it? If I weren't such a gentleman, my head would have disappeared up that skirt as soon as you opened the door."

"If I weren't such a lady, I'd mount you right here on the steps."

We both freeze when we reach the landing and see Mrs. Benson and her poodle standing there in the third-floor hallway.

"Well, don't you look like a fancy lady and gentleman tonight?" she says with that grin of hers. Alessandro starts barking, so she rushes to get him inside her apartment and we're spared an actual conversation.

We both have trouble holding in our laughter until we reach the second floor.

When she sees the stretch limo and chauffeur that awaits us outside the building, Lady Bernadette groans. "Oh brother."

"I knew you'd love it."

"I could kill you," she says to me under her breath, but she smiles graciously at the driver, who holds the back door open for us. "Good evening, sir."

"Good evening, ma'am."

He winks at me.

I open the chilled champagne bottle as soon as we're seated because I've gotta get this show on the road.

I hold my glass up to hers in a toast. "To fucking first dates and the assholes who take you on them."

She drops her head as she laughs. "To fucking first dates and the assholes you take on them." She polishes hers off in two gulps. "Will you please tell me where we're going?"

"Will you please enjoy the ride?" I open the sunroof. "You ever driven around in a limo before?"

"Not since prom."

"Baby, you ain't lived until you've driven around Manhattan in the back of a limo. Sit back, relax, and look up."

"That's what she said," my date mutters.

I had instructed the driver to play Sinatra because I had a feeling it would drive her nuts. I was right. She just shakes her head and laughs until the chorus of "I've Got the World on a String," and then she stares at me.

I smile. "We've gone from no-strings to a string. Get it?"

"Yeah. I get it. If you were really clever, you would have played Vivaldi's *Four Seasons*. That's a lot of strings."

"Vivaldi's more of a third-date move."

She finally relaxes and lies back with my arm around her shoulder, and when we can see the tops of buildings around Central Park and the midtown skyscrapers, she gets it. All of New York is still out there rushing around and making noise, but it's just us in here. Taking our time, taking it all in.

I kiss her hand, her arm, her shoulder, her dazzling elongated neck.

She's the picture of grace and elegance when she's silent and still.

Half an hour later, I inconspicuously check my phone, and our romantic, sexy, and surprisingly relaxing limo ride comes to an end.

"We're here," I say. I wait for the driver to open the door And then step out onto the curb and hold out my hand to help my reluctant date out.

It takes her several seconds to realize that we're back at the townhouse.

"Wait. What?"

I press a generous tip into the driver's hand and offer my arm to Bernadette as we head back upstairs. "M'lady."

She can barely control her excitement. "I'm gonna take my shoes off!" She hands me her strappy heels to carry while she hikes up her gown and runs barefoot up the stairs.

"Wait!" I whisper. "We're going to a dinner party at Mrs. Benson's!"

The look on her face is worth every dollar that I've spent to make tonight happen.

"I'm kidding. Proceed to 4B."

She calls me an asshole under her breath and continues upstairs.

In the time since we left, while we were driving around, I had caterers set up the dining area with a three-course meal and dessert, floral arrangements, and candles. Before I left, I'd set up a movie screen and projector that I'd rented. Only Daisy is waiting for us in the apartment when we get back. Vivaldi's *Four Seasons* is playing on the stereo. I had that set up before I left too.

Strings.

They sound pretty good with the right woman.

Especially a classy one.

"I am so fucking excited that we don't have to go out tonight!" Bernadette squeals.

She's even more excited when I tell her we don't have to eat dinner at the dining table. We load up our plates and bring them to the coffee table in the living room and sit cross-legged on the furry rug while watching *Harry Potter and the Prisoner of Azkaban.*

I swear she has stars in her eyes when she looks at me, with a huge cloth napkin tucked into the neck of her dress, eating an ice cream sundae. Daisy is curled up between us, and Hogwarts is glowing on screen. "There is literally nothing else I'd rather be doing right now. And no one I'd rather be with. Thank you."

This woman.

When she's sweet, there's no one sweeter, dammit.

Sunday is just a hazy blur of sleep and sex and laundry. I let her have the night off from dating so she can clean her apartment and "work on some things." I can only hope she's working on more beautiful dirty pictures of us.

All day long, all week, we check in with each other via text. We make and keep plans to meet up for lunch downtown almost every day. A few evenings we're able to meet up and come home from work together, arms wrapped around each other as we keep our balance, leaning against a pole on the crowded subway train.

She's so happy about me letting her stay in on Saturday night that she invites me to the Metropolitan

Museum of Art on Friday. We walk there through Central Park and eat at the dining room there after she shows me her favorite abstract paintings. Hearing her talk about art history is a huge turn-on. When I tell her about the contracts and deals that I work on as we walk home, she does a really good job of feigning interest.

It feels good and right and easy. For me, anyway. I sense her body tensing up every now and then when I mention the future, see the fleeting looks of uneasiness on her otherwise happy face.

I don't ask her what's wrong because I have a feeling that would count as *converge-sating*.

I can only hope that eventually she'll get used to dating me. For such an otherwise mature, rational. and stable person, it's odd that she seems to find the idea of a serious relationship so agonizing.

My friends think she sounds like the perfect woman—what guy would complain about a girl who doesn't constantly want to have the "where is this going" conversation and check in with their feelings? Lloyd's theory is that Bernadette escaped from some kind of new age art cult where she was forced to commit to a controlling artist cult leader and share her feelings in group therapy sessions and then the information was used to blackmail her. When I asked him if there was such a thing as new age art cults, he shrugged his shoulders and said, "Sure, why not?" I've decided to stop talking about it with my friends and just let the delightful mystery of who Bernadette Farmer is unfold before me.

CHAPTER 18
MATT

Two weeks into dating, and it looks like I'm going to get a front-row seat to Bernie's psychological makeup.

It's Saturday morning. An hour after she's left my bed for her apartment, I hear her running around. I knock on her door to see if she's okay. She is almost frantic when she tells me that she called her parents to check in on them since they hadn't been replying to her texts or emails for a few days, and the guy who's living with them answered the house phone and said that her parents are at the hospital because her dad fell off a ladder.

I've never seen Bernadette like this before. She's not crying, but I can tell how hard she's trying to keep herself together. Helping her is the only thing that matters to me now.

"I need to go. They never answer their cell phones, even if they have them on them. I have to get to the airport."

"Where are they?"

"The hospital's in Burlington. Farm's just outside the city."

"Have you bought a ticket yet?"

"No, I was about to go online for that."

"Don't fly there. Let me drive you. We can take Daisy."

"What?" She genuinely doesn't seem to understand what I'm saying.

"I can rent a car. I'll drive you."

"Matt, it takes like five and a half hours to drive there!"

"Is it imperative that you get there immediately?"

She exhales. "I guess not. I just want to be there if they need me. God! Why can't they just answer their fucking phones like normal people?"

Yeah, she needs to calm down, but I know better than to just tell her that.

"It would still take about four hours just to find a flight, get to the airport, deal with all the airport crap, and fly there."

"I guess."

"It's a pretty nice drive, right? And this way you'll be able to keep trying to call them. You wouldn't be able to when you're on a plane. Do you need to come right back, or is your plan to stay there to help out?"

"Well…I don't know yet. It depends what's going on. Sebastian's in Hudson Valley this weekend, so I don't expect him to need anything, but I can't ask you to take that kind of time out of your schedule."

"You don't have to ask. I'm offering. I don't have any meetings on Monday. Daisy and I can get a hotel room in Burlington."

"No. No, you don't have to do that. They have five bedrooms. I mean, I have no idea how many people are staying with them right now, but there's plenty of room at the house. It's not fancy or anything. I'd love for Daisy to run around the farm."

"Okay, then. Daisy can stay with you and I'll get a hotel room."

"No, I want you to stay there too." She laughs a little and takes a deep breath. "Thank you. Okay, I guess this is happening. You're going to meet my parents."

In less than half an hour, we're in a rental car headed north. Daisy's in Bernadette's lap, and I've got a premade Spotify road trip playlist on with the volume turned down low. This is not how I saw my weekend going, and I certainly hope her dad's okay, but so far I'm pretty shocked by how happy I am. My two best girls and I are on a little adventure. What more could I possibly want?

Information.

I want information.

I'm going to extract it from her in as painless a way as possible.

"So…your last name is Farmer and your family owns a farm?"

She smiles and shakes her head. "Yes. My grandfather officially changed his last name after he bought the property."

"What was it before then?"

She looks at me with a straight face and says, "Banker."

I burst out laughing. Her timing and delivery are perfect.

"I'm not kidding."

"Come on! You're telling me your name could have been Bernie Banker?"

"Laugh it up, McGovern. And don't call me Bernie."

"Why not?"

"Because. My parents named me Bernadette to offset the plain Jane-ness of Farmer, but they've always called me Bernie. I think if you make a deliberate choice, then you should stick with it."

"What if I deliberately choose to call you Bernie?" I don't think I've had so much fun teasing a girl I like since I was eleven.

She purses her lips and nuzzles Daisy's face. "I think Daisy Farmer has a nice ring to it."

If anyone's taking someone else's name, it's you who will be taking mine, Bernadette.

That thought hits me like a Mack truck that came out of nowhere. I swerve a tiny bit. She looks over at me to see if I'm okay. I keep my eyes on the road, my thoughts on track, and I remain quiet for about ten minutes after that.

I wait until we're well into upstate New York before getting into the questions again.

"You wanna tell me about your parents?"

She empties her lungs and shuts her eyes. "I guess. I don't know. I'm sure they'll tell you all about themselves when we get there. They're…"

Monsters? Weird? Unconventional? What?

"They've been madly in love with each other for as long as I can remember. And they were madly in love with each other long before I was born. But they work at it."

"How?"

"You know. They think it's important to connect deeply on a regular basis and talk about feelings." She shudders. "All the feelings. All the time. Like expressing them through art or sex isn't enough. They think it opens up the channels. I don't know. It gives me hives. They're nice, though. They're really nice. They're good parents. They just aren't good at things like email or paying bills on time."

"Because they're so busy talking about their feelings?"

"Because they're so busy being in touch with each other and nature and their art and the community."

"Are they Amish?"

She laughs at that. "I wish! They're their own brand of hippie. They just feel guilty because they had dreams of being famous, successful artists when they were young. They met in New York in the eighties. They both had very middle-class childhoods and fled their suburban lives for New York, and they were into the whole punk CBGB's scene. They stayed at the Chelsea Hotel and partied hard and made terrible art with lots of black and white and reds, you know. But then they fell in love, ran out of money, and my grandparents left the farm to my dad. So they decided to be hippies instead. You'll see. They'll tell you the story, but it's the version they want people to hear." She slaps her own cheek. "That came out all wrong. I made them sound like asshats. They're not. They're just…probably really different from your parents."

"My parents are total asshats."

"Hah! I bet."

To be honest, her parents sound incredibly interesting compared to mine.

She tries calling her mom's and dad's phones again, as well as the home phone, but nobody answers.

"Why don't you call the hospital?"

She blinks and then looks at me like I'm a genius and she hates me for it. "Oh yeah."

After ten minutes of calling around different hospitals and clinics in Burlington and being put on hold, she finds out that Steve Farmer checked out of an urgent care clinic half an hour ago. When she hangs up, she is both relieved and frustrated. She looks over at me. "I'm sorry. We're halfway there. Do you want to just keep going?"

"I definitely want to keep going. I'm glad it's not serious."

"Yeah. I mean, I guess it's not serious. I'll give them another half hour to get settled back home and try calling them again."

I reach over to squeeze her thigh. She holds my hand.

"You sure you still want to meet my parents?"

"Just try to stop me."

She stares at me, incredulous. I don't need to ask if she's ever introduced a boyfriend to her parents before. I guess in her mind, this is the string that could strangle someone. I'm not sure if it's herself or me that she's worried about. Vanessa and I didn't meet each other's families until a year after we'd moved in together. It was fine. We posed for a lot of pictures that got posted on Instagram.

I don't like thinking about Vanessa now. I'm realizing that it's the first time that I have in a while. My brain doesn't have much room for her anymore, although it does make me a little sad that it's true. How can someone I chose to live with for years just disappear from my life like this? I was so wrong about her. I moved too fast. I don't want to be wrong about Bernadette.

"When was the last time you visited the farm?"

She looks out her window. "Ages. A year and a half, I guess? I didn't make it home for the holidays last year because of work. And I never stay very long. Ever since I moved to New York, I've been a terrible daughter."

"You're not. But I'm glad we're doing this."

• • •

After filling up the tank, I come out of the convenience store with a bag full of disgusting snacks and find that Bernadette has returned to the car with Daisy, who is now curled up in her bed in the back seat. Bernadette is on the phone. As soon as I open the car door, I can hear her mother's enthusiastic (loud) voice.

Before we're back on the freeway, I've gathered that Steve Farmer fell from the third rung of a ladder this morning while he was trying to replace an exterior lightbulb. It was just a silly accident, but he has a hairline fracture in his shoulder. It hurts, and he won't be able to raise his arm for a while.

"Okay," Bernadette says. "So, he's basically fine."

"He's perfectly fine. He's just mad at himself for not watching what he was doing. How are you?"

"Actually, Mom, I'm driving to the farm to see you guys right now."

"*What?* Wait—*what?* You're coming home? Now?"

"Surprise." She rolls her eyes at me. "We're about two hours away."

"We—who's we?"

Bernadette whispers into the speaker. "I'm bringing a boy."

"Who—Tommy?" her mother asks gleefully.

"No." She looks at me while she talks. "A straight man. A very straight man. His name is Matt. We're bringing his little dog too." She covers her eyes and scrunches up her face before continuing. "Matt and I are dating."

She drops the phone into her lap when her mother starts shrieking.

"Steeeeve! Steve—come over here! No—don't move! It's fine—it's good news! Bernie! Bernie—put him on the phone! I want to talk to Matt!"

You asked for it, she mouths to me.

I nod for her to go ahead. She puts me on speakerphone.

"Hi, Mrs. Farmer. This is Matt."

"Matt! Oh I like your voice. It's so masculine! I'm Leslie, and you are so welcome to come stay with us! Bernie's room is always ready and waiting for her to visit, and the bed should be big enough for two!"

Bernadette lowers the passenger-side window and makes like she's about to jump out of it.

"Thanks, Leslie. I'm really looking forward to meeting you and seeing where *Bernie* grew up."

Don't call me that, Bernie mouths, frowning.

"Now, do you have any food allergies or preferences that we should know about? We're mostly farm-to-table vegetarians around here, but we can head over to the store if you need meat. What about your doggy—does she need anything?"

"I will eat whatever you serve me, and I brought food for Daisy. She just needs water and a place to do her business."

"Awwww, Daisy! I love the name Daisy!"

If Bernadette weren't sitting right next to me with her mouth sealed shut, I would swear that I was on the phone with *her* right now.

When Leslie starts to ask what kind of dog Daisy is and why I chose the name Daisy, Bernadette jumps in. "Mom—we should let Matt concentrate on driving, yeah? We'll see you soon. I'm so glad that Dad's okay. Love you, bye!"

She hangs up and drops her phone into her bag. "And that was just a taste."

"She sounds wonderful."

"Well, I'm glad you think so, because she's gonna get all up in your face with her wonderfulness very soon."

I guess I didn't really have a mental image of what the farm would look like. Based on the way Bernadette has described her parents, I expected it to be dilapidated in a bohemian sort of way, with a lot of homemade garden art and stoned hippies wandering around. I was right about one thing. There's a lot of handmade garden art. It's a working farm, and it's quaint and pretty well-maintained and gorgeous. It's less than ten acres from the look of it—maybe half of it's vegetable and flower crops, and the rest is pasture and woods.

As we drive up the gravel road to the big farmhouse, I see a few goats and chickens roaming around, and so does Daisy. She makes a noise I've never heard her make before. She's so excited that Bernadette doesn't even notice her mother and father have come out to greet us. I park and turn off the engine, waiting for Bernadette to get out first.

Again, her parents are not at all what I expected. Leslie is beautiful but in a very different way from her daughter. Her hair is lighter and curlier. She's thin and tan and fit, from working outside I suppose, but she does have a bit of a hippie thing going on with her long skirt and crystal pendants hanging everywhere. Steve looks more like a hip professor of art than a farmer/artist, with his round eyeglasses and black jeans. His arm is in a sling, but he looks healthy as a horse to me.

It's not until they descend upon their daughter that I get a hint of why she's so hesitant to interface with them. She looks like she's drowning in hugs and questions and positivity. I hear the words "reconnect" and "plug into nature" and "meditate on what it really means to create" thrown around before I even hear them say "hello" to her. They do an actual group hug. Bernadette is the first to pull away, of course. She turns to me. I'm holding on to Daisy so she doesn't run off and attack a chicken.

"Guys, this is Matt McGovern and Daisy."

"Welcome to Good Culture Farm, Matt and Daisy!" Steve says. "I'm Steve." He holds out his good hand to shake mine and pats Daisy on the head. "Thanks for driving our baby all this way."

"Dad."

"It's my pleasure."

Leslie's laughing so hard she doesn't seem to be able to speak. She holds her stomach. "Oh my God! Bernie! He's so handsome! It's just stupid!"

"I know."

Bernadette's mother just stands there, head tilted, regarding me. "I mean, how do you even paint this face?"

"I know!"

"You just have to sculpt him, right?"

"I guess," Bernadette says, "but there's kind of a softness underneath the sculpted features that demands a nice sharp soft pencil, don't you think?"

"Oh yes," her mother says. "Yes, I see what you mean."

"Black ink," Steve says, like that's a complete sentence and the end of the discussion.

Mother and daughter both stare at me, and it's not awkward at all.

I'm kidding. It's totally awkward.

"It's nice to meet you, Leslie." I offer my hand to shake.

"Oh, Matt! Look at us, just staring at you. This must happen to you all the time."

"Not exactly."

"It's so good to meet a friend of Bernie's—and a boyfriend, no less."

"Mom." Bernadette goes to grab our bags from the trunk, reprimanding her dad when he tries to help.

"Ohhh, and look at this little cutie! Hi Daisy! Hello little puppy dog! We should put the chickens away so she can run around."

I get the leash on Daisy and put her down on the ground. "It's okay. I'll hang on to her for now."

Leslie Farmer shakes her head and touches her heart as she leads us up the stairs to the wraparound front porch and inside their house. "This is such a wonderful surprise. After the morning we had here, what a beautiful thing to have you three visiting us. I can't wait to connect over dinner. We'll let you get settled in Bernie's room upstairs, and just so you know, Matt…we are very open about sex in this house."

"Mom!"

"I don't mean open like an open relationship. I mean if you want to have sex with our daughter while you're here, you go right ahead."

"I appreciate that."

"We're the opposite of cockblockers!"

"Don't be so sure, Mom."

"Don't listen to Negative Nelly over there. We let her have boys sleep over when she was in high school."

Wow.

"Oh my God, Mom! Zip it!"

"We taught her to be free and open about her sexuality, very early on."

"Again, I appreciate that."

Leslie Farmer winks at me and nudges my arm.

"You take the kids upstairs, Les, I'm gonna take a nap

on the sofa down here. I'm beat," Steve says as he ducks into the living room.

"Aww, Dad, you get some rest. Don't worry about us. But tell Mom to take it down a notch, will you?"

"Not on yer life."

I notice a big painting over the fireplace and know immediately who painted it. It's somehow earthy and ethereal at the same time. A vibrant fall landscape with gold tones that you just want to reach out and touch and stare at for hours. "Is that one of yours, Bernadette?"

"Yeah." She glances at it uncomfortably.

"Isn't it just fantastic? Our pride and joy."

"She painted this when she was sixteen," her dad marvels. "I wish I had half her talent. You know she's actually an artist, not just an assistant, right, Matt?"

"I sure do."

Bernadette rolls her eyes. "Here we go. Go to sleep, Dad."

We go up the creaky pine wood stairs to the second floor. The hallways are wide, the ceilings high. There are books and candles and mason jars filled with wildflowers and herbs on every horizontal surface and paintings and framed photos on every vertical one. This house is rustic and warm and lived-in. I look back at Bernadette, who has the strangest expression on her face. Like someone who's about to break a long fast by chowing down on everything that she knows will make her fat.

"Not much has changed inside the house since you were last here, I think, Bern. Just a little more dust perhaps."

"The house looks great, Mom."

Leslie holds up both arms to present Bernadette's room. It's awash in filtered golden light streaming in from the windows. I let Daisy down when we step inside, and I don't even notice the furniture. The first thing I see is the view from the picture window.

It's the forest's edge from the painting of hers, the one that I want.

CHAPTER 19
BERNADETTE

"Was this the view you looked at every day when you were growing up?" Matt asks me once my mom finally leaves us alone in my room.

"Yes."

"You really captured it."

"Thanks. Obviously it looks very different in the winter."

He chuckles. "Well, yeah."

Having Matt McGovern in my childhood bedroom is totally surreal, but he seems to feel quite at home here.

I pick Daisy up so she can look out the window too, but all I can think about is my dad.

"You don't have to entertain us," Matt says. "Go be with your dad."

Stop reading my mind!

He takes Daisy from me. "We'll go for a walk or something."

"Yeah, take her out to the pasture so she can run around. The bathroom across the hall is for us. My parents have their own. And I don't know where their resident artist is staying, but probably downstairs."

"Resident artist?"

"Yeah, they always have at least one Artist in Residence who's supposed to help out with chores, in exchange for room and board. This guy sounds like a massive tool. Anyway…you guys get settled. I'll go hang out with my dad for a bit. Dinner here is usually pretty early."

"Cool," he says, putting Daisy down. "We'll be around."

I suddenly grab him and hug him tight. "I can't believe you're here."

He strokes my hair and kisses the top of my head. "Where else would I be?"

I swallow hard. The tip of my nose tingles. Damn him. Why's he gotta be so damn perfect?

My dad is lying on one of the deep cozy sofas with his head propped up on several pillows, while I sit on a leather pouf next to him. At fifty-seven, he's still a striking and fit man, perfectly capable of handling the day-to-day running of a small subsistence farm with my mom—on top of teaching art to locals and painting for himself and hosting a summer art camp for kids. But he started complaining about aching joints and a sore back and neck a while ago. The complaining has since stopped as his recreational use of marijuana has started up again—for medicinal purposes. It's not like my parents are potheads —not at all. But they've been casual users off and on for as long as I can remember, especially when they're hosting other artists. Needless to say, it hasn't exactly improved their organizational skills.

I pick my dad's eyeglasses up from the side table and clean them with my T-shirt. He always looks older and more vulnerable to me when he's not wearing glasses, for some reason. "Are you in pain right now?"

He smiles. "I'm fine, pumpkin. Honest. I mean, it's a dull pain. They gave me an extra-strength Tylenol at the hospital. Fortunately, I didn't mess up my dominant hand."

"Yeah, but you can't do most of the things that you have to do around the farm with one hand!"

"Yeah, well... We won't be able to do the farmer's market for a while. Unless we hire someone to help out."

"What about your resident artist? That's the kind of thing he's supposed to help you with."

"We'll see. His stay here is almost up, actually. We've got a poet coming in next."

"Well, I hope he knows his way around a hoe."

"Actually, she's in her seventies."

"Dad! You're supposed to choose people who can help out around here!"

"Her poetry is beautiful and she's recently widowed. She needs a change of scenery."

"Well, then, how much money do you need in order to hire someone?"

"I don't know. I'll talk to Bill. I'm sure we can find someone in town to come around a few times a week."

"Daddy. This is why I worry about you guys. What if something happens and you have really big medical bills?"

He shrugs. "We'll sell the farm."

"But the farm is your life."

"You and your mom are my life. And my art. But I can do that anywhere. You need to find something else to worry your pretty head about, kid. We'll get by. We always have. You gotta trust that."

I look out the window and see Matt on an A-frame ladder, changing an outdoor lightbulb. My mom is nearby, playing with Daisy.

"Seriously. Isn't your Artist in Residence supposed to be helping you with things like lightbulbs? At the very least? I mean, where is this guy?"

"Elijah? He's probably in the barn, working on his project. He's a very talented sculptor. You should see his stuff. He's just a bit of a flake."

"Great. That's exactly what you need around here."

"Hey. I'm serious. We're fine. If you want a reason to keep your high-paying secretary job, we aren't it. Why don't we talk about what you're really worried about?"

I push myself up off the pouf. "Fantastic idea. I'll go see if Mom needs help with dinner."

When I was little, I was happiest when I was in the kitchen with my mom, helping her make dinner. Surrounded by the scent of herbs and spices and fresh-baked bread, the only thing I had to worry about was whether or not the food would taste as good as it smelled. Now, as I stand here slicing freshly harvested organic potatoes, I am seriously considering hacking off my own hand just to get out of this conversation.

"I just don't understand why you're so reluctant to give yourself to him completely," she says as we look out the window, watching Matt run around with Daisy in the warm golden hour light that's refracted through the trees.

"You're a couple. I see it—it's so obvious. You're a couple. You're a little family with him and that dog."

"We just started dating a couple of weeks ago!"

"Pssh! Your father and I got married after knowing each other for two weeks. When you know, *you know*. And I can see that you know, you just don't want anyone else—including Matt—to know. What I don't understand is—why? If we dig deep, we can get to the bottom of this before we sit down for dinner."

I put down the knife. "There's nothing to dig, Mom. I mean, we have nothing in common. He's a lawyer. I'm an artist. He's stoic, and I feel like a spaz around him. He's settled into his career, and I'm…let's not talk about that. Anyway, we never even would have met if he weren't staying next door to me. We're very different."

"Different!" My mother coughs out the word while laughing. "You're different from everyone on earth, Bernie! If that's your excuse, then you'll be alone forever."

"Well, maybe I should be."

"Shhh!" She immediately drops what she was doing to grab a dried sage wand (they're literally all over the house), lights it, and waves it around in front of me to clear the air. "Never say things like that—don't even think them!"

I stand still, waiting for her to calm down. She places the sage back in its bowl and gets back to making dinner. "I know you didn't mean that."

"No. I didn't." *Please, let that be the end of it.*

She smiles, all dreamy-eyed, and says, "Wasn't it Marc Chagall who said, 'All colors are the friends of their neighbors and the lovers of their opposites.'?"

Fuck, I love that quote.

"Yes. Wasn't it me who said, 'Can we please talk about

something else?' Why can't we just make awkward small talk or gossip about the people I grew up with like normal mothers and daughters?"

"Because it's a waste of time, and every minute we have together is precious."

"Geez, Mom. Are you a hippie or a Hallmark card?"

"Are you an artist or a cynic? Honestly, Bernadette. Lately, I have to wonder."

This chills me to my bones. In Manhattan I'm considered a quirky nerd. In Vermont I'm a cynic. "I don't want to be a cynic," I whisper, grabbing at my mother's arm like I need her to help me up.

She immediately drops the asparagus she was rinsing in the sink and hugs me.

"I like him so much, it scares me," I whisper into her neck.

"I know, sweet girl. He likes you too. I can tell."

"I'm just trying to enjoy the moment, because when I think about where this could be heading, I want to throw up."

"Oh, sweetie." She cups my face with her damp hands. "You were always a such hopeless romantic growing up, and you've always been so afraid of that. I don't know why. If it's got something to do with your dad and me—well, let's face it… It always comes down to the parents, doesn't it? I'm sorry. It's the opposite of what we want for you. We've been trying so hard to keep you open, but you just snap shut like a virgin's knees at a frat party."

As much as I fear my mother's words, she really does have a way with them.

"There's nothing to be scared of. Connecting at the soul level is not meant to be a frightening exercise, my dear. Between two people who love each other, it can be the lube that keeps things running smoothly, if you know what I mean."

"I always know what you mean, Mother." Even when I don't want to hear it.

At dinner, we're joined by the talented and completely useless Elijah, who is almost as bad at conveying information in person as he is on the phone. My parents regale Matt with stories of how they met and fell in love in NYC in the eighties. Their version makes them sound much more romantic and rebellious and like they deliberately chose to turn their backs on the New York commercial art world. Maybe they did. Maybe I really am a cynic.

I am very grateful that both my parents managed to wait all the way until the fresh rhubarb and strawberry pie is served before bringing up the idea of me quitting my job so I can devote myself to my own art. They ask Matt for his opinion on the matter. He looks at me before answering.

I know perfectly well that he feels the same way. He said so almost as soon as we met. But what he says is: "I think she's really smart and knows what's what, and she'll do what's right for her when it feels right." He offers me a little smile, but what he's just given me is something so big and lovely that I don't know where to put it.

My body tries to make room for it by squirting water out from the corners of my eyes.

It's humiliating.

This happens every damn time I come home to visit. I'm always so vigilant, trying to hold everything together when I'm in New York, and when I get here I usually just cry and sleep.

"Umm. I just… I need to be excused. I have to lie down for a minute," I whimper as I run out of the dining room and upstairs. The tears are just pouring down my face, and I feel like a total freakshow.

"Let her go, Matt. She's just opening up the channels," I hear my mom say. "It's a good thing. We'll let her be alone with her emotions."

Fuck these fucking emotions.

I just cried into my pie, in front of the best guy I could ever hope for.

I shut my bedroom door and dive into my bed, burying my face in the pillow that smells like lavender and fresh air and youthful romantic hopes and wishes. I let go of everything that I try to hold together when I'm marching through life in New York. I sob and I shiver because I am so in love with Matt McGovern, and I want to *be* and *do* so much more so I can have more to share with him. I want to be bold enough to tell the world that I want to be a famous painter, even if I might fail, and I want to be brave enough to look the man I love in the eye and tell him that I want to be with him even if it's not fun and easy.

I had such big dreams, lying in this bed by myself and staring up at the ceiling.

Tonight, I can only hope for something as simple and significant as the ability to share this bed with Matt and not say something sarcastic that will push him away.

Baby steps.

This is why I am always so hesitant about coming home. I get so emotional and tired when I'm here. New York doesn't give you a chance to be tired. Even when you're sleeping. On some level, you always have to be prepared to deal with a mugger or Godzilla or a beautiful man who makes you fall in love with him. I close my eyes just for a minute, not wanting to leave Matt alone with my parents for much longer. Dealing with my parents is the Vermont equivalent of being emotionally mugged by two well-meaning, excessively communicative Godzillas.

When I wake up, it's dark. My eyes have definitely been closed for more than a minute. I hear Matt and Daisy coming down the hall. I don't move, pretending to be asleep. I listen as he places Daisy in her doggy bed and removes his clothes. When he finally joins me in bed, he spoons me.

"Hi" is all he says, and that is perfect.

"Hi. What time is it?"

"Bedtime. Your dad's cool," he whispers.

I sniff the air. "Matt. Did you smoke up with my dad?"

He giggles into the pillow. Giggles! "Just a little."

I spin around to face him. "Oh my God. Did he corrupt you?"

He snorts. "Please. You honestly think I've never smoked pot before? I grew up surfing in California."

Sigh. "I honestly don't know anything anymore."

He brushes hair from my face. "Are you okay? Are your channels opened up?"

"You did not just ask me that."

"So, after you left, your dad mentioned feeling like an idiot for falling off a ladder, and then your mom got this really intense look on her face and started asking him all these questions about why he feels that way."

"Oh no."

"And he kept answering them until he kind of broke down, and then your mom got up and hugged him and sat on his lap for the rest of dessert. I kept looking over at

Elijah because it felt like we should leave because maybe your parents were going to start making out at the table, but he just sat there like he's seen it all before."

I'm basically trying to find a way to hide between the mattresses like a cat because I'm so horrified that Matt witnessed that.

"Was that converge-sating?"

"Yup. That was a patented Steve and Leslie converge-sation."

"Wow. That was…intense."

"You have no idea."

"Do they make you do that?"

"They used to. I've gotten pretty good at side-stepping it."

"Well, I promise not to make you do that. Like, ever."

"Thank you."

"Are you really sad, though?"

"Not exactly. One of the reasons it's so hard for me to visit is I don't want to leave once I'm here. I mean, I love New York. When I'm there I don't want to leave either. But it's special here."

"It is. I like it a lot."

"Really? It's not exactly SoHo."

"What's not to like? I like knowing that you grew up here. I can just picture you running around that field in your little floral handmade dresses, with your braided hair and a basket of flowers and a little pet lamb."

"I never had a pet lamb."

"This is my fantasy."

"Okay."

"Speaking of fantasies… I know your mom said we're free to have sex in this bed, but I'm kinda tired. Is it okay if we just sleep tonight?"

"Oh, Matt McGovern, Esq. I thought you'd never ask."

Spooning in bed with no sex and no talking? If this is what being in a relationship with you is, I'm all in.

I wake up with the realization of how I can best help my parents, who would never ask anyone for help. After breakfast, I pick up the phone and call their oldest friends in town, to say "hi" and to casually mention that I'm here because my dad hurt his shoulder and can't do everything that needs to be done around the farm for a while. Within fifteen minutes I have five people offering to come by every week to help them out, and I have no doubt that more offers will come in once word gets around. Of course, my parents most likely won't answer the phone, but their friends will show up uninvited eventually. It really does pay off to be a good neighbor.

Later, while my mom plays with Daisy and my dad stubbornly plants rows of beans with one hand, Matt and I go for a walk in the woods behind the house together.

"Can I just say something?" he says, after minutes of only the sound of birds and our footsteps. "It's not really my place, but in case you want someone else's perspective... I don't think you need to worry about your parents so much. They seem pretty functional to me. And really happy."

"You're just saying that because my dad's your bong buddy."

"We did not use a bong."

I shake my head. "Do you have any idea how many

times the power got turned off when I was growing up because they forgot to pay the utility bill? I always did my homework at the library after school because I never knew if I'd be able to use the Internet at home. But you know… we always had fresh eggs and homemade soap and high-quality art supplies, so I didn't have much to complain about."

"I've heard much worse stories."

"I know. I'm not even complaining about my childhood. It was great. It's just weird being more responsible than your parents."

"They don't exactly seem irresponsible to me. They're just a little flaky… I know you don't want to talk about your job, but…"

"I'm thinking about it."

"About quitting?"

"Not yet. I'm ready to take a good look at my finances and figure out how to make the transition. It's not going to be easy going from working for one of the most successful artists in New York to starting out on my own again. I'm not young and foolish anymore. It was fun when I first moved to New York, but I was a broke-ass idiot. I just need to take baby steps."

He nods. "It's not so scary here in the woods, though, is it?" he says, looking around at the trees and squeezing my hand.

"It is at night when you're a little girl."

"Then don't go out alone at night."

He looks down at me, like being with him is the answer to everything, and maybe it is. I'm about to throw him down and put my mouth on his mouth when he says, "I have to tell you something. I saw your sketchbook.

When you had the flu. Those drawings of us? They're really beautiful."

"Oh..." Amazingly, I don't burst into flames or run away screaming. "I'm glad you think so."

"I don't think I've ever inspired anyone to draw before."

"I'm sure that's not true. But you have inspired me. A lot."

I stop in front of a tree, lean back against it, and pull Matt toward me. He rests one hand above my head against the tree trunk, pushes my hair behind one ear, and leans down to kiss me soft and slow. I can taste Vermont maple syrup on his lips and tongue, and I could stand here kissing him until it snows. It doesn't matter if we're in bed or a laundry room or a crowded subway train or a forest—when Matt McGovern kisses me, I'm exactly where I need to be.

"I want you to have the painting," I tell him, "when we get home."

"Really? *Into the Woods* is mine?"

"Yes. If you want it. You've definitely earned it."

I may not be able to tell him that he has my heart so completely, but I can give him this.

"I want it," he says. "I've always wanted it."

CHAPTER 20
BERNADETTE

A couple of weeks after we return home from the farm, Matt invites me to have lunch with his parents in the middle of a workday. He brings it up early that same morning while we're both getting ready to leave for work—I assume because he knows that it will give me less time to fret about it in advance. It's a good call on his part.

"Oh great. Yeah. I should be able to make it. Thanks. Are they going to be in town long?"

"Just overnight, actually. They were originally going to fly direct to London, but they decided to break up the flights and see me. You'll like them. Or not. Ever had lunch with three lawyers before?"

"Uh, only in my dreams. Are they going on vacation?"

"Yes. They're meeting up with Dolly and her boyfriend in London." He watches me for a reaction as he says, "And then Dolly will be coming home right after that."

Cue record scratch sound effect.

This is news to me.

"Oh right. Cool." That seems like the appropriate thing to say.

I knew that Dolly would be coming home eventually, of course, but I had gotten so used to having Matt and Daisy next door that I'd actually forgotten that it's not a permanent situation. Matt never talks about apartment hunting, and he certainly doesn't seem to have time to do it.

He puts on his jacket, kisses my cheek, and puts Daisy's leash on her while heading for the door. "I'll text you later."

Part of me is wondering if I should offer to let them stay with me until he finds a place, because he surely won't want to stay in 4B with his aunt. I'm sort of proud of myself for having this idea and thrilled that it doesn't induce any nausea or heart palpitations whatsoever. I plan to bring it up to him tonight when we're both home from work.

Meanwhile, back in Tribeca…Sebastian has been really weird around me, ever since the party. He's keeping me very busy with organizational tasks—updating and checking his catalogues of work and art books and valuables for insurance purposes. Most of the time when I'm in his office, he's in his studio, but occasionally when he's in the office with me, I'll catch him staring at me wistfully. He always looks away without saying anything, which makes it even more awkward. He keeps taking phone calls in another room for privacy—something he didn't used to do. I assume it's because he's talking to a woman he's dating and he doesn't want to do it in front of me, but I really don't care.

I just wish everything could go back to the way things were with us—minus the obsessive crush part—so I can get on with slyly working out a plan to leave this job.

When I poke my head into his studio to tell him that I'm leaving for lunch, he starts asking me where I'm going and who I'm meeting with and when I expect to be back. He needs to talk to me this afternoon, he says, so I need to be back by three at the latest. I'm wondering if he suspects that I'm looking for another job, because he's not usually this neurotic. Or rather…he's not usually neurotic about *me*.

I get to the midtown restaurant fifteen minutes after I'm supposed to meet Matt and his parents there. They are already seated and his parents are sipping on their gin and tonics. Matt introduces me to them as "Bernadette, who I told you about…" So, I have no idea what he told them about me. I assume he didn't happen to mention the no-strings thing, and I don't let myself wonder whether or not he referred to me as his girlfriend. Mr. and Mrs. McGovern are perfectly nice and polite to me, regardless.

They could not be any more different from my parents. As suspected, Matt and I are not descended from the same species. Pierce and Margaret McGovern are both Santa Barbara lawyers with sun-kissed skin, who spend their weekends sailing, golfing, and playing tennis. Pierce has the whitest, straightest teeth I've ever seen, and Margaret looks like a Banana Republic ambassador in her sheath dress, ballet flats, and perfect jean jacket that was probably ironed.

You can't paint these people. You'd just have to sharpen your colored pencils to a point, steady your hand, and come as close to perfection as possible.

Now that I'm looking at Matt with his parents, though,

I'm thinking that there's some truth to what that lady at the dinner party said about him. He certainly is genetically gifted, as his parents are both very attractive and fit, but they wouldn't make you do a double-take when they walk into a room. They wouldn't make me want to laugh or slap them. The thing that makes Matt so darned gorgeous is the way he carries himself. He's hot on a metaphysical level.

That said, they are clearly Matt's parents. Pierce exudes reliability and has the same brand of stoic charm, while Margaret displays the warmth that her son reveals to the lucky few. I also catch glimpses of Dolly in her when she teases her husband and son.

I like them.

I don't think they knew what to make of me at first, especially when Matt tells them about the farm, but once Margaret asks me what it's like to live next door to her sister, all of the McGoverns are entertained by my carefully curated anecdotes. It's nothing like how easily my parents welcomed Matt into their home—the McGoverns are polite but guarded. When Margaret mentions that she still follows Vanessa on Instagram, it doesn't seem to occur to her that it would make me uncomfortable. She just comments on how striking she looks with bangs, and I don't disagree.

Matt holds my hand under the table whenever we aren't using our hands to eat, silently reassuring me. He's really good at this dating thing. Anita was right. I need to tie this guy down with all the strings.

I nearly choke on my linguini when Margaret asks Matt to tell her more about his new apartment.

Matt squeezes my thigh. "I just found out right before you got here," he tells me. "I just found a place this morning. Lloyd's cousin is a broker, and he called to say he had a listing that goes on the market later today. He gave me the chance to look at it first, so I rescheduled a meeting." He looks really excited and happy. "They've already approved my application. It's perfect, so I knew I had to move fast. It's a garden duplex—two beds, two bath, really good space, nice light, with a small, fenced-in backyard. And it's on a great street in Park Slope…" He swallows those last two words.

I suddenly feel like I'm coming down with the flu again.

Fucking Brooklyn.

I've lost so many friends to Brooklyn. That borough is ruining my life.

I could go hang out with them there; I know I could.

I could live there; I know I could.

It's only a half hour from downtown Manhattan by subway, but it's not super convenient to get there and back from the Upper West Side. It can sometimes take almost an hour, by subway or car. I could get out of my comfort zone. If I've learned anything this past month, it's that getting out of my comfort zone feels good, at least when Matt's there with me.

I just don't know if he'll still be with me or not, and that makes me very uncomfortable.

"Wow, that sounds perfect," I manage to say. "Daisy will love having a little garden of her own."

"When do you move?" Mr. McGovern asks.

"This weekend," Matt says as he looks at me. "Before Dolly gets back."

"Well, cheers to starting over," his mother says as she raises her nearly empty glass. "When things fall into place like that, it's because it's meant to be."

Matt's parents ignore my trembling hand when I raise

my glass, like the well-bred rich white people they are. By now my own parents would have rubbed CBD oil on the bottoms of my feet and badgered me about what I'm so nervous about until I'd cried. I can't meet Matt's gaze anymore, and the hand he rests on my leg no longer feels reassuring, so much as it feels like he's letting me down easy.

When Matt kisses my cheek as we say goodbye at the restaurant, he tells me we'll "talk about everything after work." I don't have time to ask what "everything" is, because I need to get back to Sebastian's place before three. I can't believe I was going to ask him to stay with me. Turns out he can't wait to get out of that building.

Location, location, location.

You'd think that it would matter less on such a small island as this, but it matters even more when people are looking to spend as few New York minutes as possible getting to where they need to go.

The question now is: do Matt and I *need* to be together? Without the neighborly convenience, do we make sense together at all?

My illustrious boss is waiting for me in front of the front door to his apartment when I get back. He's talking on his phone, probably just getting some fresh air. But still. It's weird. He is relieved to see me and brings me to the living room. We never sit together in the living room.

He plants me down on the sofa and takes a seat on the

heavy wood coffee table across from me, leaning forward and sighing.

"I have some news," he says.

Great! More news!

"What's up?"

He rests his hand on my knee, and I only tense up a little bit. "I bought a house in Hudson Valley."

"You did?"

"Yes." He pushes his glasses up the bridge of his nose and then runs his fingers through his hair in one sweep. I've always found it so sexy when he does that. Right now I like it because he has released my knee. "It's in Catskill," he continues. "Well, we haven't closed yet, but I just found out that the inspection went well today, and I'm paying cash, so it will be mine very soon."

"Yours…as a vacation home?"

"Mine as a new home." He sighs. "I'm moving there."

Fuck this day.

"I'm going to sell this place." He doesn't seem as excited as Matt did about his new place. He's more sad. He looks around. I can tell he's feeling nostalgic. "I'll find a small apartment to keep in town as a pied-à-terre. I will miss this place, but I want to live in Hudson Valley. I can't breathe here anymore. It's why I wanted to have that party for my friends here. I had to say goodbye for now, to my New York life. I need to start a new chapter in my life." His hand is on my knee again. "And I still want you to be an important part of the story. You've always been such an important part of my story, Bernadette, since you started working for me, but it was too hard for me to see you, with my head so far up my ass. I apologize for that."

"Ohhh, you don't have to apologize for anything. I've

loved working for you." My voice is cracking. Here come the nose tingles. "This has been a great job."

"It can still be a great job, Bernadette. Come with me. Catskill—all of Hudson Valley—is a wonderful place for artists. You'll love it, I know you will. You have to. I don't know how I'll get along without you."

"But I don't… I don't know anyone there. Where would I…"

He sits on both of his hands now and looks down at the floor. "You can live with me." He looks up to check my reaction before proceeding. I feel some flushed cheeks and an intense eye spasm coming on. "It's a huge five-bedroom house on three acres. Come. I'll show you the website." He gets up to grab his laptop from the office.

I can't move, so he returns to the sofa with it. I don't think I've breathed since he said the words *"Come with me."* He is not the man I wanted to utter those three little words to me today.

"You can have your own wing," he says gallantly as he brings up the real estate website. "There's a pool and spa and a pond and a garden and a stunning view of the mountains."

He ain't kidding. The house is nearly four thousand square feet, on three acres of land. Aside from the luxury pool and exterior kitchen, the surrounding area does remind me a lot of Vermont.

"I need you with me, Bernadette. I'll pay you more. I understand what it would mean for you to have to pick up and move, but…I can pay you more attention out there too."

"I don't… I don't understand exactly what you mean."

He places the laptop on my lap and puts more distance between us on the sofa. "I don't either, I'm afraid. All I have are my feelings and longings and confusion. I see how you look at me differently lately. Is it too late?"

"Too late for what?"

"To start over. You and me. I don't know how to approach this." He waves at the space between us. "There are boundaries, and I've always wanted to be respectful of them. But I need you to know that I think about crossing them. Do you understand?"

"Sebastian, I… This is a lot to take in."

"I know. I know, and I'm sorry about that. You have time to decide about the move, of course. But I do need you to come with me to the new house on the weekend. It's empty. I'll need help finding people to decorate and set everything up the way I like it. You know what I need. I need you to help organize and orchestrate things. I don't need you to pack or anything, of course, I'll hire people to do that." By that, he means *I'll* hire them.

"You need me to go with you to Hudson Valley this weekend?"

"Are you unavailable?"

"Um, no. I mean, I'm not unavailable."

"Good. I'll drive. We'll get two rooms at the inn that I've been staying at. It's really wonderful. As Anita would say, it's so quaint you'd just shit yourself. Or if it makes you uncomfortable…"

"No, it's fine. That's fine. I can go. On the weekend, I mean."

Fucking Sebastian Smith.

What is happening?

My crush has been oh so crushed. I was besotted with him for years, and now I'm not. So why do I feel the need to go home, put on my Fleetwood Mac, and listen to "Landslide" over and over while weeping? I've been so preoccupied with Matt that I'm just now realizing the youthful admiration I had for my boss is dead and gone. What's left is a professional respect and, to be honest, annoyance that I had wasted so much time obsessing over him.

Yes, it was an obsession.

There, I said it.

And yet…I am his work wife, and while it would be difficult for him to find a replacement for me, it would be damn near impossible for me to find another job like this if I decide that I still need a job like this.

I am so tired all of a sudden.

When Matt texts me to let me know that he's already in the Upper West Side because he had a meeting uptown, I tell him I'll be home soon. It seems to take about a month to get from Tribeca to my building this evening for some reason. The train runs late, everyone and his cousin is out walking around, and tourists are finding the exact perfect spot to stop and take pictures right in front of me.

I hate everything.

When I turn the corner onto my street, I stop in my tracks.

The statuesque woman with the great hair who's exiting my building is definitely Vanessa. She doesn't see me as she crosses the street. She looks…not happy, exactly, but optimistic. And the opposite of me. She's the glowy Instagrammable cherry on the shit-cake of my day.

I wonder if Matt called her to let her know that he's moving to Brooklyn.

I wonder if he asked *her* to move there with him.

It doesn't make any sense that he would, after the past

month we've spent together, but not much about this day makes any sense to me so far. Maybe his parents hated me. Maybe after I left the restaurant, his parents encouraged him to get back together with Vanessa.

I trudge up to the fourth floor, just wanting to get this over with. When I get there, I see Matt in the hallway, approaching my door. He's holding a small envelope, about to bend down to place it through the crack. When he sees me and registers the look on my face, he slides the envelope into his back pocket.

"Hi," he says hesitantly.

"Hi."

"You're back."

"Yes."

"Good."

Oh God. It's come to this. This is all we have left to say to each other.

"I saw Vanessa," I blurt out. I keep my eyes locked on his, expecting him to look away or reveal something that I don't want to see—guilt, regret, shame. Instead, what I see is relief. What I feel is anything but that.

CHAPTER 21
MATT

"I'm glad you saw her," I say. "I wasn't sure how to bring it up."

Bernadette looks so fragile and defensive right now. It seemed like the best time to mention that Vanessa suddenly decided to stop by was *never*. The truth is, she wanted me to know that things didn't work out with Todd. She wanted to let me know that she regrets the way she ended things. She wanted me to know that she still cares about me.

"Thanks" is what I said to her. *"I've got a lot going on right now, so you'll have to excuse me, but I appreciate you coming by."*

I was being polite. She told me she'd be in touch. She may have read it as me keeping things close to the vest, as usual. The problem with being stoic and expressionless all the time is that the people who think they know me well don't realize that sometimes that means I actually don't have any feelings for them.

But Bernadette's just standing there, with her keys in

one hand and her other hand on the door to her apartment, waiting for me to say more.

"Did you talk to her?" I ask.

She shakes her head.

"She just texted that she was in the neighborhood. She finally dropped off a few little things of mine that I left at the apartment. I mean, at her apartment."

This doesn't appease her to the degree that I had hoped it would. I shouldn't have to tell her that nothing happened. She should know that I wouldn't let anything happen.

"Nothing happened," I say. It comes out sounding more defensive than I'd intended. "Are you okay? You look really tired."

"Yeah. I am." She starts unlocking her door, not looking at me. "This day has really kicked my ass."

I'm about to ask her what I can do to make it better, but she continues.

"I found out that I need to work this weekend. So I won't be here. When you guys move out."

"Work, huh?"

"Out of town. Hudson Valley."

And now my ass is getting kicked. I actually feel like she just sucker punched me. "You're going to Hudson Valley with Sebastian? For the whole weekend?"

"Just overnight. I think. It's—he bought a house. I have to help him arrange some things. I'm going to be pretty busy for a while. Hang on, let me get something."

She goes inside her apartment without inviting me in. So I get to stand here in the hallway, thinking about her spending the night out of town with Sebastian Smith. I won't hear her next door when she gets home. I won't be the guy who's always calling and texting her to check up on her. I'm not that guy. I may be Emoji Guy for her, but I refuse to be the guy who begs for reassurance.

She comes back out into the hallway, offering me a little bag from a pet boutique, with tissue paper bunched up around whatever's inside it.

"It's a little jacket and winter booties for Daisy. For when it gets cold out. They were half-off. In case…well, I just saw them and got them for her because they were cute."

"Thanks." I don't take the bag from her. "Do you want to see Daisy? Give this to her yourself?"

She lets out a little sigh and nods.

I let her into my aunt's apartment. Daisy gets up from her dog bed in the living room as soon as she sees Bernadette and comes over to her, her entire body wagging. I watch my soon-to-be ex-neighbor give my dog all of the affection she doesn't seem to think I deserve right now. Tears are streaming down her face while she whispers sweet nothings to Daisy, as if it's the last time she'll ever see her.

"It's just Brooklyn," I grumble. "It's not that far. You're still going to see her…" As soon as I say it, it hits me that she may have already decided that she won't.

She wipes her face with the back of her hand and nods. "Were you going to give me a note? Under the door?" She asks me this like it's some sort of a challenge.

I remember that I put it in my back pocket. "It just says to let me know when you're home."

"Oh." She looks down at Daisy, and she seems to come to some sort of decision. She takes a deep breath before saying, "Sebastian is moving to Hudson Valley. He's going to be based there. And he asked me to go with him. I don't know what I'm going to do." She finally looks up at me.

Her eyes go wide. "Matt, unclench your jaw. You're going to crack your teeth!"

Emoji Guy is dead. "He's asked you to move with him to Hudson Valley, and you're going there with him this weekend, to spend the night. Did I get that right?"

"Yes and no. I mean, yes, but it's not how it sounds. I don't… I don't feel the same way about him. The way I used to."

I do like the sound of that.

"Do you feel the same way about Vanessa? The way you used to?"

"No, I don't."

"Good."

For a second, it feels like this is going to turn into an actual conversation. The kind that people have when they're in a relationship. She rubs Daisy's head one last time before standing up.

I have to ask… "I thought you were going to get back to your own painting career."

"I was. I am, but—"

"But you're actually considering moving to Hudson Valley with Sebastian Smith?"

"I can't *not* consider it, Matt. I've worked for him for years. He asked me to move there with him, so I'm going to consider it. That's all. If I don't move with him, I'll be unemployed a lot sooner than I thought I would be. And I can't just quit until I help him find and train my replacement. That's what I was planning to do, but now I'd have to do it sooner. I have a lot to think about."

I feel myself shutting down just as quickly as she is. I'm having a flashback to all the conversations with Vanessa that led to me moving out. "Yeah. I get it. You need your space."

"Yeah. That's me." She shakes her head. "I need my space. Like I said, I expect I've got a lot to do for work. I'll have to reschedule his whole summer and organize…a lot. So…if I don't see you before—good luck with the move. I'm going to go cry in the shower now."

I can see her swallowing a lump in her throat. She makes a sad little chipmunk sound as she heads for the door.

I hate that I'm about to ask this, too. "Do you want your painting back?"

She spins back to face me. She's not sad anymore—she's angry. "What? I gave that to you. I made a deliberate choice to let you have it. Are you telling me you don't want it anymore?"

"I still want it."

"Good. Then you better keep it."

"I will."

She calms down and covers her face. "What's happening?"

I can't stand this. I go over and put my arms around her. All I can say is, "Don't go." I don't want her to go now. I don't want her to go to Hudson Valley on the weekend. I don't want her to *move* to Hudson Valley.

The phone in her pocket vibrates.

Of course it does.

She pulls away and reaches for it, shaking her head.

I can see that it's Sebastian calling.

Of course it is.

"I have to take this. I'm sorry." She answers the phone as she walks out.

And we're back to that. Sebastian's calling—end of discussion. It's her job, I get it. But I would have let an after-hours call go to voice mail for her. I would have done so much for her, it scares me.

I can't believe I was about to leave her a note asking her to move to Brooklyn with us. It was a crazy idea. Seeing Vanessa just made me realize how much I prefer being with Bernadette, but that doesn't mean either of us are really ready to move in together. Does it? I just didn't think that my moving would mean that we were done doing whatever it is that we've been doing.

She did tell me that she'd never fall for me, right from the start. She did say that if someone makes a decision, they should stick with it, and I guess she really meant it. I should have asked her if those clear boundaries were also geographical and limited her to engaging in intimate acts within this particular borough.

I can't even do what I'd normally do to blow off steam right now—blast classic rock while blasting my abs and arms in the comfort of my own home and then try to soothe my dog by singing to her. Because I don't want Bernadette to hear any of it. I don't want to go to my old gym because I don't want to risk running into Vanessa. City of eight and a half million people, and I'm only trying to avoid two of them, but it means I have to go back to the office to work out.

This is what the McGoverns do. When there are emotions to be processed, we get moving. My parents have never had a fight. They just play tennis and golf until one of them feels like a winner. I used to surf. Now I work out on land. By the time I'm done working through this mess of feelings, I'll have a ten-pack.

When Daisy and I leave the townhouse for the last time, Bernadette is gone.

We didn't cross paths at all the last couple of days, and I didn't even hear her next door. I was so busy getting utilities and everything else set up at the new place, arranging to have my stuff moved out of storage—because I never ask my assistant to do personal stuff for me (like some asshole bosses). It was when I was ordering a new bed online that it really hit me just how strange it would be, to be living on my own again. Just my dog and me. Not that Bernadette was ever officially living with us, but it did feel like it for a while.

It's only been a few months, so it's surprising to me just how much this townhouse has come to feel like home to me. I don't think Daisy will miss all of the stairs, though. I leave a gift for Dolly after making sure there are no dog smells or stains left anywhere. I even slipped a thank-you card under Mrs. Benson's door.

I don't let my aunt know that I won't be giving her spare key directly to Bernadette. I leave it in an envelope and slide it under Bernadette's door on Saturday, with a note that has my new address and a photo I had printed of her with Daisy in the park. There were a million things I thought about writing in the note, but in the end, it was just ***This is where we'll be*** and the new address.

"This is where we'll be moping around and thinking about you" is what I could have written.

"This is where we'll be playing sad guitar and missing you."

"This is where you should be."

Daisy looks up at me, whines, and shakes her head, as

if to say: *"You fucking pussy. Not to be a drama queen, but you're letting your one chance at real love slip away because you're afraid she doesn't want you as much as you want her. If you weren't the guy who feeds me, I'd just pee on you."*

Women.

Can't live with 'em, can't live next door to them, can't imagine what life will be like without Bernadette in it.

But it looks like I might have to.

CHAPTER 22
BERNADETTE

FROM: DOLLY KEMP <doloreskemp123@yahoo.com>
TO: BERNADETTE FARMER
<thisisbernadettefarmer@gmail.com>

Dearest Bernadette—salutations from the great city of Miami (LOL just kidding)!

I'm sure my handsome nephew has kept you up-to-date, but I wanted to personally let you know that I'm at Marty's place now and will return to 4B tomorrow. This may not affect you at all, as you may be spending nights in Brooklyn now, for all I know. I have my key, of course, so there is nothing you need to do.

I really have missed our townhouse and neighborhood. I look forward to seeing you again and catching up on juicy no-holds-barred girl talk (that's a threat *and* a promise)! My sister and brother-in-law liked you very

much when they met you at lunch, FYI. The McGoverns may not be exuberant people like you and I are, my dear, but they do know a good thing when they see it (eventually).

See you when I see you—but you'll probably hear me running around screaming "it's good to be home!" first.

xx Dolly

Well, I guess she didn't get the message.

Although, I barely got a message from Matt either. Just a picture that made me burst into tears as soon as I saw it and a hot pink Post-it Note with his new address on it. This is more than I usually get from a guy when a no-strings thing has ended but so much less than I wanted from Matt McGovern, Esq.

I don't know why I feel so hurt that he didn't bring up the idea of me moving to Brooklyn. I don't even mean *moving in with him*. I mean, it would have been nice if he had just asked if I'd be interested in moving to a place in Brooklyn so we could live closer to each other. But that's crazy. We haven't known each other long enough for that. Right?

I know I should have brought the idea up myself, but I felt so blindsided after Sebastian's news and then seeing Vanessa, and now that he's moved it just feels like it's too late. It has only been a few days since he moved, but too many New York minutes have passed, and the fact that he didn't bring it up says a lot.

And yet, Sebastian *has* asked me to move in with him.

A few months ago, I probably would have done backflips all the way to Hudson Valley. I did love Catskill when we visited on the weekend. He was a perfect gentleman when we spent time together. It *was* work, and he *is* a nice boss. He didn't cross any boundaries because I think I made it pretty clear to him that I wasn't open to it anymore. If he's at all heartbroken, he's doing a great job of hiding it.

I, on the other hand, feel like people can just tell that I'm one country song away from bursting into tears. I can't believe how quickly Matt went from *there* to *not there*. But when I think about how unemotional he seemed, having moved away from Vanessa after living with her for years, it makes sense that it would take him three seconds to get away from me. And I'm so mad at myself for being angry and sad about everything when I'm the one who didn't want to get attached in the first place.

I should have stuck to the rules.

I should have stuck to Netflix.

But it's impossible to go back to the way things were. This bedroom, this bed, feels so empty without Matt McGovern in it, or at least on the other side of the wall from me. Even my Apple TV Netflix app is pissing me off by constantly rearranging my carefully curated list of shows and movies like some shitty houseguest. I can't find anything anymore. All Matt ever did to piss me off was rearrange my life and steal my heart.

It's shameful how fast that heart races when I feel my phone vibrating in my pocket and how I feel the whole weight of the world on my shoulders when I see that the wrong person is calling me. It's Anita again. This is the third time she's called in the last two days, and I let it go to voice mail because I assume that she wants to talk about Matt. I don't have the energy to have a conversation with her about hormones and penises right now.

It's late, and I spent the whole day at Sebastian's place making very specific labels for moving boxes and hiring the most expensive, highest-rated moving company in the city. Everyone is moving and coming and going and I've just been sitting on my bed feeling sorry for myself, so I force myself to get up and check on Dolly's plants to make sure they're still in good shape. Also to make sure there's no evidence of my sexcapades with her nephew—not because I think it would bother her but because I'm afraid she'll ask me to describe every last detail when I see her.

It is so weird to be in 4B now that Matt and Daisy aren't here. I may have to move just so I can get away from the lingering scent of Matt's cologne. I better make this fast, or there is a good chance that Dolly will come home to find me curled up in a ball under the guest bed comforter, sniffing it. I stick my finger into the soil of all the potted plants in the living room and kitchen—all moist and healthy. Matt must have remembered to water them before he left.

What a guy.

The plants in Dolly's bedroom and bathroom are all good—that leaves the one in the guest bedroom. The door is closed all the way. I knock first, as if there's a chance maybe Matt's hiding in there, waiting to jump out and yell, "Surprise! I couldn't leave you!" I laugh at the very thought of it because it would be so unlike him.

When I open the door, I try not to look at the bed, just head for the fig tree. But something else catches my eye—a hot pink Post-it Note that's dangling from the wall behind the painting over the bed. My painting. I recognize Matt's neat, controlled handwriting and see the words *fucking hot.* Pulling it from the bottom of the painting reveals the whole note: ***You're so fucking hot.***

Did he leave me another note on a Post-it and forget to put it in the envelope? I mean, it had better be for me and not his aunt. I find myself smiling, but I hope that's not all he wanted to say to me. I notice that my painting is hanging a bit crooked. When I angle it to straighten it, I hear something rustle behind it.

I lift the canvas from the hook and find dozens of notes stuck to the wall.

And here we thought I was the nutty one…

I pluck one note at a time.

Thank you.
You're good in bed.
You're good out of bed.
I think about you all the time.
I like thinking about you.
I'm glad I met you.
I don't know if it would have been better if we'd met years earlier, or months later, but I'm glad I know you now.
I want to know more about you.
I want you to know more about me
I want a lot when it comes to you, Bernadette. It surprises me. You surprise me.
I wish you were here in bed with me now.
I wish you were in bed with me all the time.
I want to crash through this wall between us.
I want to break all of your rules.
I want strings.
I'm getting attached.

You're already the best girlfriend I've ever had, and you don't even want to be.
You are so talented, and I wish you were painting again.
Your paintings are mysterious and beautiful and calming and exciting, just like you.
You were so stunning in that dress, the first time I saw you.
I wanted so badly to kiss you that time when the power was out.
I want to kiss you right now, dammit.
Bernadette. Come back to bed.

I can barely read the words anymore because tears are squirting out of the corners of my eyes like windshield wiper fluid. These are definitely the best sentiments I have ever seen written on a Post-it Note. But I have no idea when he wrote them. Obviously it was before he saw Vanessa again, before I told him about Hudson Valley.

What I do know is that he felt these things at some point.

What I do know is that despite how wonderful he is, I'm still somehow afraid of all the things I feel for him.

What I do know is that I need to get back to my first love and become my whole self again. I need to find the artist that I buried, back where it was born, and finally open the fucking channels so that I can love Matt fearlessly and with my whole heart. The way that he deserves to be loved. With all the colors and shades and tones and textures.

If he ever wants me again.

CHAPTER 23
MATT

It has been a full week since I moved into this place, and I haven't even seen my neighbors yet. I like it as much as I can like a place that has absolutely zero Bernadette Farmers in it. I really think she'd love Park Slope. If you manage not to trip over all the baby strollers, you can really appreciate the historic brownstones and down-to-earth bohemian vibe. Sitting here, staring at her *Into the Woods* painting, both subdues and exacerbates the longing to be with her.

I've always been able to compartmentalize and disappear into my job when I don't want to think about something else, but I'm not about to go to the office on the weekend just to get away from these thoughts. Not yet, anyway. Whenever I'm home, Daisy begs me to let her out into the little garden area—I'm pretty sure it's not because she wants to be outside but because she can't stand to hear me play "Lover, You Should've Come Over" by Jeff Buckley on my guitar one more time.

As I quietly sing the last lines, when I get to "Oh, love

I've waited for you/Lover you should've come over," I realize just how passive these words are. Am I really the guy who waits for love? I am now able to grasp just what a stubborn ass I'm being, doing the same thing that I did with Vanessa—just giving her space—when I don't feel the same way about Bernadette as I did with Vanessa. I want her. I want her in my space. I always have. I'm sure as I've ever been sure of anything that I always will.

I pick up my phone, watching Daisy perk up in her outdoor bed through the patio door. She stares up at me, and it's like she knows I'm finally calling Bernadette. She gets up and comes to the door. I let her in. She looks up at me hesitantly: *"You better say the right thing this time, buddy."*

It goes to voice mail after four rings. I don't usually leave messages unless it's a business call. What the fuck is the right thing to say to a voice recording at a time like this? I clear my throat. "Hi, it's Matt McGovern, Esquire. I just wanted to say that I hope you let me know if you're ever in the neighborhood here, in Brooklyn. We'd love to see you… Actually, fuck that—we'd love to see you no matter what neighborhood you're in. I'd love to see you. I *need* to see you. I want to talk to you. Call me."

I hang up and look down at my dog. She blinks and shakes her head. I know what she's thinking: *"You're going to have to do better than that, Loverboy. This is the woman who bought me winter boots* in the summer."

I text her all the sad-face emojis before leaving food in Daisy's bowl and ordering an Uber to the Upper West Side.

• • •

Brooklyn Bridge is hilariously jammed today, and I'm kicking myself for not taking the subway, because it's nearly an hour later when we finally get to where I need to be. By the time the Prius has turned the corner onto her street, I haven't gotten a response to the call or text, but I know what I want to say to Bernadette. I just hope I'll get the chance to say it to her face. Hopping out of the car, I'm at the front door of the townhouse in three long strides.

She doesn't answer the buzzer after the first or second time I've ringed her. She might be in the basement doing laundry. I hope she's in the basement doing laundry and not making out with her boss by some lake or hiding in her apartment and ignoring me.

I try my Aunt Dolly's buzzer, on a whim. I'm not even sure if she's back in town yet.

"Who is it?" My aunt sounds so tough through the intercom, as if only thugs would be buzzing her on a Saturday morning.

"Aunt Dolly? It's Matt."

I hear her sigh. "Oh, Matt. Good. I know why you're here. Come on up, my dear."

When I reach the fourth floor, my aunt is standing by her open door. She is wearing a 70s-era pantsuit that probably used to belong to Diana Ross. It has been a while since I've seen her in person, and I'm surprised by how happy I am to see her. She holds out her arms for a hug.

"My darling boy," she says, patting my back. "You look like crap."

"I haven't been sleeping much this past week."

She nods knowingly. "Thank you for the teapot. It's lovely. Bernadette isn't here."

I reach out for the doorframe to brace myself. "Did she move to Hudson Valley?"

"No, silly. She isn't going to work for Sebastian Smith anymore."

Once again, when it comes to Bernadette, I release a breath that I didn't even realize I'd been holding.

"She took a job at a gallery. She'll be working for my friend Anita. Come inside."

I do. It's strange, being here with my aunt. I've had sex so many times in her apartment, and no matter how old I am or how much she encouraged it, I feel like a guilty teenager. But I can't really think about that now.

"Oh. You know Anita?" Of course she does. My aunt knows everyone.

"Yes, why? Do you?" She wrinkles her brow at me, probably wondering if I've slept with that woman.

"Not really. I met her once. When I was with Bernadette. So, she's working for Anita now?"

She leads me to the sofa in the living room and takes a seat next to me. She's talking to me like I'm a little kid who's finding out he doesn't get to go to camp this summer or that there's no Santa Claus. It's doing nothing to calm me down. Inside my brain, I'm screaming.

"Not yet. She starts next month. She still has to help Sebastian transition to his new home and find him another assistant, and Lord knows that won't be a walk in the park. I only know this because she sent me an email right before I got home. She said that she'll be out of town until next week and it might be difficult to reach her."

My insides clench up again. "Do you think she's in Hudson Valley?"

My aunt looks at me with an expression that I so rarely see on her or anyone's face when they look at me: pity.

"No, I don't. Now, I don't know any details of why you two aren't together anymore, because Bernadette is nothing if not discreet. But she did say that she's unclear as to where things stand with the two of you. I know you're not exactly a spoiled golden boy, Matt. You work hard, you're a good guy, but you haven't really had to fight for anything in your life. If you want to make it work with Bernadette, you're going to have to fight for this one."

It's possible, very possible, that my aunt understands me better than my parents do.

"Way ahead of you, Aunt Dolly."

"Crossing the Brooklyn Bridge on a Saturday is a nice gesture, but that's not going to cut it."

"I'll cross all the bridges for her."

She smiles, her lips pursed. "That's the cheesiest thing I ever want to hear you say, but good for you."

"Can you look after Daisy for one night?"

"It would be my great honor."

"Okay. I'll bring her back here on my way to the airport."

"You think she went to the farm?"

"I'm sure of it." I'm up and nearly out the door when I remember to say, "Oh hey, and thanks. For introducing us."

"It's my pleasure. Thanks for buying new sheets for the guest bed." She winks.

That's my cue to leave.

For a guy who spent most of his New York life sticking to the lower half of Manhattan up until a few months ago, I think I deserve some kind of romantic medal for going back and forth between Brooklyn and the Upper West Side twice in one morning and then to LaGuardia for an afternoon flight.

I can't believe I'm rushing to the airport, like the end of a fucking movie that I'd never watch, but I swear all I can hear is cheesy music swelling in my ears and all I can see is a montage of all my favorite moments with Bernadette. There are a lot of them. And not all of them are naked, either.

It takes less than two hours to fly into Burlington, Vermont, but it feels like two years. When we land, I turn on my phone as soon as I can, but there's still no message from Bernadette. I know in my soul that she's at her parents' farm, and I know they get shitty cell phone reception there, and I know in my heart that she's probably in some barn painting something amazing and I just need to get to her.

I panic when I get into the cab because I don't know where to tell the driver to go. I don't even have the number for her parents' landline. I could call my aunt to see if she has it, but even if she did there's no guarantee that anyone would answer.

"Do you know where Good Culture Farm is?" I ask the driver, because I might as well ask.

"No," he says. "Do you?" He doesn't offer to look it up. He must be from New York.

Then I remember that I put the farm's address into my Waze app when we drove there. The driver tells me he can't drive that far out of the city, and that's when I know for sure that he's from New York. So I have to get back out, go back into the airport, and rent a fucking car.

I remember the cell phone reception got really spotty as we got nearer to her parents' place, so I expect to lose the signal every now and then, and I also recall that every damn country road that led off the main one we took to the farm looked the same to me, but I'm prepared to drive down every one of them until I find her.

In Vermont, in Manhattan, or Brooklyn—all roads lead to Bernadette.

CHAPTER 24
BERNADETTE

I've been working on a painting in the paint barn for forty-eight hours, with only a few hours of sleep each night. It's not even all that big, just 18x24, but it has been years since I've done figures on a canvas. I'm working off a photo of Matt and Daisy on my phone, one I took of them when they were running around out in the field, backlit by golden rays of sunlight. There's movement and stillness at the same time. It's so beautiful, it takes my breath away, breaks my heart, and fills me with joy all at once. That's a lot to try to capture in a painting, but I'm determined to do it. There are darker colors seeping through lighter colors to the surface and a lot of blending in with gold to smooth the edges of different colors together so that they quietly come alive in the place where they meet.

Of all the things my parents have said to me that drove me nuts, the one thing I will never hear them say is "You need to stop working on that painting." My dad comes out to offer advice or praise, and my mom brings me fresh berry lemonade and meals. They know exactly why I'm here and why I have to do this now, and I'm so grateful. The days are long here in July, and as I stand here holding a brush and palette, wearing my T-shirt and overall shorts, with my hair up in a crazy bun and paint all over me—I feel really bad about criticizing my parents for letting the day-to-day things slide. It's really hard to step away from a project when you're in the zone. I had forgotten how it feels.

This barn is completely set up for painting, with easels and drop cloths and every size and type of canvas, all the paints and brushes, lots of different kinds of lamps, and great natural light during the day when the door is wide open. I'm about to step away to get some fresh air and check my phone, when I see a shadowy backlit figure approaching. I'd know that shadowy figure and sexy gait anywhere; I just can't tell if I'm hallucinating from all the paint fumes or not.

"Matt?"

"I am so fucking glad I found you."

When he steps inside, he comes into focus, and literally everything else fades away. I drop my paintbrush and palette and run to him, jump up and wrap my legs around his waist. He kisses my lips so sweetly, like he's kissing a delicate wound that needs to heal.

"Is Daisy here?"

He laughs. "She's with my aunt. I'm happy to see you too, you nut." He finally looks at me in that way he looked at my painting the first time he was in my apartment. Like he recognizes me as something that he absolutely must have in his life. And for the first time, I feel like even though we're so different, I was made for him.

"Matt. I've missed you so much. I'm so sorry for not telling you how I feel."

"I'm sorry I held back too. I told you I wasn't going to hold back anymore, but then I thought you might not want me."

"Oh, I want you." I kiss him all over his stupidly handsome face. "I love you," I say. "I love you. I love you!"

"Dammit, I wanted to be the one who said it first. I had a whole speech planned, and I forgot it as soon as I saw you. I love you. I love you." He gives me one firm kiss on the mouth to punctuate my new favorite sentence. "I love you. I hated being in a different borough from you. I don't even want one wall between us. I want to go to sleep in the same bed as you every night. You and Daisy. Move in with us. There's plenty of room, and you can use the second bedroom as a studio until you can afford another space."

I don't know… Maybe it is the paint fumes, but I almost pass out when I hear him say this. Oh, who am I kidding. It's Matt McGovern who makes me light-headed. He lets me down, arms still wrapped around me, holding me tight.

"I want to. I want that more than anything. Thank you for asking. But are you sure you want to live with me?"

"Are you sure we haven't already lived together up there on the fourth floor?"

"Yeah, but I'm painting now. It's different. It's good, but I might be crazy."

"I've always thought so."

"No, but I mean really bananas, like staying up all night and being a total asshole when I'm in the middle of a project and an even bigger asshole when I *can't* paint."

"Okay. Well, great news—if we decide we hate living together, you can just move out."

I laugh. "I guess it really is that simple, isn't it?"

He finally notices my painting on the easel. "Wait, what is this? This is beautiful."

"It's not finished yet."

"Is it for me?"

I can't help but smile at that question. I may never stop smiling, in fact. "It's for us."

"Does it have a title?"

"It's a secret. I'll tell you after…"

"After what?"

"After we fuck in my bedroom," I whisper, pulling him out of the barn.

He pauses for a second. "Are your parents home?"

"They're probably working in the other studio, and anyway, you know it wouldn't matter to them."

"You people are my kind of crazy." He breaks into a run, and I take a mental picture because I want to paint this image of us sprinting to the bedroom to have sex. I want to paint everything, and it's all because of him.

I start pulling Matt's shirt off before we've reached the door to my room. His skin is damp and taut and giving off so much heat. He releases my hair from its bun and rakes his fingers through the length of it. Every cell in my body is pulsating with the need to touch and be connected to this man in every possible way. When he shuts the door behind us, I unzip his jeans and reach for his beautiful hard cock like a hysterical starving woman unwrapping a Dove ice cream bar.

But then, when he's unhooking my overalls and they drop to the ground, I realize that we need to slow this down. This is about more than lust. This is about us coming together for real from now on.

It's going to happen. It's happening now. I'm going to converge with him on every level, even if it's the only time we ever do this. I'm going to say everything that needs to be said with my body and with words until there's nothing but love and understanding and sweat between us.

Matt gives me a look, and I know that he knows what we're about to do here. He gives me that little cowboy nod of his and grins. He kisses my forehead. "Nothing ever happened with Vanessa after I met you. You know that, right?"

I kiss his bare chest, right over his heart. "You know that nothing ever happened with Sebastian, right? I've never been in love with anyone before. It's only you."

"I think everything that I thought was being in love before was really just a longing for this feeling I have for you."

He lifts me up and drops me onto the bed. As he pushes my T-shirt up my stomach, he kisses around my belly button and asks, "So you're going to work for Anita? Is that a good thing?"

I laugh. "It will be, I think. She promised not to make a pass at you. I think she actually went out with your friend a couple of times."

"That's news to me," he says, his mouth ever so slowly making its way up to my breasts. "You do know that I make a fuck-load of money, right? I mean, I'm not a millionaire, but if you have your savings and you don't want to work for a while, you don't have to."

I hold on to his head. I love the thoughts that live in that head of his, even when I have no idea what they are. "I love you for offering that, but I need to make money on my own. I think I'd get too anxious if I felt like I depended on you like that."

"Okay. I understand."

"Anita called to offer me a part-time job as soon as she heard that Sebastian's moving out of town. It's just organizational stuff that her regular assistant isn't good at and cataloging collections. But I can make my own hours, which is perfect because I'll be painting too."

"I'm glad." A kiss to my ribcage, and then he hovers there over my cleavage, looking up at me. "I don't have a talent, you know. I'm good at contracts and conference calls and explaining laws to people. But I want to be great at being here for you. So you can be a dreamer again and shine on your own."

"My anchor."

"Yes."

Lord, when this man finally talks, every word from his mouth takes my breath away. "Matt. I don't know what I did to deserve you, but I will do everything I can for you. Every day. Top of my Will-Do list."

Mmmmmm is all he can say to that. His tongue swirls around my nipple, and I arch my back to offer myself up to him. It's when he consumes me like this that I feel the frenzied need inside him, and it turns me on like nothing else ever has.

"I want you to have all of me," I whisper. "I'm going to give you everything, every dark neglected corner, all the parts that don't work properly yet."

"I'm taking all of you," he growls. "I'm going to find every place you try to hide in and stay with you there until you aren't afraid of anything anymore." He reaches down into my panties and groans when he finds the warm, wet place that's aching for him.

"I'm not going to try to change you. I don't want you to force yourself to talk if you don't want to."

"You already have changed me," he says emphatically, pushing down his own underwear. "I'm not just the guy my parents raised anymore. I'm the guy who lives for you. I need to be inside you now."

"Get in there right now. God, I can't wait to live with you so we can do this all the time."

"I'm going to wear you out, Bernadette Farmer."

"I'm going to crash through all the walls, Esquire."

He enters me slowly, and it's only been a week and a half or so since this has happened, but I swear he has grown since the last time, and I gasp. I gasp because I not only see, but I feel a burst of colors. All the colors, as they fade to black and then explode like fireworks when he thrusts and makes that sound that I love. The throat sound that means he can relax now because he's where he needs to be.

There are no boundaries.

The only rule is we're all in.

"The painting I'm working on is called *Love at First Sight*," I whisper breathlessly. "I fell in love with both of you as soon as I saw you and every time after."

"I knew it," he says. "Fuck, I love you. I'll never stop loving you." He picks up the pace, and there's nothing left to say with words now.

We did it.

We converge-sated.

And now we're going to come together for real.

EPILOGUE – MATT

Three Years Later

I still haven't gotten over how quiet it is in our little corner of Park Slope in the middle of the night.

I walk down the hall to the master bedroom, light on my feet so I don't wake anyone. Lately, I've really started to enjoy watching Bernadette Farmer while she sleeps. She has been a spectacular whirling dervish of productivity for months, always making and giving and doing, and when she's finally unconscious I can just quietly marvel at this person she's become. Falling in love with her was a relatively quick trip, but watching her grow and push her own boundaries and get out of her comfort zone has been a journey that's seemingly without end. I never dreamed I'd be the kind of person who could inspire anything, but being the inspiration she needed to get to this place is one of the things I'm most proud of. Even when she feels like she's a crazy mess, I'm quick to remind her that it's a beautiful mess and I wouldn't want her any other way. That's when it's time for me to get her between the sheets so I can remind her what *good* feels like.

I rub Daisy's belly as she stretches out at the foot of the bed, snoring.

Bernie slowly opens her eyes and tries to raise her head off the pillow.

"You get her back down?"

"She just looked up at me, laughed, slapped my face with her tiny hand, and went right back to sleep."

"Hah. Sure she did. Get back in bed."

"You need to sleep." I slide back under the covers, coming face-to-face with her in our little world where everything always makes sense.

"I'm trying. I'm too excited. Aren't you excited?" She wraps one leg around me, pulling me in even closer and pressing herself against me in a way that still makes me hard as a rock, every damn time.

"Of course I'm excited, but I also feel like it's going to be like every other day for us. All the days are special."

"You cornball." She touches my face and stares into my eyes.

"Yeah. Go the fuck to sleep."

I've been taking the night shift this month because Bernadette's been so busy preparing for her solo show, which opened at Anita's gallery earlier tonight. It was a great success. I expected nothing less. It's her second solo show in two years. The first opened two years ago, in Hudson Valley. *Sebastian Smith Presents: Bernadette Farmer* was nothing short of a triumphant debut and got her on a Top 30 Under 30 Artists in New York list. Not that she cares about that sort of thing. The exhibition was called "Come Back to Bed." The paintings and drawings were erotic (inspired by our sex life and relationship—you're welcome), but she also brought in elements of the nature and landscape that she grew up with. It brought her a lot of sales and commissions and allowed her to quit her part-time job for Anita and paint full-time.

Later today, we'll drive up to the farm in Vermont, where her parents have been busy preparing for guests.

Tomorrow we'll finally get married, at the edge of the woods, with our friends and family, our dog, and our baby girl.

Harriet Dolores Farmer McGovern was born five months ago. Our first, and probably not the last, co-creation of ours, she was a welcome surprise. As always, Bernadette initially flipped out and got mad at me when she found out things weren't going to go as planned. I calmly reassured her that we would be fine, and then she put everything on hold so she could paint a mural in what is now the baby's room. Once she was done with it, she was mentally prepared for anything the little alien monster could possibly throw at us. Bernadette is infinitely more maternal than she thought she would be, though I never had any doubts.

I knew I wanted to marry this woman as soon as I saw her in that barn wearing overalls. Everything we said and did in her childhood bedroom after that just confirmed it for me. But I didn't propose to her until she told me she was pregnant. She said yes immediately but didn't want the stress of a wedding while she was pregnant. Once Harriet was born, she wanted to wait until after her gallery opening. I feel like I've been waiting forever to make it official, so one more day isn't going to kill me.

The one thing I never knew I wanted is the thing that has owned my heart since the moment I knew she was a possibility.

Like everything that springs forth from my bride, our daughter is breathtakingly beautiful, mysterious and recognizable all at once. She keeps me on my toes and doesn't take any shit from me. She always has this look on her face when she's staring at me, like: *"Seriously? Are you for real?"* Ever since she was born, whenever someone calls her "Harry," she cries. Ever since she was born, people have practically begged us for their turn to babysit whenever the nanny has time off. Tommy and his new boyfriend look after her most often since they live the closest. Lloyd likes to hold her whenever I bring her to the office. Even my aunt crosses the bridge just so she can squeeze those fat cheeks. She's brought out a side of my parents that I never thought I'd see—the emotionally expressive one. And Steve and Leslie Farmer are suddenly really good at answering their phones and responding to texts and emails when there are pictures of their grandchild attached.

Everything blends together and works somehow, like the colors in Bernadette's paintings.

"I love you," she says quietly as she drifts off to sleep. "I'm gonna marry you tomorrow."

"Is that a threat?"

"When I threaten you, Esquire, you'll know it."

"I love you," I whisper, kissing the top of her head. "When I marry you, Bernadette, it'll be forever."

THE END